JADE'S EROTIC ADVENTURES

BOOKS 46 - 50

LESBIAN EROTICA BUNDLES
BOOK 10

VICTORIA RUSH

VOLUME 10

LESBIAN EROTICA BUNDLES: BOOKS 46 - 50

COPYRIGHT

For the uninhibited...

WANT TO AMP UP YOUR SEX LIFE?

Sign up for my newsletter to receive more free books and other steamy stuff.
Discover a hundred different ways to wet your whistle!

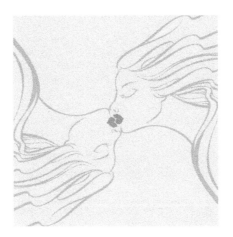

Victoria Rush Erotica

BOOK 46

THE KISS

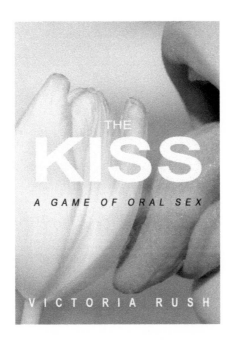

THE
KISS

A GAME OF ORAL SEX

VICTORIA RUSH

1

When I received a new invitation to a party at my friend Madison's house, I couldn't wait to open the message. She always hosted the most interesting and sexy events, and with the cryptic subject heading *Kissing Game*, I could already feel my heart pounding as I began to read the message.

Dear Jade,

You are cordially invited to a party at my place this Saturday evening, starting at 9 p.m.

As with my previous events, there will be an exciting game designed to loosen everyone's inhibitions and get our juices flowing.

I don't want to give too much away, except to say you're likely to pick up some new pointers for spicing up your love life.

So get ready to mix it up with friends and foes alike, because in this game, there's no telling who or how you'll be paired up.

Be there or be square,

Maddy

P.S.: Make sure you're scrubbed clean, and I do mean everywhere, because no area of your body will be off limits!

Holy cow, I thought after reading her message. *What in God's name has she dreamed up this time? No area off limits? Mixing it up with friends and foes?* I had no idea what she was planning, but she was right about one thing. It was definitely going to get my juices flowing.

As my mind began to wander about the hijinks she had in store, my hand slipped under my panties, imagining who might soon be kissing me all over my naked body...

W hen I arrived at Madison's house on the night of the party, she escorted me to her living room, where a group of people sat cross-legged around a large mattress covered with satin sheets. I recognized some of the faces in the crowd, but there were also quite a few new people I hadn't met before. With an even sprinkling of men and women, I scanned the crowd as everybody made small talk introducing themselves.

In addition to my friends Lily, Bonnie, and Emma, there was the sexy neighbor couple from the last party, Brad and Laura, plus my old friends from work, Ryan and Marco. But there were two new faces in the crowd that attracted most of my attention. One was a gorgeous African-American stud who looked like a young Denzel Washington, and the other was a stunning Asian girl who reminded me of the kick-ass actress, Lucy Liu. Rounding out the group was my transgender friend Shae and the full-figured Christina Hendricks lookalike from my tribbing workshop, Paige.

This should be interesting, I thought, squirming excitedly on the floor as I surveyed the beautiful assembly of men and women.

When the last guest arrived and was seated in the circle, Madison placed large wine goblets beside each of us, then she sat near the foot of the bed, passing two bottles of wine in each direction. After everyone had filled their glass, she pulled a packet of playing cards from her pocket and smiled at the group.

"First, I'd like to thank everyone for coming to my party," she said. "I know I was a little coy in my invitation about what I had planned, but those of you who've been to my previous parties know that's half the fun. Not knowing who you'll be paired with or what you'll be asked to do makes it all the more interesting."

Then she raised her glass, nodding to each of the participants.

"So, before we get started, I'd like to make a toast: to new friends and new discoveries!"

"Cheers to that," Emma said.

"Amen," the handsome African-American newcomer, Linc, said.

"Okay then," Maddy said after everybody took a large gulp of wine to loosen up. "You're probably wondering what kind of kissing game I've cooked up and how we can make such a seemingly innocent act a little more interesting."

She opened the packet of cards then placed the deck face-down between her legs.

"As always," she smiled. "Most of the fun is in the expectation and the surprise. But instead of using a spinning wheel this time to determine the match-ups, we're going to use a deck of cards."

She began pulling cards off the top of the deck and spinning them toward each person around the circle, and as they reached out to catch their card, they peering at it with a puzzled expression.

"Here's how it's going to work," Maddy smiled after everyone received a card. "The person with the highest card will be the one giving the kiss in each round, and the one with the lowest card will be the one receiving the kiss."

There was a brief moment of silence in the group, then Ryan raised his hand cautiously.

"Are we going to be kissing each other in the usual manner?" he said. "I mean, insofar as being restricted to kissing on the *lips*?"

"Well, that's where it gets interesting," Madison grinned. "The person with the high card will also get to choose where on the other person's body he or she wishes to kiss. And as I suggested in my party invitation, there is no area off limits. Subject to the agreement of your partner, of course. As always, this is a full consent zone."

"Are we going to be doing this fully *clothed*?" the full-figured redhead, Paige, said, winking in my direction.

"That's up to the two of you," Maddy nodded. "Depending on the area targeted, you might find the experience more titillating, in a matter of speaking, if you choose to expose a little skin."

"And this so-called *kiss*," Brad said, peering at his wife, Laura, to clarify the limits of the game. "Are we limited to lips-only contact, or are we allowed to engage certain *other* oral body parts to heighten the experience?"

Madison paused for a moment, smiling at Laura.

"If that's how you and your wife kiss, closed-mouthed like in those old black-and-white movies, then knock yourself out. But if you want to make it more interesting and exciting, then I encourage you to take a page out of the French playbook and bring a little tongue action into the equation."

Everyone chuckled at the subtle dig at Brad's kissing technique, then the pretty Asian girl, Mei, raised her hand.

"Exactly how far are we allowed to go with these kisses?" she asked. "What if we start to get, you know, *aroused* by the experience? How will we know when to stop?"

"Something tells me you'll know when the time comes," Maddy smiled. "Like I said in my message, there are no limits with this game. I encourage each of you to explore the full range of possibilities until you're fully satisfied."

"So, there'll be no hourglass or egg-timer this time?" Marco chuckled.

"I'm not going to stop you just when things begin to get interesting," Madison nodded.

"What if we're handed an ace?" Shae said, turning her card around to reveal an ace of hearts. "Does that count as a low card or a high card?"

"I'll leave that up to the holder of the card," Madison smiled. "In that case, you can decide if you want to give or receive your kiss with the next lowest card holder."

"Mmm," Shae hummed, peering around the circle at the flushed faces of the already excited participants. "I'm starting to like this game already."

2

"Let's get started by everyone revealing their cards," Madison said.

Everybody flipped their cards around, with both Bonnie and Shae showing an ace and Emma showing a two.

"What do we do if we have the same card?" Shae said, frowning as she peered at Bonnie's high card.

"Well, since this is a game all about *kissing*," Maddy smiled. "We'll give hearts the highest rank, then diamonds, then spades, then clubs. Since you've got the highest card, Shae, you can decide if you wish to give or receive this turn."

Shae peered around the circle to see who had the next lowest card and when she saw it was the cute blonde, Emma, she grinned.

"I think I'll elect to be the one giving this time," she said.

"And which body part would you like to kiss in this instance?"

"Are you sure I only get to kiss *one*?" Shae said, running her eyes over Emma's slender but curvy figure.

"Those are the rules," Maddy nodded. "We've got to save some of the other parts for the future rounds if we want to keep it interesting."

"In that case," Shae said, smiling toward Emma. "I think I'll choose her lips."

"Which ones?" Emma said, lifting an eyebrow.

"It's tempting," Shae said, glancing between her crossed legs. "But I want to start by kissing that pretty face of yours."

"Okay," Madison said, nodding toward the two girls. "Why don't the two of you make yourselves comfortable on the mattress so the rest of us can enjoy the show?"

Emma catwalked onto the middle of the bed, sitting upright with her arms extended behind her, then Shae slunk up next to her, resting beside her hips.

Shae peered at her partner for a moment, then she turned her head, kissing Emma gently on the side of her neck under her ear. Emma moaned softly, and I glanced expectantly toward Madison. Normally, she enforced the rules like an overprotective den mother, but this time she simply smiled at the two women, nodding for them to continue.

Shae continued kissing Emma's neck downward with soft kisses, and Emma lifted her chin, exposing her throat while Shae nibbled on it like a lion cub play-fighting with her sibling. With everyone looking on in rapt attention, I wondered how many of the guys were making mental notes about how to warm up their lovers with the tender display of foreplay. I wasn't sure how many of them even knew that Shae was transgender. Being a true hermaphrodite, she had fully functional male and female sex organs, but her hourglass figure and delicate facial features made her look one hundred percent like a feminine sex goddess.

"Are you getting as turned on as I am watching this?" Lily whispered, sitting next to me.

"Fuck yes," I panted. "I've been on the receiving end of those kisses, and I can tell you firsthand that Shae knows how to use every weapon in her arsenal to drive a woman crazy."

"It's too bad the roles weren't reversed," Lily nodded, squirming restlessly on the floor. "Cause I'd love to see some of those *other* body parts in action too."

"Something tells me this won't be the last we'll see of her this evening," I smiled.

As Shae began to slowly kiss her way up the underside of Emma's chin, she shifted into a kneeling position, raising one leg and straddling Emma's hips. The closer she moved toward her mouth, the wider Emma parted her lips, eagerly anticipating Shae's touch.

But just as she reached the bottom of her lower lip, Shae pulled away a few inches, just enough for them to feel their hot breath on each other's skin. While Shae tilted her face from side to side, she brushed her lips softly against Emma's opening, intimating about she intended to do next.

"She's giving a master class in kissing," Lily sighed. "I only wish the *guys* I dated knew how to do this half as well."

"Perhaps you should bring a few of them along next time," I chuckled. "The more we can educate, the better."

After teasing Emma with soft butterfly kisses for the better part of three minutes, Shae opened her mouth, clutching Emma's upper lip and sliding her tongue softly under the rim while feeling the ridges of her teeth. Emma tilted her head higher up, encouraging her to press deeper inside, but Shae seemed determined to go slow and explore every crevasse of the girl's soft and pliant cavity.

While Emma began to move her hips sensuously on the heaving mattress, Shae pulled one of her knees down, forcing Emma's legs apart as she slid her thigh up toward the crotch of Emma's tight jeans. When she pressed her leg against her cleft, Emma moaned into Shae's mouth and Shae raised her right hand, running her fingers softly through Emma's hair as she continued nibbling and sucking on her upper lip.

"Holy fuck," Lily panted next to me. "What I'd give to have that girl kissing my *pussy* like that right now."

"If you play your cards right," I smiled. "You might just have a chance later this evening."

As Emma began to rock her hips against Shae's pressing thigh, Shae lowered her head to suck on Emma's lower lip. While everybody looked on in mesmerized silence, I noticed a few of the men adjusting their package, obviously turned on by the erotic sight of the two women kissing so lustfully.

By now, Emma's mouth was wide open as Shae sucked, nibbled, and probed her with her tongue. When she pulled Shae closer toward her, pressing their tits together, Shae adjusted her leg to the outside of Emma's hips, sitting down over top of her crotch as they ground their pubises together. Shae lifted her other hand to the opposite side of Emma's head and pulled her face harder toward her, thrusting her tongue deep into her opening while they mashed their lips tightly together.

As the two women began kissing each other passionately and moaning into each other's mouths, Shae traced a line around the side of Emma's face with the tips of her fingers, starting above her eyebrows, then down over her soft cheekbones and along the crease of her jaw. When her hand reached the underside of her chin, Shae placed her fingers around the front of her neck, squeezing her throat as she began to kiss her more forcefully.

After a few minutes, Emma pulled away, gasping for air as she peered into Shae's eyes with flared eyes. I wasn't sure if it was because Shae had been partially cutting off her air supply or Emma just wanted to show her partner what effect she was having on her. Either way, she wasn't the *only* one approaching the peak of her excitement while I noticed many of the other participants moving their hands between their legs as they watched the action unfolding on the mattress.

"Have you guys had *enough* yet?" Madison interjected, trying to tamp down the escalating tension in the room.

"Fuck no," Emma said, grabbing Shae's head with both of her hands and pulling her hard toward her. "We're just getting started."

As the two lovers continued twirling their tongues inside one another's mouths, they started to rock their hips together rhythmically. I noticed a bulge in Shae's pants and wondered if her hardening tool was providing some direct friction on Emma's clit under her tight jeans. But the reaction of the two women soon answered my question. As they began moaning more loudly and grinding their hips harder together, it was soon apparent that they were moving ever closer toward a mutual climax.

"Fuck *this*," Lily said, unbuttoning her jeans and thrusting three fingers under her soaking panties. "I can't wait any longer for my turn. I need a piece of this action right now."

"No kidding," I nodded, joining her in stimulating myself while we watched the sexy pair on the mattress.

By now, Emma and Shae were rocking their hips vigorously together, and I wondered why they hadn't removed their clothes, since Madison had given her approval to do so at the beginning. Whether it was because they knew they were only supposed to be touching their lips together or because they were already too far gone to interrupt their hot lovemaking session, I wasn't sure. But one thing was for certain – it wouldn't be long before the two of them reached the height of their passion.

As their moaning notched up in volume and frequency, they wrapped their arms around one another's backs, pulling their bodies harder together, then they began shaking in each other's arms, groaning and panting while they bit each other's lips tightly. It must have taken almost a full minute for each of them to come down from their powerful climaxes and when they finally finished shaking and convulsing, Shae pulled away to gently kiss the sides of Emma's swollen lips while she ran her fingers through her hair softly.

"Now *that's* what I call a kiss," Lily said, still playing with her pussy with her hands down her pants.

"Yes," I panted alongside her. "Who needs to be naked when you have a lover like *that* giving you all of her oral attention?"

When the two women finally separated and stood up to return to their previous places in the circle, I noticed the crotch of Emma's jeans had a wide stain in the front. But it was the front of *Shae's* pants that attracted most of the attention around the circle. Her enormous engorged cock was pointing forty-five degrees up toward the side of her hip, bulging prominently under the tight confines of her equally wet jeans.

"Holy shit," I grunted. "If that's how hot it gets from kissing only *lips to lips*, I can't wait to see what happens when we get to kiss some of the other interesting body parts."

3

When the girls returned to their places in the circle, Madison smiled as she watched the men adjusting themselves in an obvious state of arousal.

"I hope you all enjoyed that little demonstration of oral love," she said. "I don't know about you guys, but *I* certainly picked up a few pointers for elevating my game."

"Definitely," Lily panted, zipping up the front of her jeans.

"Well, we're just getting started," Maddy nodded. "There's still a lot of other body parts to explore. Are you guys ready for the next round?"

Everybody nodded and returned their cards to Madison, then she shuffled the deck, tossing a new one to each participant. When they revealed their numbers, this time Laura held the high card and Paige had the lowest one.

"It looks like Laura will be the one giving this time, and Paige will be the one receiving," Madison said. "Have you decided which body part you'd like to kiss, Laura?"

Laura turned her head to examine Paige's full-figured body wrapped up in a tight t-shirt and jeans, then her eyes bulged, staring at her huge melons.

"Um, I think I'd like to kiss Paige's *breasts*," she hesitated. "That is, if she doesn't mind my being so forward."

Paige placed her hands under her tits and playfully pushed them together, smiling back at Laura.

"Of course not," she purred. "I've been dying to unshackle these things all day. It'll be my pleasure."

"Mine too," Laura said, turning to wink at her husband before she shuffled over to the middle of the mattress.

As Paige crawled toward her on her hands and knees, everyone in the room stared at her magnificent round ass, looking more like it belonged on the back of a thoroughbred *mare* than the sexy redhead. When she sat down next to Laura, her partner paused for a moment to inspect her Rubenesque figure, then she pressed Paige's back down onto the mattress. She climbed on top of her, straddling her hips with bent knees, then she leaned forward, slowly sliding her palms up her torso. When she reached Paige's big globes, she curled her fingers around the edges, massaging and teasing her while the redhead panted below her.

"Mmm," Laura grunted, peering over in the direction of her husband, who was looking on in a catatonic trance. "I bet you wish I was built like *this* goddess, don't you?"

"You're perfect just the way you are," Brad lied. "But I'm enjoying your worshipping her from this position at the foot of the altar."

Laura leaned forward to whisper something in Paige's ear and they both chuckled. Then she began kissing her way down Paige's upper body until she reached the top of her mounds, pausing to bury her face in Paige's deep cleavage. I watched her back heaving as she breathed in the perfume of Paige's decolletage, and for a moment, I was transported back to our last encounter at Laila's tribbing workshop, where I got to play with them firsthand.

After a few seconds, she lifted her head, nibbling toward the tips of Paige's mountains, stopping at the top to bite each of her thick nipples until her t-shirt was soaked with two dark rings of saliva. Laura sat up for a moment to admire her handiwork, then she shook her head in disbelief.

"Jesus, girl," she panted. "Those have to be the most magnificent tits I've ever seen on a woman. Can you share your secret for building a bosom like that?"

"I suspect it's mostly genetics," Paige chuckled. "But if you're not afraid to put on a few extra pounds, some of that additional weight will migrate to your bustline eventually."

Laura turned back to glance at her husband and grinned.

"What do you say, dear?" she said. "Would you like me to gain a few extra bra sizes if it means I'll be plumper everywhere *else*?"

"All the more to love," Brad smiled.

"Well, I don't know about the rest of you guys," Laura said, peering at the other participants around the circle. "But I'm dying to see what these girls look like untethered."

She turned her head to glance at Paige, and smiled.

"May I?"

"By all means," Paige nodded. "I've been waiting all this time to feel those lips on my skin."

Laura reached behind Paige's shoulders and pulled her up into a sitting position, then she pulled her t-shirt over her shoulders and reached behind her back to unclasp her bra. As she pulled the straps around to the front and let the brassiere fall to the side of the mattress, everyone around the circle gasped. Paige's giant breasts looked almost as big as a cow's udder, with thick, protruding nipples to match.

"Oh my God," Laura panted, gawking at them like a twelve-year-old seeing his first centerfold. "They're exquisite. And *firm*. And natural..."

"Of course," Paige said, kissing Laura on her flushed cheeks. "Are you just going to *stare* at them or were you thinking of touching them? This is a *kissing* game, after all."

Laura peered into her hazel eyes for a moment then she lowered her head, unable to resist the siren call of Paige's protruding bullets. She drew them hard into her mouth like a suckling pig, and Paige moaned, arching her back to press her mounds harder against Laura's face.

"Damn," Lily said next to me, watching the pair with dilated pupils. "That is one magnificent set of tits. You know I lean more toward *men*, but you wouldn't have to twist my arm to persuade me to rub myself against that voluptuous body if I had the chance."

"Well, it's still a card game," I smiled. "You've got as good a chance as any."

While Laura sucked and nibbled on each of Paige's hard teats in turn, she squeezed her small hands around her huge orbs like a schoolgirl caressing a Greek statue. I peered around the group, noticing everyone's mouths parted slack-jawed as they squirmed on the floor beside the mattress, wishing it was their turn to worship the gorgeous redhead instead of Laura.

After a few minutes, Laura grew tired of bending down to lick Paige's breasts, and she pressed her back down onto the mattress, straddling her waist between her thighs. She took a minute to appraise the shape of Paige's breasts resting with the full force of gravity weighing down on them, then she shook her head, marveling at how tall and upright they were, even when she was lying down.

"I wouldn't have believed these were real if I hadn't felt them with my own *hands*," she said, staring at Paige's bosom like she was admiring a masterpiece in an art gallery.

"Not to mention your *lips*," Paige smiled, pulling Laura back down toward her. "Don't forget your lips."

Laura lowered her head toward Paige's chest and her long hair brushed over her mounds, then she paused halfway to tilt her head from side to side, caressing Paige's dark medallions with the tips of her strands.

"Mmm," Paige purred. "That feels heavenly. Caress my nipples with your silky hair."

"That's not the *only* body part I'd like to caress them with," Laura smiled, glancing in Madison's direction to make sure she wasn't going too far astray.

Maddy peered back at her for a moment, shaking her head slowly.

"We've already given you plenty of extra license using your hands and other parts to caress her," she said. "But as long as you stay fully clothed, I'll give you a little more room to maneuver."

"Well, in *that* case," Laura said, leaning down to press her breasts covered in a silk blouse against Paige's bare tits.

"Yes," Paige groaned, rolling her body on the mattress to feel Laura's tits rubbing against hers. "I can feel your hard nipples tweaking mine. I only wish I could return the favor–"

"The night is still young," Laura grinned, leaning down to kiss Paige passionately on the mouth.

"Ahem," Madison said, clearing her throat. "As much as I'm sure you two would like to engage certain other body parts, this is supposed to be about kissing Paige's *tits*. There's still plenty of skin to titillate and excite lower down."

"Indeed there is," Laura said, raising up and scanning Paige's heaving chest. "But are you sure we've got enough time to give those beautiful mounds proper attention? Because I could spend all *day* kissing and lapping up those lambchops."

"How about five more minutes?" Madison said, noticing some of the other group members touching themselves impatiently. "We've still got a few more rounds to go through, and from the look of things, I think a few of the other participants are eager to have their turn in the spotlight."

"We better make the most of it then," Laura said, shifting her hips further down over Paige's pelvis and spreading her knees wider apart. "You said as long as we keep our clothes on, anything's fair game, right?"

"Within reason, yes," Madison nodded.

As Laura lowered her head back down toward Paige's bulging teats, she began to grind her pussy over the front of her jeans, creating a widening wet spot along her seam.

"Yes," Paige panted, rolling her hips in tandem with Laura. "Rub your pussy against my clit. If you keep licking my nipples like that, I'm going to come soon."

"Mmm," Laura grunted, twirling her tongue around Paige's

thumb-sized berries like she was licking a lollypop. "I haven't had this much fun fully clothed since I first laid eyes on my husband."

Brad peered at his wife, grinding her pussy against Paige, then he reached into his pants to straighten out his straining cock.

"Um, I'm pretty sure we never had quite that much fun with our clothes on," he chuckled.

"You don't mind, baby?" Laura said, keeping her eyes focused on Paige's hardening tips.

"Are you kidding?" he said, rolling his fingers over his dripping crown. "You're not the *only* one who's enjoying this show right now."

I smiled as I watched the rest of the group caressing their nipples and stroking their crotches while they gazed at the duo grinding and rocking their bodies together on the bouncing mattress.

"It looks like Maddy's allowing a little more stretching of the rules than usual," I said, elbowing Lily.

"Yeah," she panted, twirling her fingers under the front of her jeans as she stared at the sexy couple in front of us. "Thank God, because those two aren't the *only* ones who need to get off right now."

As Laura and Paige began to grind their hips harder together, Laura started to squeeze Paige's tits tighter between her hands, licking her nipples like a hungry baby. It didn't take long for the two of them to begin groaning louder as they neared the peak of their excitement.

"Yes, baby," Paige panted, tilting her head up to watch Laura sucking her teats. "Suck my nipples harder. I'm going to come soon."

Laura pressed her face harder down onto Paige's tits, then Paige grasped the back of her head while she arched her back in mounting ecstasy.

"God, yes," she hissed. "Yes, yes, yes – *guhhh!*"

As Paige started to convulse in pleasure under Laura's rocking hips, Laura angled her hips forward, pressing her cunt harder against Paige's wet crotch. I saw the wet spot in her pants darken as she squirted into her jeans, holding onto Paige's teat for dear life.

"Mhhh," Lily moaned beside me, starting to shake along with the others around the circle who also had their hands down their pants.

Up to this point I'd been so focused on soaking up Paige's magnificent figure that I'd completely ignored my own mounting arousal. But I was so worked up that it only took a few seconds of touching my dripping pussy to come along with everyone else.

"Jesus," I panted after recovering from my brief but intense orgasm. "This is almost as much fun *watching* as participating in the action. It looks like Maddy's hit another home run. Pretty soon, her parties are going to become so popular, they'll be first come, first served only."

"Yeah," Lily sighed, leaning back against her outstretched arms to recover from her own powerful climax. "And there's no telling who'll be the first to come."

4

"Wow," Madison exhaled deeply, when Paige and Laura returned to their places in the circle. "Who knew kissing could be so much fun?"

"It helps when you have a canvas like *that* to work with," Laura said, smiling toward Paige.

"And when you have a master like Laura applying the brush strokes," Paige grinned.

"Something tells me there'll be plenty more masterpieces yet to come," Maddy nodded, noticing the bulges in the pants of many of the men sitting around the circle. "Shall we get started with another round?"

"Yes please," Brad grunted.

After Madison collected the cards and reshuffled the deck, she passed everyone a new card. This time the new girl, Mei, got the high number and Brad held the lowest.

"It looks like we're going to mix it up a little this time," Maddy smiled. "Mei holds the high card and Brad has the lowest, so it's Mei's turn to choose which body part she wishes to kiss."

Mei peered toward Brad, noticing his large erection straining against his tight jeans, then she smiled at Laura.

"I think it's only fair since his wife enjoyed a little extra-curricular activity in the last round that he gets an equal degree of attention. I'm hungry for some cock about now – that is, if Brad's feeling up to it."

"Oh, I'm feeling *up* for it alright," he smiled, turning to peer at Laura. "That is, if my wife doesn't mind my freeing my python."

"Knock yourself out, dear," Laura chuckled. "Maybe I'll pick up a few techniques to keep things interesting in the bedroom."

As the two players crawled toward the center of the mattress, I noticed Laura's eyes darting over Mei's sexy figure with a tinge of jealousy, and I wondered if it was such a good idea that they'd come to the party together. When Brad and Mei sat down beside one another, Mei slid her hand between his legs, caressing his throbbing member overtop of his moist jeans, then she glanced over at Madison.

"You said at the beginning that we could expose a little *skin* when we do this," she said. "Am I allowed to take off his clothes?"

"In the target area, yes," Maddy nodded. "So long as you keep the rest of your bodies covered. Mouth to penis only, those are the rules."

"Okay then," Mei said, peering at Brad's straining crotch. "Let's get you out of those tight pants. I think that snake of yours needs a little room to breathe."

As Mei slowly unbuckled his belt, I noticed Laura's face growing tenser, and I wasn't sure if it was because she was becoming envious of the other woman's attention, or because she was trying to suppress her own arousal at the thought of watching her husband having sex with the pretty Asian.

When Mei unzipped Brad's fly, he raised his hips then she pulled his trousers down over his ankles. When his dick flopped up and slapped against his belly, many of the women around the circle bulged their eyes, admiring his impressive package. Standing eight inches in height and at least six inches in circumference, his circumcised rod stood tall and proud, already glistening with a layer of precum oozing over his crown.

"Mmm," Mei said, kneeling between his legs and sliding her index finger up the underside of his pole from the base of his balls to his tip. "That looks delicious."

When she reached the sensitive skin on the underside of his glans, his dick twitched, emitting a drop of precum over the top of his flaring helmet.

"And I see you've already added some marinade to make my meal even more appetizing."

She leaned down, lifting her sexy ass in the air, and extended her long tongue, swiping it slowly up the length of his cock as she'd done with her finger. But this time, when she reached the head, his cock flapped excitedly, bouncing against his hard abs like a flagpole in a heavy wind.

I noticed that the position of the pair on the mattress had placed the angle of Brad's legs directly facing Laura, and as Mei continued to tease his cock with her tongue, Laura angled her body, trying to get a closer look at what Mei was doing. I smiled, realizing it probably wasn't an accident the way Mei had positioned herself, trying to block her view.

"Let the games *begin*," I nudged Lily beside me. "I'm not sure Laura's going to enjoy this quite as much as her husband."

"What's good for the goose is good for the gander," Lily chuckled, staring at Brad's impressive pecker.

As he arched his back to give Mei freer access to his pulsing tool, Mei tilted her head while she drew circles over his darkening crown, slopping up his rivers of precum with the flat side of her tongue. When she began flicking it against his sensitive frenulum, he tilted his head back, moaning in pleasure.

"Looks like this isn't her first rodeo," I nodded to Lily.

"Mmm," she hummed approvingly. "Something tells me she's had a little practice doing this before."

"Are you taking notes?"

"Yes, while my quiver is still wet."

After a few minutes of teasing Brad with the tip of her tongue, Mei pushed Brad down onto the mattress and raised his knees, spreading his legs apart. Then she lay down on her stomach with her head in front of his crotch, lapping at his balls like a puppy dog. I noticed that Brad was freshly shaved in his perineum, and I wondered how much of his manscaping had been motivated by his anticipation of this evening's events as opposed to his usual marital routine. Either way, I noticed his wife looking on in rapt attention, now that she had a clear view of the show.

While Mei lapped and tugged on his scrotum with the tips of her teeth, he flexed his buttocks, raising his cock higher in the air as it flapped excitedly over the shaved stubble of his mound.

"That is one *fuckable* dick," Lily sighed, squirming on the floor next to me.

"You're not going to touch yourself this time?" I said.

"I don't want to miss one second of this performance," she nodded. "Besides, my fingers would be a poor substitute for that magnificent organ."

As Mei threaded her hands behind Brad's knees, the further she pushed his legs up toward his chest, the lower she began licking and nibbling toward his anus.

"Um, *hello*," Madison interrupted. "I hate to put a damper on your fun, but you're moving a little far astray from the target area."

"It's all part of the same erogenous zone," Mei protested, pausing her head.

"That may be true," Madison nodded. "But that *particular* erogenous zone you're moving toward has its own set of inducements. I'd like to save that one for its own dedicated attention later on, if someone so wishes."

"Fine," Mei huffed, pretending to be upset. "I guess I'll just have to focus on certain *other* areas. Am I still allowed to touch his balls?"

"I think those are connected close enough to the main attraction to count as part of the package," Madison smiled, peering toward Brad. "What do you say, Brad? Is it okay if Mei caresses your balls in addition to your penis?"

"If you *insist*," he chuckled.

Mei raised up on her knees and rested her ass on her feet, then she grabbed his dick with two hands and slid her mouth over his knob, engulfing his pole halfway down his length. As she gripped the base of his shaft with her fists, Brad pumped his organ in and out of her mouth, flexing his buttock muscles while he groaned loudly.

"*That's* what I'm talking about," Lily panted. "I'd let that stud cum in my mouth any time."

"I don't expect he'll be long for this world," I nodded, appreciating Mei's multi-pronged attack on his purple phallus.

As Brad began to hump Mei's face more vigorously, she lowered her hands and clasped his balls while his face began to flush more deeply. But just as he seemed ready to erupt, she suddenly pulled her face away from his organ, and it flapped wildly, inches away from her lips. At first, I thought she'd pulled away because she didn't want him coming in her mouth, but as she peered into Brad's eyes with a sly smile, she bobbed her head back down over his dick, tickling his perineum with the tips of her fingers while he grunted in delirious pleasure.

As his pleasure escalated toward its inevitable climax, Mei shifted one hand to the base of his erection while squeezing his balls tighter with her other hand. As he gradually lifted his hips off the surface of the mattress, she stepped up the pace of her bobbing head, twisting it from side to side to provide an extra degree of stimulation over his sensitive glans.

Suddenly, he reached out to grasp the back of Mei's head, and he howled like a wolf as his knees buckled and his buttocks quivered in the midst of an orgasm that seemed to last forever. The whole time he was shaking, Mei kept her mouth over his pulsating organ, gulping to swallow down his enormous load. When he finally stopped shaking and moaning, he fell back onto the mattress and flopped his arms out to the side, breathing heavily.

I glanced over in the direction of his wife, noticing her hands were down the front of her pants, jilling herself rapidly as she shook in simultaneous pleasure.

"I guess Laura wasn't as jealous as I thought at the idea of another woman sucking her husband's cock," I said to Lily.

"Yes," Lily nodded. "I have a feeling this isn't the *first* time those two have enjoyed a little two-way swinging action."

"hew," Madison said, pretending to wipe her brow after Brad and Mei returned to the circle. "Is it getting warm in here or what? That was some pretty hot kissing."

"I think there was a lot more than just *kissing* going on there," Laura said, elbowing her husband hard in the ribs.

"Well, as long as the one administering it uses his or her *mouth*, as far as I'm concerned, anything's fair game."

Madison glanced at the satin sheets, noticing a large wet spot in the middle of the mattress.

"Why don't we all take a little bio break before we start the next round?" she said. "You might want to top up your liquid courage before we resume, because something tells me it's going to get even more titillating moving forward."

While everybody took a moment to freshen up and top up their wine glasses, Madison changed the sheets and collected the cards. I noticed Brad and Laura took a little longer than the others to return to the circle and when they did, their cheeks looked flushed.

"I guess Laura couldn't wait any longer for her turn at the other end," I smiled to Lily.

"That was some seriously hot foreplay in the last round," she nodded. "If *my* husband were here, I'd have taken him to a private room too."

While Madison reshuffled the deck, she peered around the group.

"I hope everyone had a chance to clean up and prepare for a new round," she said. "Because there's still quite a few unexplored places still to kiss, and I for one am looking forward to some interesting new combinations."

After everyone received their new card and turned them around, it was Ryan who held the highest card while the hot African-American newcomer, Linc, held the lowest.

"Oh goody," Lily smiled when she saw the outcome. "I've been waiting for some hot boy-on-boy action."

"This should be good," I nodded. "I know Ryan's hard-core gay, and from the looks of things, the new guy seems pretty straight."

"Okay," Madison said, looking at everyone's cards. "It looks like Ryan drew the high card and Linc has the lowest. Which body part would you like to kiss this time, Ryan?"

Ryan paused for a moment as he peered at Lincoln's broad shoulders and muscular thighs.

"You know I can never pass up an opportunity to worship another pretty cock," he smiled.

"What do you say, Linc?" Madison said, glancing at her new guest. "Are you up for a little man-to-man oral satisfaction?"

"Um–" Lincoln hesitated, peering around the circle as if he was embarrassed to hook up with another man.

"Oh, come on," Madison said. "You're among friends here. You know what they say, you should try everything at least once. You never know if you'll like it until you give it a try."

Lincoln tilted his head, then sighed deeply.

"I guess if I'm the one on the *receiving* end, it can't hurt," he said with a lopsided smile.

"Oh, I'm pretty sure it won't *hurt*," Ryan chuckled, sashaying over toward the center of the mattress with a Cheshire Cat grin on his face.

When Linc sat down cautiously beside him, Ryan caressed his

shoulders, then slid his hands sexily down the side of his V-shaped torso.

"Are sure I can't take off the *rest* of his clothes?" Ryan said, peering toward Maddy with a wrinkled forehead. "Because I'm pretty sure I'm not the *only* one in this room who'd like to see this stud fully uncovered."

"I suspect you're right about that," Madison said, glancing around the circle at the drooling women admiring Lincoln's muscular physique. "But rules are rules. It'll have to be just his pants."

"Pants it is," Ryan grinned, peering into Lincoln's flushed face with a devious smile.

As he began unbuttoning the handsome African-American's fly, I noticed the front of his jeans bulging, and when Ryan pulled them down to his knees, his thick organ flopped out, pointing off to the side. Everybody could see the sinewy muscles and ligaments of his lightly shaved mound above his caramel-colored, semi-erect dick, and I was sure they were all thinking the same thing.

"Shit," Lily hissed next to me. "Why do the *gay* guys have all the fun?"

"Something tells me it's not just the gay guy who's going to enjoy this little episode," I said, noticing Linc's dark dick slowly lengthening and rising as Ryan cupped his balls and tickled the curly black hair over his pubis.

As he continued to tease Linc around the base of his penis with the tips of his fingers, Lincoln's organ continued to rise until it was standing straight up, extending two full inches above his navel.

"Oh my God," Lily gasped, staring at Linc's flapping totem. "How will he even get his lips around that thing?"

"I'm pretty sure Ryan's had his share of well-equipped lovers," I nodded. "Just watch and enjoy."

When Linc's cock had reached its fully engorged length, Ryan wrapped his two hands around his soda-can-thick shaft and pulled the skin down, exposing his huge, bulging crown under his foreskin. He took a moment to admire Lincoln's impressive package, then he lowered his head to suck on the glistening bulb like a boy with a lollypop. Linc closed his eyes and tilted his head back, trying to conceal his growing pleasure.

"I wonder what it feels like to get head from a man for the first time?" Lily said, squirming excitedly on the floor.

"I dunno," I smiled. "But from the looks of things, this isn't the first time he's fantasized about it."

"Well, they say everyone's at least a *little* bit bi," Lily nodded.

"I think *any* red-blooded dude would turn gay for a moment if they could get their hands on that magnificent piece of meat."

While Ryan rolled his tongue expertly around the rim of his partner's erection, Linc slowly raised his body up onto his knees, pressing his hips further forward toward Ryan's face. Recognizing the signal that he was enjoying his ministrations, Ryan slowly lowered his lips over Lincoln's pole until he engulfed it all the way down to the base.

"Holy *fuck*," Lily grunted. "How can he even do that? That thing must be halfway down his throat!"

"Most gay guys learn how to relax their throat muscles when they go down on their partners. It's really just a matter of learning how to control your gag reflex."

"I don't see how I wouldn't gag on that firehose. He'd fairly rip me apart with that giant dagger."

"I guess it's a good thing you weren't chosen as his partner then," I chuckled. "Because something tells me Ryan's about to put on a master's class for giving head."

When Ryan swallowed the whole length of Lincoln's dick, Linc placed his hands over the back of his head and looked down, thrusting his hips hard against Ryan's face. I smiled knowing Linc had probably never received a blow job like this before, and his eyes flared while he bucked Ryan's face like a wild animal. Ryan reached around his back to grab his powerful flexing buttocks, and Lincoln began grunting more loudly, getting ready to empty his load down Ryan's throat.

But just as he was about to erupt, Ryan lifted his head off Lincoln's cock and grinned up at him while Linc gazed back with a puzzled look. Ryan didn't say a word, then flipped over onto his back while he straightened his dick under his tight jeans as he peered up at Lincoln's tight balls and sweaty crack.

"I want you to fuck me *this* way," Ryan said, smiling up at the muscular Adonis.

"*Fuck* you?" Linc said, pinching his eyebrows together. "How do you mean?"

"The same way you were before, just from a different angle," Ryan said. "This way, you'll be fully in control."

Ryan tilted his head back, then opened his mouth as wide as he could, nodding for Lincoln to insert his dick in his mouth. Linc peered at his unusual position for a moment, then he spread his legs further apart and pointed his instrument into Ryan's willing mouth, slowly inserting it deeper and deeper while Ryan relaxed his throat. Within seconds, he'd inserted his entire length down Ryan's gullet as he began humping his face, watching his partner eagerly swallowing his manhood.

"Holy fuck!" Lily gasped next to me. "I've never seen anything like that before."

"Welcome to the world of gay sex," I chuckled, watching Ryan's hips dry-humping the air while Lincoln skull-fucked his head.

Linc leaned forward and placed the palms of his hands beside Ryan's hips, watching Ryan's erect dick bulging under his pants, then he looked up, peering in Madison's direction.

Madison paused for a moment as if reading his mind, then she nodded quietly. While Ryan continued rocking his hips, Linc unbuttoned his jeans to free his straining hard-on, and when it popped up, Lincoln lowered his head without hesitation to suck on his head voraciously. He couldn't take as much of Ryan's dick as was being reciprocated on the other end, but with Ryan's smaller penis, he was able to get at least half of it in his mouth.

"It seems like Lincoln likes dick more than he's let on," Lily smiled.

"Like you said," I nodded. "Everybody turns a little bit bi when the right opportunity presents itself."

As I glanced around the circle at the rest of the group, I noticed virtually every guy had their hands down their pants, rubbing their hard cocks while the women seemed just as turned on, circling their clits. Even *Madison* seemed aroused by the spectacle, rubbing her wet crotch as she watched the two men sixty-nining one another.

It didn't take long for them to approach the height of their pleasure while they pounded each other's faces, and as they began to hump each other harder and faster, their moaning grew progressively louder until they both grunted loudly, pressing their dicks hard against each other faces. When Lincoln came, his buttock muscles contracted tightly as he rammed his spear balls-deep against Ryan's chin while Ryan moaned in delirious pleasure, emptying his own burgeoning load into Lincoln's moaning mouth.

After they both finished climaxing, Lincoln pulled his dripping tool out of Ryan's mouth and zipped up his pants, nodding silently to his partner. When they both returned to their previous places in the circle, you could hear a pin drop in the room while everybody stared at the two of them with equally flushed faces, utterly awestruck at what they'd just witnessed.

6

"Like I said," Madison interjected after a few seconds, breaking the awkward tension in the room. "Things were going to get a little more interesting the further we moved along. I don't know about the *rest* of you guys, but that was one of the hottest things I've ever seen. Kudos to both men for showing us how much fun two people can have when they let their guard down a few inches."

"I think it was more than just a *few* inches," Bonnie chuckled, still staring at Linc's bulging jeans.

"Who's ready to push it one step further?" Madison smiled.

Everyone raised their hands and she tossed them a new card, and this time Marco displayed the high number while Bonnie held the lowest.

"Mmm," Madison hummed. "We haven't had any boy-on-girl kissing yet. Looks like you're going to be the one in charge this time, Marco. What body part of Bonnie's would you like to kiss?"

Marco peered toward Bonnie and she smiled back at him, slowly spreading her legs apart.

"It seems we've missed one body part so far," he said, staring at the wet spot in her crotch. "If Bonnie's game, I'd love to give her pretty kitty some oral attention."

"What do you say, Bonnie?" Madison said, turning toward her sexy friend.

"I thought he'd *never* ask," Bonnie chuckled, running her eyes over Marco's slender, athletic physique.

When they joined together in the middle of the mattress, they sat upright on their knees facing one another, staring into each other's eyes. Marco leaned forward a few inches and angled his head, pretending to kiss her softly. While she closed her eyes awaiting his touch, the other women squirmed uncomfortably, wishing they were the ones on the opposite side of the handsome Latino's sensuous caresses.

"I hope you're not going to tease me like this when you go further down," Bonnie panted, opening her eyes to glare at Marco in mock outrage. "Because it's not going to work if you just stare at me and *breathe* on me the entire time."

"We'll have to see about that," Marco smiled, reaching down to unbutton her jeans.

As he lowered her zipper, she tilted her head upward, and Marco blew softly on her neck. While he tugged gently on her jeans, she rocked her hips from side-to-side, until they dropped down to the bottom of her knees. Marco placed one hand behind her back and slowly lowered her onto the mattress, then he gently pulled her pant legs down over her ankles, one at a time.

"This guy's obviously had some practice doing this before," Lily said, breathing heavily next to me.

"It looks like he's in no hurry to get down to business," I nodded, feeling my own panties dampening while I watched his sexy display of foreplay.

"Slow is good," Lily panted. "Especially with a Valentino like that doing the kissing."

After Marco pulled Bonnie's jeans down over her feet, he spread her ankles apart then kneeled between her legs, slowly sliding his palms up over the top of her trembling legs. When he reached the bottom of her panties, he threaded his thumbs under the lower seam, sliding them up along the crest of her hipbones, pausing when he reached the waistband. But instead of pulling them down over Bonnie's writhing hips, he leaned forward to kiss her stomach softly, nibbling on the waistband with his teeth as he pulled it teasingly away from her skin.

"Yes," Bonnie cooed, mesmerized by his expert technique. "Pull my panties off with your teeth. I want to feel your soft lips on my pussy."

But instead of pulling off her briefs, he slid the tip of his tongue under the waistband, sliding it toward the edges of her hips, dampening it with his warm saliva.

"Fuck yeah," Lily grunted, pressing her fingers under the front of her pants. "Those aren't the *only* panties he's making wet right now."

"I'm pretty sure *every* woman in this room is moist watching this guy work his magic," I nodded, squirming along with the rest of the girls while I watched the curly locks on the back of Marco's head while he teased Bonnie with his tongue.

As he pulled her panties ever-lower with his teeth, he swiped his thick stubble over the smooth surface of her shaved pubis while she raised and rocked her hips against his face, practically begging him to plant his mouth over her aching pussy. When he finally revealed the slit at the base of her mound, all the men in the room groaned, adjusting their hardening dicks as they watched Bonnie writhing on the mattress.

"I hope all those other guys are taking some cues from this Casanova," Lily groaned. "Because if they were even half as good at pleasing a woman as he is, they'd have a steady stream of them breaking down their doors in no time."

"Madison wasn't kidding when she said we were going to pick up a few pointers for spicing up our love life," I nodded. "I've already picked up a bunch of new moves I want to try out on my next lover."

After Marco pulled Bonnie's panties down below her knees, he gently raised each of her feet, pulling her panties off her legs, one leg at a time. Then he placed her undergarment on the mattress beside her feet and slowly raised her knees, shifting his body closer toward her junction. With Bonnie now exposing her dripping pussy inches from his face, he leaned down, kissing his way slowly up the inside of her thighs.

But instead of moving toward her apex, he kissed around the edges of her pussy, breathing in her sweet musk while gently pressing her legs further apart. By the time her knees were up around the sides of her chest, her flaring snatch was gaping wide open, dripping rivers of lubrication down over her perineum and under the crack of her ass.

"Jesus Christ," Lily panted next to me. "If he doesn't start sucking that pussy soon, I'm going to go over there and do it *for* him."

"All in due course, my dear," I smiled. "Most of the fun is in the journey, not in the destination."

"Tell that to poor Bonnie. She's likely to burst a gasket if he doesn't stem that hemorrhage pretty soon."

As if reading her mind, Marco tilted his body down and lowered his face to the base of Bonnie's slit, lapping up her juices with the flat side of his tongue like he was licking the side of a dripping ice cream cone. When his tongue passed over the top of her flaring bulb, she groaned, tilting her hips upward, begging him to suck her harder.

But he seemed determined to build up her tension before focusing on her glistening fruit, poised at the top of her folds like a ripe apple waiting to be plucked. While everyone rubbed their crotches staring at her flaring gash, Bonnie rolled and rocked her hips, begging Marco to take her into his mouth. By the time he finally pursed his lips and placed it over her burning gland, she'd already reached the peak of her excitement. When he began sucking her jewel and rolling his tongue over the nub with gentle figure-eight motions, she grabbed his ears, pulling him harder toward her dripping snatch.

"Fuck, yes," she groaned. "Suck my clit, Marco. I'm going to come so hard in your mouth. I haven't been kissed like this in such a long time."

Marco simply nodded softly while keeping a steady rhythm on

her nub as she raised her hips higher and higher over the surface of the mattress. He placed his hands under her buttocks to help support her weight, and when she finally came, her hips buckled wildly while she screamed at the top of her lungs.

"Yes," she howled. "Suck me, baby. I'm coming in your beautiful mouth. Oh God, you know how to make love to a woman. *Ngahh!"*

While Bonnie came hard in Marco's mouth, I noticed all the other men and women around the circle groaning along with her as Lily flapped her knees against mine, jerking her body in simultaneous pleasure. By the time everyone finished groaning in mutual ecstasy, I was sure Madison's neighbors would be calling the cops by now, wondering just what kind of moral degeneracy was going on inside her darkened living room.

7

"Now *that's* how to make love to a lady," Madison smiled after Marco and Bonnie returned to their places. "Who else feels like adding Marco's number to the speed dial on their phones?"

When every woman's hand shot up, Madison chuckled while shuffling the cards in preparation for the next round.

"We still have a few guests that haven't participated yet," she said, peering over in Lily's and my direction. "Here's hoping we can get the *rest* of you as well stimulated before the evening is over."

She flipped the cards one at a time around the circle, and when everyone revealed their number, this time Emma held the high card and I held the lowest one.

"Mmm," Madison smiled. "I've been waiting for this match-up all night. Have you decided which of Jade's body parts you'd like to kiss this time, Emma?"

Emma peered over toward me, and I grinned, reading her mind. Ever since our all-girls' camping trip last summer, I'd been dying to have the pretty coed back in my arms and under my hips.

"As much as I'd love to kiss every inch of her sexy body," Emma said, running her eyes over my figure. "There's one spot that I've been fantasizing about most of the night."

"Well, if you two want to take your positions on the mattress," Madison nodded. "I'm sure I'm not the only one excited to watch a woman make love to another woman."

After Emma and I crawled onto the mattress, she sat behind my back, curling her legs gently around my hips. I could feel her cool breath on the nape of my neck, and as she brushed my hair to the side and began kissing me softly, I felt goose bumps rising on my skin. She technically hadn't yet revealed which body part of mine she wanted to focus on, and I smiled watching the rest of the group peering at us with a curious expression as Emma softly caressed the back of my neck.

But as she began kissing me slowly down the center of my spine, she pushed me further and further forward, until my shoulders were resting on the floor with my ass pointing up toward her face. As she began unzipping my jeans and pulling them down my legs, at first, I thought she intended to focus on my anus. But as she pulled my pants further down toward my knees while kissing my buttocks, I leaned further forward, tilting my dripping pussy up toward her face.

She paused for a moment, staring at my glistening snatch, then she rolled over onto her back, sliding her face under my splayed legs and resting her head in the cradle of my bunched-up jeans. While she peered up at me from between my legs, I smiled at her, running my fingers through her soft, corkscrew hair. As she turned her head to kiss the insides of my slippery thighs, I slowly lowered my steaming pussy onto her beautiful rosebud lips.

When I felt my vulva make contact with her mouth, I gasped, remembering what it felt like to touch her for the first time in the privacy of our two-person tent up at the lake. Emma nibbled on my outer labia for a few minutes, pinching me teasingly between her front teeth, and I groaned watching her pretty face buried in my warm snatch. While she licked and nibbled me closer toward my burning clit, I tilted my hips forward, resting the crack of my ass over her chin.

I glanced around the circle, noticing the rest of the group stimulating themselves once again, then I peered back at Emma and smiled.

"Yes, baby," I purred, stroking her hair. "Kiss me the special way you do. Let's show these guys how to properly go down on a girl."

Emma nodded, then reached around the sides of my hips to pull my crotch harder down toward her face. I tried spreading my legs further apart, but the jeans bunching around my knees restricted my movement, so I sat further back, pressing my dripping cunt harder onto her face. When she felt my hard pubis pressing against her jaw, she retracted her lips while I rubbed my hardening clit against her teeth.

At first, I was happy to hump her face as my pleasure continued to build, but before long I wanted to feel her lips on my clit, and I raised myself up a few inches to let her peer at my erect gland. While I rolled my hips tantalizingly above her raised head, she tried to lick me with her tongue, but instead I held my snatch barely out of reach, dripping my juices onto her face.

She smiled back at me, rolling her tongue around the edges of her mouth, then she pulled my hips back down over her face, sucking my hard nub into her mouth. While she slathered my bean with her tongue, I clenched my fists in her hair, leaning further forward, pressing my weight harder down onto her. Since we'd done this before, she didn't panic, instead, threading her hands upward under my brassiere to squeeze my breasts as I began to rock my hips harder against her glistening face.

Somehow, she looked even prettier with my shiny lubrication coating her rosy cheeks, and as I moved ever closer to a climax, I smiled watching the rest of the group jerking and jilling themselves while they watched Emma eating my cunt.

"Shall we give them a little extra surprise for their viewing pleasure?" I whispered to Emma, humming happily as she lapped up my juices.

She nodded and I waited for just the right moment, then when I passed over the point of no return, I lifted my hips six inches above her head, gushing hard jets of fluid all over her blinking eyelashes. There was something incredibly erotic about cumming all over her pretty face, and while I grunted in delirious pleasure a few feet above her, she groaned in unison with me, enjoying my impromptu shower almost as much as I did.

8

When I returned to my place in the circle, I didn't even bother pulling up my pants, soaked as they were from my drenching orgasm. Instead, I placed my wet clothes on the floor beside me, crossing my legs while I peered back at the rest of the group with a bare midriff.

"Alright then," Madison said, adjusting herself distractedly at the foot of the mattress. "I'd say that gives a whole new meaning to the expression *wet kiss*. Why don't we all take another short break while I change the sheets? I think we've got time for one final round."

While she changed the bed linens, Lily and I chatted casually, awaiting the next pairing.

"It seems everyone's had a turn on mattress except *me*," she frowned. "My chances aren't looking good."

"I dunno," I said, watching Maddy collecting the cards. "It's funny how Madison seems to be picking us off one at a time. I think maybe she's holding a few cards up her sleeve."

After everybody resumed their positions, Madison paused as she peered around the circle.

"It's certainly been an interesting night," she smiled. "What do you guys think? Have you picked up a few extra kissing techniques this evening?"

"Damn right," Lily said. "I just wish I could experience it *first-hand* like the rest of the group."

"If you play your cards right," Madison said, reshuffling the deck in her lap. "You might still have a chance."

She tossed everyone a new card, and when Lily picked hers up, I peered over her shoulder, noticing she held an ace of hearts.

"Looks like you got your wish," I smiled.

"Yeah," she nodded. "Now I just have to decide whether I want to give or receive."

When everyone else showed their cards, this time it was Shae who had the lowest number.

"You said you wanted the roles *reversed* earlier," I said, watching Shae eyeing Lily up while she squirmed excitedly on the floor. "Here's your chance to give her girl cock a little extra oral love."

"Okay," Madison said, peering at everyone's card. "It looks like Lily holds the high card and Shae has the lowest. And because you have an ace, you get to choose whether to give or receive this time, Lily. Have you decided how you'd like to play this turn?"

"Um-hmm," Lily nodded, staring at Shae's crotch in her tight jeans. "But I'd like to keep it as a surprise until we come together on the mattress."

"Works for me," Maddy smiled, turning toward Shae. "How about you, Shae? Are you ready for a no-holds-barred final round?"

"I'd have it no other way," Shae winked. "With my special set of features, I'd rather Lily wait to view my buffet before taking her first bite."

When the two women crawled to the center of the circle, they kissed softly for a few moments, then Lily pressed Shae down onto the mattress, kneeling over her in a sixty-nine position while she began to unbutton Shae's pants. When she pulled them down over her hips and Shae's large cock sprung out, some of the participants gasped, not realizing the pretty girl was actually transgender.

While Lily dragged her jeans down over the bottom of her legs, Shae dry-humped her stomach, squeezing Lily's ass from behind. Lily placed her hands under Shae's knees and bent them up softly, then she leaned down to lick the tip of Shae's dripping dick with the end of her tongue. Shae groaned and lifted her hips off the mattress, and Lily lowered her head, tracing a line down the underside of Shae's instrument with her tongue.

When she planted her face between her thighs, we heard a strange slurping sound, and everybody peered at one another with a surprised expression. But it didn't take long for the enigma to be revealed, as Lily slowly pulled Shae's knees toward her, tilting her hips upward to reveal her glistening gash. Instead of the usual testicles nestled under her cock like most transgender she-males, Shae was a true hermaphrodite, with a fully functioning set of both male and female sex organs.

As Lily curled her hips further forward and lifted her ass higher off the mattress, Shae spread her legs wide apart, revealing her bouncing hard-on and her dripping vulva for the whole room to see. Everybody groaned at the incredible sight of the sexy ladyboy displaying her bifunctional sex organs, and it didn't take long for them to pull off the rest of their underclothes and begin stimulating themselves unabashedly while they watched Lily kissing and sucking Shae's perineum.

Although Lily was technically kissing more than one body part, Madison didn't seem to mind, pulling her own pants down to the bottom of her knees while trilling her pussy as she took in the erotic show with the rest of us. When Lily pulled Shae's upturned ass further toward her, she licked her tongue along the full length of her slit, teasing her until she reached her pink pucker. Without any hesitation, she rolled her tongue along the outside of the rim, flicking the tip into her crevasse while Shae moaned and rocked her hips in delirious pleasure.

I wasn't sure if Lily knew exactly what she'd gotten herself into when she started this match-up, but from the look of the huge wet spot in the crotch of her jeans, she was apparently just as turned on as the rest of us, jerking and trilling ourselves as we watched the two lovers curled up in an upright sixty-nine position.

While Lily continued to rim Shae's sphincter with the tip of her tongue, she reached under her hips with her right hand and grasped Shae's dripping cock in her fist, jerking her off while licking and teasing her slit. Shae grabbed Lily's ass perched above her head, and reached around, beginning to unbutton her jeans. Lily shimmied her hips to help her pull her pants down, then she lifted each of her knees to allow Shae to pull them all the way off her legs.

By now, everybody's lower body was fully exposed, including my own while we shamelessly rubbed and fingered ourselves in a fever pitch of excitement. The sight of the two women licking each other's pussies was impossible to resist, especially with Shae's big phallus dangling between her legs. Although they had both far exceeded the game rules by touching more than the one target area, nobody including Madison seemed to mind as we groaned and panted along with them in simultaneous pleasure.

While Lily squirmed over Shae's face, pumping her dick with her right hand, she continued to lick and tease her dripping vulva and flaring sphincter with her tongue. It didn't take long for both women to begin squealing and grunting in mounting pleasure, and as they approached their climax, I peered around the circle, noticing the rest of the group gaping their mouths open in escalating pleasure, teetering on the edge of their orgasms.

When Shae started to shake her legs and her big dick began to squirt thick ropes of cum down over her stomach, no one could hold back any longer as Lily and the rest of us began jerking and convulsing in mutual ecstasy. I noticed even Madison hunched over, jerking heavily as she peered ahead at the erotic sight of the two women kissing and sucking one another in unbridled passion.

Jesus, I thought after everyone finally came down from their highs, slumping forward in exhaustion. *How will Madison ever top this wild and exciting party?*

But something told me this wouldn't be the last of her sex parties, and my pussy twitched at the thought of what she might have in store for us next time...

BOOK 47

PLEDGE WEEK

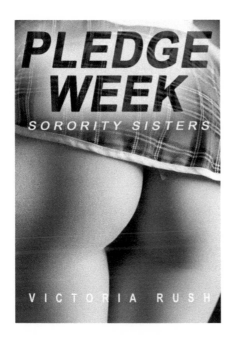

1

When Abby drove onto the campus of Emory University with her parents, her eyes widened in wonder. With tall stately buildings, lush mature trees, and broad open courtyards, it seemed a world away from her boring suburban subdivision on the outskirts of Chicago. As she watched the young students strolling across the grounds, her heart skipped a beat, realizing this would be her first time living away from her parents.

Home-schooled since she was a child, she'd chosen Emory partly because of its Christian Methodist roots, but also because it was far enough away for her to stretch her legs and gain a degree of newfound independence. As much as she'd enjoyed being spoiled as an only child, she was eager to experience the world outside her cloistered home life.

When the car pulled up in front of the Alpha Sigma Chi sorority house, she peered through her window at the large Victorian mansion. A group of girls wearing cut-off jeans were sitting together on the front steps, and when Abby opened her side door, the heavy Georgia humidity hit her like a ton of bricks.

"Wow," she said, pulling her light cashmere sweater away from her sweaty skin. "It looks like I've overdressed."

Abby's father got out of the other side of the car, circling around to the trunk to remove Abby's heavy travel bag.

"I'm not so sure about that," he said, wrinkling his forehead at the scantily clad girls lounging on the steps. "I think you're dressed just fine for the occasion. Remember your upbringing. Just because you're leaving home doesn't mean you have to lower your moral standards."

"Yes, Daddy," Abby huffed, pulling her laptop bag out of the trunk.

"Let the poor girl breathe, Frank," Abby's mother said, glaring at her father with a disapproving stare. "She's just stepped foot on the campus, and you're already trying to smother her with your rules and expectations."

"Humpf!" Frank grunted as he limped toward the front steps carrying the heavy bag.

"Is this the Alpha Sigma Chi sorority house?" he said, pausing in front of the group of women.

"It's pretty hard to miss," one of the girls nodded, pointing up to the stylized symbols emblazoned over the eavestrough at the top of the house.

"It's all Greek to me," Frank muttered, shaking his head.

"This is our daughter Abby's first week on campus," Abby's mother said, stepping forward. "Can you point us toward her room?"

"Ah, yes, Abby," the girl said, rising up and walking down the steps while she peered at Abby's tight sweater hugging her curvy figure. "My name's Taylor and I'm the chapter president. If you follow me, I'll be happy to show you the way."

As Abby and her parents followed Taylor up the steps, Abby's pupils swelled staring at Taylor's tight round ass, barely concealed under her cut-off shorts. Everybody else in the house seemed similarly dressed, wearing either flip-flops or bare feet on the hardwood floor, skipping from one room to the next while chatting noisily with their roommates. As much as Abby had been looking forward to meeting boys on campus, her summer fling with the next-door neighbor Jade had opened her eyes to the pleasures of lesbian sex. By the time they got to her room, her tight jeans were already soaked in the crotch.

"You can drop your bags here," Taylor said, pointing into an open room with a bunk bed and two small desks. "Your roommate hasn't arrived yet, so you get your choice of the top or bottom bunk. I'll come around a little later to get you set you up with the first day's activities."

After Taylor disappeared upstairs, Abby slid her duffel bag under the lower bunk then placed her laptop bag on the desk closest to the window.

"She seems nice enough," Abby's mother said, looking out the window. "And your room has a nice garden view."

"It's a little more cramped than my room at home," Abby nodded. "But I think I can make it work."

There was an awkward silence as Abby's parents glanced at the empty walls, unsure how to say goodbye.

"Well, you don't need us hanging around any longer than necessary," Abby's mother said. "We'll let you unpack and meet some of the other girls. I'm sure you're eager to make new friends and get the lay of the land."

"Um, yes," Abby said, pulling open the lower window to bring some fresh air into the stifling room. "Thank you for bringing me all this way. You really didn't need to drive all the way from Chicago..."

"Nonsense," Abby's father said, wrapping his arms around Abby. "We couldn't send our baby girl off to college on an airplane."

"Be sure to drive safe on the way back," Abby smiled. "I'll send you a note in a few days to let you know how things are going."

"That would be helpful," Abby's father said. "And don't forget to keep your wits about you with all these oversexed boys running around campus. There's going to be a lot of temptations now that you're all alone."

"Yes, Daddy," Abby sighed, not ready to tell him she was far more likely to lose her innocence to her sexy housemates than some college stud. "I've got my sorority sisters to keep me protected from the big bad wolves."

After Abby finished unpacking her belongings, Taylor stuck her head in the door while she passed by in the hall.

"How does it feel to be a free woman finally?" she said, stepping into the room.

"A bit strange, actually," Abby smiled, turning around to face Taylor. "This is my first time on my own, or even at an independent school."

"Yes," Taylor said. "I remember reading in your sorority application that you were home schooled. It must be quite a leap, jumping from constant supervision to being on your own."

"Well, it looks like I won't be entirely on my own," Abby smiled, motioning to the empty upper bunk. "Plus, I've got all my sorority sisters to keep me company."

"You do indeed," Taylor said. "And it all starts tonight with the initiation ceremony. Everyone will be convening downstairs at eight p.m. to welcome you and the other freshmen into the club."

Abby paused for a moment as she appraised the college senior. Taylor had a thick shock of shimmering brown hair falling over her tight halter-top shirt hugging her large, pointed breasts. Her thin bra barely concealed her dark medallion-sized nipples, and her exposed belly button seemed to be practically begging her to lower her gaze toward her slender, tanned thighs.

"That seems like an unusual term for a group of first-year students in a sorority," she stammered.

"Oh, we've got plenty of other names for you," Taylor smiled. "Frosh, plebes, virgins. By the end of the night, I'm sure you'll have a much clearer picture of your role in the hierarchy."

"Virgins? Hierarchy?" Abby said, pinching her eyebrows. "It almost sounds like you'll be making blood sacrifices."

"Well, there will be sacrifices of a sort," Taylor grinned. "And maybe even a little shedding of blood. But not to worry, it will all be in good fun."

Taylor peered down at Abby's sweater, lingering longer than

usual at her upstanding tits, tightly harnessed by her old-fashioned bra.

"Though you might want to wear some more casual clothes to the event. Like a t-shirt and some shorts. It's likely to get a little messy..."

2

After Taylor left her room, Abby changed out of her cashmere sweater, pulling on her new Emory College t-shirt. She looked in the dressing mirror to compare her look to Taylor's, shaking her head at how artificial her breasts looked, constrained by her tight bra. When she removed her bra and pulled her t-shirt back over her shoulders, she nodded at how much sexier she appeared with her breasts hanging naturally. The outline of her nipples was concealed by the stenciled letters, but whenever she shifted position, her breasts rolled from side-to-side, creating a sensuous, airy feeling.

"Much better," she said, shaking her tits playfully while she smiled at herself in the mirror.

"Hello?" a girl said, tapping softly on the open door. "Is this Abby's room?"

"Yes," Abby said, turning away from the mirror and crossing her arms over her chest while her cheeks reddened in embarrassment.

"Taylor said I was bunking with you," the girl said, pulling two heavy suitcases behind her into the room. "Where should I put my stuff?"

"There's a dresser next to the bed," Abby nodded, motioning

toward a chest of drawers. "I've taken the first three drawers for my clothes, but there are extra shelves in the closet if you need some extra space."

"Thanks," the girl said, extending her hand toward Abby. "I'm Willow."

"Abby," Abby said, noticing how clammy her hand felt surrounded by her new roommate's fingers.

As Willow began to unpack her clothes, Abby checked out her slender but athletic figure. She looked to be about her height, but with more slender hips and small but perky breasts. Her auburn hair was tied up in a long, braided ponytail, and when she turned around, her braid swung around her neck, dangling sexily between the cleft in her cleavage. She had little freckles dotted over the bridge of her nose, and her emerald-green eyes reminded Abby of the pretty actress Emma Stone.

"Did you manage to find a spot for everything?" Abby said, feeling the warmth in her face from her attraction to the girl.

"Barely," Willow chuckled. "This place is a lot smaller than my room back home. I'm not used to sharing my space with anybody."

"Same here," Abby nodded. "But something tells me we'll be sharing more than just this small space before long."

Willow peered at the neatly pressed beds and squinted her eyes.

"Have you chosen which cot you'd like to sleep in?" she said.

"I can go either way," Abby grinned, making a thinly veiled reference to her lesbian leanings.

"Where are you from?" Willow said, collapsing onto the lower bunk to stake her claim.

"Chicago," Abby said, sitting on the desk chair opposite the bed. "Well, Naperville, officially. It's a suburb on the west side."

"Tulsa," Willow smiled, sitting back against the wall and propping up one knee. "Looks like we're both a long way from home."

Abby stole a brief glance between Willow's legs, noticing the camel toe produced by her tight jeans and a small wet spot in her crotch.

"I guess this will be our new home for the next eight months," she grinned.

"What does a girl do for food around here?" Willow said, leaning forward to break the escalating tension in the room. "I'm famished after the long drive from Oklahoma."

"The closest dining hall is a few blocks away," Abby said. "But I noticed a kitchen on the main floor. Maybe we can grab a quick bite before the initiation ceremony starts."

"Initiation?" Willow said, pinching her eyebrows. "What's that all about?"

"Your guess is as good as mine," Abby said. "All I know is that the sisters are meeting downstairs at eight p.m., and that the new pledges are expected to attend."

"Maybe we can get some details from the other girls," Willow said, jumping off her bunk. "Let's go check the place out."

When Abby and Willow entered the open-air kitchen, they saw a group of seniors sitting around a small table in the corner. The older girls peered at them for a moment, then returned to their idle chatter, ignoring the newcomers. Willow opened the large double-panel fridge and peered inside, noticing a stack of cardboard boxes with different food labels. She squinted at the labels, then turned around to address the group in the corner.

"How does this work, exactly?" she said to the girls. "Do we just grab whatever we find in the fridge, or is there some kind of procedure for ordering what we want?"

"If you're on the regular meal plan," one of the girls said, looking up briefly. "You're entitled to ten meals per week. Write your name on the box you want and our food coordinator will check it off the list."

Willow stuck her head back in the fridge and sorted through the boxes, noticing that almost every one already had a student's name scrawled on the outside.

"Beef stroganoff, chicken casserole, shrimp tempura..." she said. "Looks like all the good stuff is already taken."

Abby picked up two clear plastic containers containing pre-assembled salads.

"These two aren't taken yet," she said, pulling them out of the fridge. "Which do you prefer, the Cobb or the Caesar?"

Noticing that all the chairs around the small table were already occupied and that the seniors didn't seem interested in asking them to join their group, the two girls sat on the open stools facing the large kitchen island. While they nibbled on their salad, Willow's eyes flickered as she darted her eyes back and forth between the senior's table and theirs.

"Looks like we're going to be the junior members on the totem pole," she whispered to Abby.

"I suppose we have to earn our privileges around here," Abby nodded. "Kind of like being in the army."

"As long as we don't have to deal with a drill sergeant," Willow chuckled, peering at the head senior out of the corner of her eyes. "At least we have our own room to escape the icy stares of these sisters."

Abby munched on her salad for a few moments, then glanced back in the direction of the other group.

"How long have you guys been members of Alpha Sigma Chi?" she said, hoping to ease the friction in the room.

There was a long silence, then the girl who'd spoken first looked up.

"Three or four years, depending," she said.

"So, I suppose you know all the protocols by now," Abby nodded. "What does a girl do for fun around here? I mean, between all the trudging to classes and cramming for exams."

"We kind of make it up as we go," the girl said, grinning at her friends. "Starting with the first night of pledge week. That's always good for a few laughs."

"What does that involve exactly?" Abby said. "Taylor said it was likely to get a bit messy..."

The girl peered at her seat mates while they jiggled their shoulders in silent laughter.

"Let's just say you'll be wringing out more than the usual Atlanta humidity from your clothes before the night is over," the girl smiled.

As she lowered her head to continue eating her meal, the rest of the girls snickered while they peered up at Willow and Abby with sinister smiles.

"What the fuck?" Willow whispered to Abby, glancing at her with a worried expression.

"All I know is we're supposed to wear light clothes to the party," Abby said, shaking her head softly. "Maybe we'll be meeting your drill sergeant after all..."

3

———

As the hour for the initiation ceremony approached, Abby and Willow grew increasingly anxious about what they were getting themselves into. Heeding Taylor's warning, they both chose to go braless under their chest-hugging t-shirts, wearing torn jeans and slippers on their lower halves to protect their more expensive clothes. When they entered the dimly lit basement, they noticed a large wading pool filled with mud, where six girls stood in line as the rest of the seniors rested in beach chairs around the circle, sipping pina coladas.

"Now that we're all here," Taylor said, motioning for Abby and Willow to stand next to the other girls. "We can start the initiation process for our new pledges. As you all know, it's a great honor for someone to become a member of Alpha Sigma Chi. But in order to do so, they must first pass a sequence of tests to prove they're worthy."

Willow turned her head to glance at Abby with a worried expression, and Abby reached out to clasp her hand.

"Each of you will need to pass a series of progressively more difficult challenges," Taylor continued. "Only those who make it to the final challenge will be offered bids to join our organization."

She turned her head, nodding toward the muddy pit.

"Your first challenge is the mud wrestling ring. If any part of your body other than your feet touches the floor of the pit at any time, you'll be immediately disqualified."

There was a long pause while the eight pledges peered at one another, still unclear about the rules. Willow peered over her shoulder at the slick mud lining the pool, then slowly raised her hand.

"So do we just stand there trying not to fall?" she said.

"Of course not," Taylor grinned. "That would be far too easy. You need to fight to earn your position in the hierarchy. You're no longer babes under your parents' protection. Out here in the real world, only the strong survive."

The new girls looked at one another with wide eyes, afraid to step into the filthy pool.

"Well, what are you waiting for?" Taylor said. "Get in there and put your game face on. May the best woman win."

Abby kicked off her slippers and started rolling up the bottom of her stretchy jeans, glancing up at Taylor.

"What's the prize for the winner?" she said.

"The winner of each round will earn a special house privilege," Taylor said. "For this first round, the prize is first dibs on meal choices during your first week."

Following Abby's lead, the other girls pulled off their shoes and rolled up their pant legs, stepping gingerly into the tub as they spread out their arms to counterbalance their weight over the slippery surface. One of the girls quickly fell backwards onto her back, sending a spray of sticky mud up over the other girls' clothing. The seniors sitting around the perimeter cheered and raised their glasses, sipping their cocktails through their straws.

"Well don't just stand there," Taylor shouted at the girls. "The sooner you learn about the bell curve, the better. Only so many of you will earn high enough grades to move on to the next semester. Show us that you're worthy of moving on to the next round. Start demonstrating some initiative!"

The girls peered at one another for a moment, then they tentatively placed their hands on one another's shoulders, gently tugging and pulling on each other's bodies. As their feet began to swish around on the slippery floor, they spread their legs, hunching over to keep from falling.

"Seriously?" Taylor said, mocking the girls. "Is that the best you can do? You look like a bunch of toddlers learning to walk for the first time. You're in the school of hard knocks now. Stop acting like pussies, and start acting like Alpha Sigma Chi warriors!"

As the pledges began pushing and shoving each other more aggressively, the seniors around the circle egged them on, calling them names and encouraging them to fight dirty. When Abby twisted her body and sent her partner flying into the mud, another loud cheer rose from the group. She looked around her, noticing Willow struggling to stay on her feet while her larger partner grabbed her shirt, sliding her around the ring. Suddenly, another girl approached Abby from behind, trying to pull her backward, but Abby bent her knees to regain her balance, then she wrapped her arms around the other girl's waist, pulling her off her feet and dropping her with a loud splat into the mud.

Within a few minutes, there were only four of the original eight girls still standing. While Abby grunted and wrestled with her latest partner, she heard Willow squeal when her larger partner grabbed her ponytail, yanking her down into the mud.

"Hey!" she yelled, sliding her foot over her partner's, sending her toppling into the pit. "Why don't you pick on someone your own size?"

The girl peered at Abby's dirty t-shirt clinging to her braless torso and smiled.

"With pleasure," she sneered, lunging toward Abby as she side-stepped the bigger girl.

While the final two contestants grabbed each other's shirts and began sliding around the pit, the noise in the room reached a fever pitch as the seniors began shouting and egging the players on. Abby's opponent was at least six feet tall, with an athletic basketball player's frame, and the only way she could keep from falling was to grab onto her torn t-shirt for support.

But when the other girl squeezed Abby's swinging tits with her sharp fingernails, her eyes flared open in anger, and she grabbed the girl's arm, rolling her over her back as she flopped down into the sticky mud with the rest of the girls. When Abby turned around to face Taylor, heaving and panting in exhaustion and covered from head to foot in dripping mud, the seniors stood up out of their chairs, clapping enthusiastically.

"Well, that was a gladiator-worthy performance," Taylor nodded, smiling at Abby. "Congratulations on being the last woman standing. But now we need to get you girls cleaned up. We can't have you traipsing around the house looking like that. What do you say sisters, should we tidy these girls up now?"

"Absolutely," the senior from the kitchen smiled, placing her cocktail glass beside her chair.

"Would you like to have the honor, Reece?" Taylor said, smiling at the senior.

Reece walked to the opposite wall of the basement and lifted a hose curled up on the floor next to a plastic tarpaulin hanging on the wall, then she curled her finger toward the girls in the pit, signaling for them to join her.

"It's time to get you freshies washed up," she grinned. "Come over here so I can wash you down properly."

When the girls lined up in front of the tarpaulin, Reece adjusted the nozzle on her sprayer, then she squeezed the trigger, sending a strong jet of water toward the women. As they blinked and sputtered while she hosed each of them down, the rest of the sisters cheered and laughed, staring at their soaking clothes clinging to their shivering bodies. While Taylor walked up and down the line to inspect the group, Abby glanced down, noticing her nipples standing at attention as they darted the front of her clinging t-shirt.

"You poor babies," Taylor grinned, carrying a stack of neatly folded terrycloth robes. "You must be freezing in those wet clothes.

Who'd like an Alpha Sigma Chi robe as your prize for surviving the first challenge?"

While everybody nodded enthusiastically, Taylor took a step back, shaking her head.

"You can't very well put a dry robe over wet clothes, can you?" she grinned. "You're going to have to strip down if you want to move onto the next stage of your initiation."

The girls peered at one another for a moment, then they slowly pulled off their clothes, stepping into the soft robes while Taylor handed them out, wrapping them tightly around their bodies.

"Doesn't that feel much better?" Taylor said, peering at the logo of the sorority, prominently displayed over the left shoulder of each robe. "What do you say, sisters, do you think the girls are ready for the next phase of their initiation?"

"They seem to be suitably dressed for the occasion," Reece nodded, pulling eight armchairs into a straight line next to the dripping tarpaulin. "I think it's time we took a closer look at what these girls have to offer."

While the rest of the sorority seniors pulled their chairs up in front of the line of empty chairs, Taylor bent down to open the lid of a wooden chest lying on the floor, pulling out a battery-operated Magic Wand vibrator.

"This next test might be a little more difficult to resist," she smirked, staring at the naked legs of the eight dripping girls peering back at her with wide eyes.

4

"What do you expect us to do with those?" Abby said to Taylor.

"Oh, come now," Taylor smiled. "Don't tell me you've never used a vibrator before?"

Abby nodded, recognizing the Magic Wand device from her neighbor's bedside night table. After the two had shared a brief but intense summer fling while spying on each other through their adjacent bedroom windows, Jade had introduced her to her extensive toy collection.

"Well yes, but–" Abby said.

"You don't actually expect us to use those while the whole group is watching?" Willow interjected.

"Of course," Taylor grinned. "That's half the fun. Of course, the other half is what you'll experience while you're being watched."

Taylor bent down and pulled eight hand-held Magic Wands out of the chest, passing one to each of the girls. They paused for a moment, not yet ready to touch themselves in front of the other women, staring at the long, oversize instrument.

"Now, I know what you're thinking," Taylor said. "Some of you may not have ever used one of these before. You may not even have had sex in front of another person before. But let me assure you, it's a sublime experience using one of these magical devices. Nothing will get you off as quick or as hard as a Magic Wand."

"How does it work exactly?" a shy girl said.

"If you look at the handle," Taylor nodded. "You'll see three blue buttons. The one nearest the flexible head turns it on, the one in the middle adjusts the speed of the vibrations, and the one on the bottom changes the pulse pattern. Go ahead, turn yours on and experiment with the different settings."

The girls turned on their devices then they placed their hands over the vibrating head, widening their eyes.

"It's a little different from other vibrators you may have tried," Taylor said. "This one has more of a deep, rumbling vibration, as opposed to the soft buzz you may be used to. Try adjusting the speed and experimenting with the different patterns. I think you'll find it's quite a versatile device."

The girls moved their fingers to the adjacent buttons, and as they flicked the switches, the sound of the devices changed from a steady rumble to a pulsating drone, slowly ramping up and down in volume. As the loud buzzing echoed through the basement, some of the girls shifted their feet impatiently on the cold concrete floor, growing increasingly excited about touching their more sensitive areas.

"Pretty hot, huh?" Taylor smiled, noticing the red flush in their faces. "Of course, it's a lot more interesting when you feel it vibrating against certain other parts of your body."

"I don't know," the shy girl said, peering at the lineup of seniors sitting a few feet away in their beach chairs with their legs crossed. "This doesn't feel right..."

"Nobody's forcing you to do anything you don't want, Olivia," Taylor said. "This is a full-consent organization. If you don't want to have sex in front of other girls, we understand. Of course, I can't guarantee that you'll be offered a bid to join our sorority at the end of the process..."

"What are the rules?" Abby said, trying to take some of the pressure off Olivia. "If we decide to do this, how do we advance to the next round?"

"This one will be a timed contest," Taylor grinned, taking a large hourglass out of the chest. "If you can last fifteen minutes without coming using the vibrator, each of you will earn another privilege."

"How will you know if we come?" Willow said, shaking her head.

"Oh, we'll know alright, won't we girls?" Taylor smiled, looking over her shoulder at the lineup of seniors eagerly awaiting the start of the contest. "These spotters aren't here just to enjoy the show, but to keep a close watch for any sign of climax."

"And we can use any setting we want?" Abby asked.

"To start with," Taylor nodded. "But at various intervals, you'll be asked to ramp up the speed as we demand."

"What's the prize for the winner?" Willow said.

"You'll get your choice of dorm room for the next semester," Taylor smiled. "Except mine of course. That's reserved for the chapter president."

"And what happens if we can't stop ourselves from coming?" Abby said.

"You'll be punished appropriately," Taylor grinned. "But don't worry, it won't be anything too serious. You'll just have to submit to a different type of sex toy."

Abby peered into the toy box, noticing some large wooden paddles with the Alpha Sigma Chi symbols etched on the side.

"Are we allowed to cover ourselves up while we do this?" she said.

"You could, but then you could conceal your orgasm from the rest of us. You'll need to open your robes and place your feet on the edge of your chairs so we can watch. I think you'll find the experience quite liberating."

The girls peered at one another for a moment, then Abby cocked her head to one side and raised her eyebrows, smiling at Willow.

"I'm game if you are," she said.

"I suppose it can't hurt," Willow nodded.

"Oh, I think you'll experience a whole range of feelings before you're finished this exercise," Taylor grinned.

5

The girls sat down in their wooden armchairs and gently parted their robes. Abby stole a glance down the line, peering at each of their exposed pussies, noticing that everyone had a furry patch on her mound except herself. Some of the girls had trimmed their bush down to a narrow 'landing strip', but only Abby had a completely shaved, bald pussy.

Thanks, Jade, she grunted to herself, remembering how her neighbor had shaved her pussy while they shared a bath. Suddenly, she felt self-conscious as the only new girl in the group who'd obviously had sex with another partner.

"Very nice," Taylor said, pulling up a chair a few feet in front of Abby and Willow, who were sitting side-by-side in adjacent chairs. "Now, raise your legs and place your feet on the edge of your seats so we can see your pussies. Don't be shy, we all like to share at Alpha Sigma Chi."

The girls slowly raised their knees one leg at a time until they rested their feet over the edge, clasping their thighs tightly together to protect their modesty.

"Mmm," Taylor purred, turning her head slowly as she inspected the exposed vulvas of each girl. "Isn't it a beautiful sight, ladies? Every flower so pink and unique. Every petal a different shape, every pistil a different size. We should celebrate our unique features while we share our feminine beauty with our fellow sisters."

"Very pretty," Reece nodded, pulling her chair alongside Taylor's. "I can't wait to sink my teeth into some of this fresh meat."

"Okay, girls," Taylor smiled, turning over the hourglass and placing it on the table between her and Reece. "Now it's time for the fun part. Turn on your vibrators and see what it feels like to rub your pussy with something other than your finger."

Each of the girls pressed the On button on the side of their vibrators, then they slowly lowered them to the base of their mounds. Some of them jerked when they felt the powerful vibration rubbing against their private parts, while a few others moaned as they began to spread their legs apart.

"Yes," Taylor nodded. "Isn't it exquisite? Enjoy the sensation and try experimenting with the different settings. You'll notice the head of the wand is flexible, so you can press it as hard as you wish against your sensitive folds."

Since Abby already had experience using the Magic Wand with Jade, she knew exactly how to use it and where it would deliver the most pleasure. But she was determined not to succumb to Taylor's dare and resist the temptation to lose herself in the mounting pleasure beginning to radiate across her pelvis. As she lowered the pulsating knob below her tingling clit, she peered over at Willow, sitting next to her with her legs spread wide apart.

"Unghh," Willow moaned, holding the handle with two hands while she pressed the bending tip hard against her nub.

Abby peered at the sand falling through the middle of the hourglass, then she glanced back at her roommate.

"You're not going to last very long using that technique," she chuckled.

"I'm not sure I want to win this contest," she grunted. "It seems to me that the losers will be the ones having the most fun."

"Maybe," Abby smiled. "I didn't want to lose you as my roommate, anyhow."

"What about you?" Willow panted, sliding further down in her chair as her dripping juices began to pool on the seat between her legs. "You shouldn't fight it."

Abby could feel her clit throbbing as she watched Willow's face contorting, and she spread her legs wider apart until her knees touched Willow's at the side of their chairs, then she dragged the rumbling head up over her bulb.

"Mhhh," she groaned, watching Willow's nipples hardening.

"There now," Taylor purred, adjusting her position as she watched the eight pledges writhing in pleasure on their seats. Even Olivia seemed to have overcome her shyness, spreading her knees far apart for the whole group to see while she moaned and massaged her vulva with the big stick.

"Okay girls," Taylor said, noticing the sand in the hourglass passing the halfway point. "It's time to ramp up the pleasure. Tap the middle button to increase your vibration speed to the next level. Let's see which one of you has the most control."

When the girls turned their handles around and tapped their speed buttons, the buzzing sound in the room notched up a few decibels. The noise of their collective moaning rose in lockstep, and Abby peered down the line, noticing their knees flapping in and out while they twisted in their chairs.

"Fuck yes," Taylor groaned, reaching over to grab Reece's crotch over her jeans. "That's what I'm talking about."

"Something tells me this group is going to be one of our best yet," Reece nodded, raising her hand to pinch Taylor's nipples through her thin tank top.

Taylor glanced at the hourglass once again, realizing there was only a few minutes left before time ran out.

"You're doing great, ladies," she said. "But now it's time for the ultimate test. I want you to tap the speed button two more times to set it to the maximum intensity. And no cheating, you must place the vibrating head directly over your clits now. Let's see who has the right stuff."

While the buzzing sound in the room escalated to the level of a thousand cicadas, the girls began to moan more loudly as they quivered in their chairs.

"Oh God, oh God," Olivia grunted from the far end of the line. "I can't hold it any longer. Eeiee..."

Abby glanced in her direction and noticed her body jerking in hard spasms as she held her Magic Wand tightly between her legs with two hands while the seniors clapped and cheered in approval. Then, one by one, each of the other girls squealed and jerked violently in their chairs, unable to resist the mounting pleasure spreading over their hips. Willow was the second last one to come, staring at Abby's bald pussy as she groaned loudly, pressing her chin down hard against her chest while her mouth gaped open in ecstasy.

Abby tried to resist the urge to climax, but watching her pretty roommate's tits flushing and feeling her knees knocking against hers quickly put her over the edge. As she closed her legs and clenched her teeth, trying to conceal her contracting pussy, she suddenly jetted a hard stream of juices out of her opening, soaking Taylor and Reece, who were watching with rapt attention only a few feet away.

"Damn, Reece," Taylor sighed, wiping the droplets off her face. "Looks like we've got a ringer in our new class of recruits."

"Yeah," Reece groaned, pulling Taylor's hand harder against her wet crotch. "And I think I've selected my next candidate for the next round of the initiation..."

6

———————

"Well now," Taylor said after all the girls stopped quivering in their chairs. "It looks like none of you demonstrated the level of self-control expected of an Alpha Sigma Chi member. And for that, you'll need to be punished."

Taylor pulled the large paddles out of the chest and handed them to the seniors, who lined up in a row next to the chairs.

"Now you'll need to walk the gauntlet while your sisters teach you a lesson."

Abby peered at the seniors who were eagerly slapping their hands against their paddles, then glanced back at Taylor.

"You're going to hit us with those paddles?" she said.

"It's not like you've never been spanked before," Taylor smiled. "This is just the grown-up version of what your parents did to you when you were younger. It can be quite titillating, if you put yourself in the right frame of mind."

"How do you want us to do this, exactly?" Willow said. "Do we just walk down the line to accept our punishment?"

"Oh no," Taylor grinned, laying a padded mat on the floor in front of the seniors. "That would be far too simple. You need to assume the position of underclasswomen and crawl on your hands and knees through the gauntlet."

Willow peered at Abby with a surprised expression, and Abby frowned, shrugging her shoulders.

"It shouldn't be too bad," she said. "This will likely be the worst of it. We just need to suck it up to get through this."

"Right then," Taylor said. "Get in position at the front of the line, starting with Olivia and ending with Abby. Leave your robes on the chair."

Olivia pulled off her robe and walked up to the front of the line where Reece was waiting with a sinister sneer, then she kneeled down on the mat and Reece slapped her cheeks with a loud smack. She squealed and lurched forward on the mat, where the next senior paddled her ass. With each blow, her cheeks reddened deeper, until she scurried off the end of the mat, holding her stinging buttocks with both hands.

As each pledge kneeled down and received their punishment, Abby watched the look on the faces of the seniors, who seemed to take perverse pleasure in striking each of the girls harder than the last. When Willow lined up in front of her and bent down to expose her ass, Abby noticed her pussy glistening in excitement. As she waddled down the line on her hands and feet, rivulets of lubrication ran down the insides of her thighs, belying her arousal from the humiliating spectacle.

By the time it was her turn, Abby was at a fever pitch of excitement, her pussy already dripping from her powerful orgasm using the Magic Wand vibrator. When she bent down in front of Reece, the older sister walloped her butt hard enough to send her sprawling on the mat, while the rest of the seniors laughed and cheered. She pulled herself back up and slowly cat-walked down the line, biting her lips with each smack to her ass.

As much as each slap stung her skin, she found the experience strangely stimulating, reveling in the thought of all the girls watching her quivering ass and exposed pussy. When she reached the end of the line, Taylor issued the final blow, striking her low enough for her to feel the sting of the paddle on her throbbing vulva.

"There now," Taylor grinned when Abby stood up beside the rest of the girls, holding up her paddle to reveal the wet spot in the middle. "That wasn't so bad, was it? From the look of things, I'd say some of you actually enjoyed the experience."

"Not as much as you apparently," Abby grunted, sliding her hands over her burning cheeks.

"I have to admit," Taylor nodded. "It was kind of fun watching your tight butts shaking and wiggling while we slapped your asses. But it's not like each of us haven't experienced what it's like to be on the other end of the paddle. All of us went through the same initiation process as you girls, and we're the stronger for it."

"So, what now?" Willow said, massaging her sore red ass. "Are you going to tattoo us with the sorority letters to show that you own us?"

"That's not a bad idea," Taylor smiled, nodding toward her sorority sisters. "But I think we've already placed a strong enough mark on your bodies."

Then she reached into the chest on the floor and pulled out a harness with a long pink dildo attached to the front, dangling it in front of the girls.

"No, for this next ceremony, we'll be demonstrating that we own you in an entirely different kind of way."

7

"**Y**ou've got to be kidding me," Abby said, looking at Taylor with an incredulous expression.

"Oh, come now," Taylor said, stroking the end of the pink phallus with her fingers. "With that pretty shaved pussy of yours, don't tell me you've never been fucked with an artificial dick before?"

"Not one as big as that," Abby said, remembering how Jade and her had used a long English cucumber as an improvised double-dildo during their summer affair.

"I think you'll find this one is even better than the original," Taylor said, bending the dildo down then letting it snap back up in the harness. "Unlike a regular man's cock, this one stays hard until you've gotten all the pleasure you need."

"And what's the prize if we survive this contest?" Abby said.

"You'll have your choice of administrative role in the house. The job of social director is up for grabs this year. You might even have a chance to plan the activities for the next initiation ceremony if you're lucky."

Abby's pussy suddenly pulsed at the thought of introducing some new games at the next ceremony. Her experience with her older lover had taught her there was a new world of wonders having sex with another woman, and she reveled at the thought of teaching the new girls some of the things she'd learned.

"Is there any particular way you want us to do this?" Willow said, staring at the oversize dildo with wide eyes. "I mean, position-wise?"

"Just like with a regular cock," Taylor nodded, "you can get fucked in pretty much any position with one of these things. But the sisters will undoubtedly want to demonstrate their dominant position in ladder. In this case, you'll be kneeling on your chairs while they take you from behind."

"When will we know when it's finished?" Abby said. "It's not like that thing ends with a bang like a regular cock."

"Actually," Taylor smiled. "These particular dildos have a built-in feature that a regular boy's doesn't."

She flicked a button at the base of the phallus and suddenly the dildo started shaking in her hand.

"Just like the vibrators you used in the last exercise," she said, "this one also rattles. Except this time, both you and your partner will have a chance to reach the peak of pleasure."

Olivia shuffled her feet anxiously, crossing her arms over her bare chest while she furrowed her brow.

"What if we've never..."

"Been fucked before?" Taylor smiled. "Well then, you're in for a treat. Getting fucked by a woman is an entirely different experience. We know what a woman likes, and when to be gentle and when to be rough. Just lay back and enjoy the experience. You seemed to like the last one plenty enough."

"What if some of us aren't ready to lose our virginity this way?" Abby said, mindful of the relative inexperience of the other girls.

"You can always say no," Taylor nodded. "If you don't want to participate, we will abide by your wishes. Of course, I can't guarantee–"

"Yeah, yeah," Abby interrupted, knowing what Taylor was going to say. "You can't guarantee we'll be accepted into the sorority. You sure have a funny way of showing your affinity with your sisters."

"What better way than joining together in carnal delight?" Taylor grinned. "We're just getting started. Wait until you attend one of our slumber parties as a full member. There's more than one reason our sorority is called ASX."

"So I'm beginning to see," Abby smiled.

"Alright then," Taylor nodded. "Let's get this next ceremony started. It's only fair that the other the sisters have a chance to enjoy themselves as much as you have so far. It's time to climb up on your chairs and assume the position."

The pledges looked at one another for a moment, then they slowly crawled onto their chairs, placing their knees on the edge of the seat and their hands over the backrest for support.

"Who wants first dibs on the fresh meat?" Taylor said, pulling some more strap-on dildos out of the chest.

Seven sisters quickly stepped forward, including Reece, who moved behind Abby to stake her claim while she fastened the harness around her hips. Taylor strapped the last one over her hips, then positioned herself behind Willow, standing next to Reece.

"Are you sure you girls are ready?" she said, peering down the line of upturned bare asses. "This is your last chance to withdraw if you still want to protect your virginity."

There was a long pause in the room, then Reece began slapping her dildo against the side of Abby's ass, making a loud smacking sound.

"Let's see if we can prime that pump for some more action," she grunted, grabbing the end of the buzzing dildo and sliding it slowly up and down Abby's dripping lips. "I want to see you gush all over my dick while I watch you come this time."

When she thrust her phallus deep into Abby's hole, the chair tilted forward, and Abby had to push back to counterbalance her shifting weight.

"Yes, baby," Reece hissed as she began to pound Abby's ass. "Sink my cock into your pretty cunny. You've got the sweetest ass I've seen in a long time."

This wasn't the first time Abby had felt a vibrator inside her pussy, nor the first time she'd been on the receiving end of a strap-on dildo. But it was definitely the first time she'd been fucked in front of this many women and the first time she'd witnessed other girls her age having sex for the first time. As she glanced down the line of chairs, she peered at the expressions on the girls' faces while they got pounded from behind with their vibrating penises. As their bodies rocked back and forth and their chairs slid noisily on the wet concrete floor, their faces flushed while they groaned loudly, obviously enjoying their first experience with lesbian sex.

"Holy fuck," Willow grunted next to me. "Taylor wasn't kidding when she said this is better than being fucked with a regular cock. I only wish all my boyfriends' dicks could vibrate like this."

"Oh yeah?" Taylor groaned behind her. "You like getting fucked by a chick? There's a lot more where this comes from. Now hold still while I come in your sweet pussy. I'm getting close..."

Abby glanced behind her, noticing the reddening faces of the seniors plowing their dildos into their charge's asses. It was obvious the vibration from the strap-on dildos was stimulating their pussies as much as their partners, and as they grabbed the girls' asses with their curling fingers, their mouths began to yawn open as they approached orgasm.

"Fuck, yes," Reece grunted behind Abby, digging her fingers harder into her ass. "I'm going to come so hard in your pussy. Let me see you spray your juices all over my balls when you come."

It was obvious that Reece was getting overly excited channeling the role of a man fucking the new girl, and Abby was getting just as turned on by the sights and sounds of the women groaning in tandem while the eight chairs rocked and squeaked on the floor.

"Oh fuckkk," Willow growled next to Abby, gripping the back of her chair tightly with her fingers. "Come with me, Abby. I want to feel you shaking next to me again."

"Yes, Willow," Abby groaned, feeling the pressure inside her releasing like a dam.

As she clamped down over Reece's dildo and curled her hips forward, her legs started quivering as she sprayed a waterfall down the inside of Reece's legs. When Reece felt her coming, she rammed her dick as hard as she could against Abby's shaking ass, pressing the base of the dildo hard against her twitching clit.

"Oh gawd," she hissed, hunching over Abby's back as her legs trembled in the midst of the most powerful orgasm she'd experienced in a long time. "We have got to do this more often."

"With the new girls, you mean?" Taylor gasped, clasping Willow's ass as she also started coming. "Or with the rest of the sisters?"

"I don't care," Reece panted, reaching around to squeeze Abby's swinging tits. "As long as I get to play the role of the man."

8

"There, now," Taylor said, peering down the line of bent-over girls still quivering from their powerful orgasms. "Are your asses feeling a little better now?"

"Mmm," Olivia purred.

"I'm sure our fraternity brothers will appreciate our breaking you in for them," Taylor smiled. "But this initiation ceremony is all about celebrating our sisterhood. And there's still quite a few sisters who haven't had their turn sharing in the spoils."

"What more could we possibly do?" Abby said. "Haven't you humiliated us enough already?"

"There's still many more ways you can demonstrate your worth to the club," Taylor grinned, peering over her shoulder at the other seniors. "Isn't that right, ladies?"

"Damn straight," one of them said, stepping out of her jeans and pulling off her panties.

"For this next phase of the ceremony," Taylor continued. "You'll demonstrate your sexual talent using a different part of your body. This time it will be the seniors sitting in the chairs while you pay homage with your tongues."

Six naked sisters stepped forward, taking the place of the girls on the chairs, spreading their knees wide apart to expose their glistening vulvas. As the pledges knelt before them, Taylor and Reece took the final two positions, with Abby and Willow positioned in front of them.

"It looks like some sisters have more privileges than others," Abby smiled, peering up at Taylor.

"Privileges are earned at our sorority," Taylor nodded, running her fingers through Abby's hair. "The more experience you gain, the higher everybody rises in the pecking order."

"So, what privilege do we earn for completing this exercise?" Willow asked.

"If you do a good enough job servicing us, each of you will earn a hundred house points, which you can use as credits toward meal plans and other prizes."

"Who decides if we've done a good enough job?" Abby said.

"Those on the receiving end, of course," Taylor smiled.

"What if we don't have experience doing this sort of thing?" Olivia said, peering at her partner's dripping vulva with bulging eyes. "I've never been with a girl this way–"

"Surely you've had plenty of practice touching yourself?" Taylor said. "The only difference is that this time you'll be stimulating the sensitive parts with your lips and tongue instead of your hand. Plus, your partner will provide some additional guidance with her verbal input. That's one of the advantages of joining a sorority, learning from your sisters while sharing in the communal experience."

Abby and Willow glanced at one another and smiled. The initiation ceremony so far had been far more intimate than either one had anticipated, but they'd both found it tremendously stimulating, and both of them were looking forward to being alone together to finish the experience.

"Alright then, girls," Taylor nodded. "It's time to get down and dirty. Assume the position and start eating pussy!"

As each of the girls moved their faces closer to their partners' pussies, the seniors placed their hands behind their heads, pulling them closer. When their lips touched their wet vulvas, the seniors moaned, spreading their legs wider apart. Abby already had experience going down on a woman thanks to her experience with Jade, and she was thankful for the expert instruction she'd received learning how to please a woman. But she was in no hurry to get Taylor off, wanting to tease and torment her as payback for her domineering role so far. She nibbled on Taylor's outer labia, sliding her tongue up and down the inside of her inner lips, pausing next to her twitching clit.

"Fuck, yes," Taylor panted, running her fingers through Abby's hair. "You know how to turn a girl on. Suck my pussy with your pretty face."

But instead of moving closer toward Taylor's throbbing gland, Abby shifted her head lower, sliding the tip of her tongue down over her perineum toward her anus, circling her tongue over her sphincter while Taylor groaned and writhed in her chair.

"God damn, girl," she grunted, pulling Abby's head harder against her snatch. "You've obviously done this before. Keep licking my pucker, that feels incredible."

But as Taylor began writhing in ecstasy from the attention of Abby's tongue on her sensitive rosebud, Abby pulled her head back again, nibbling on the insides of her thighs.

"You're such a tease," Taylor groaned, grabbing the back of Abby's head and pulling her toward her steaming twat. "Eat my cunt, bitch. You're driving me insane."

"Mmm-hmm," Abby nodded, straightening her tongue and driving it deep into Taylor's dripping tunnel.

As she pulled her head forward and back, Taylor stared down at her while she tongue-fucked her pussy.

"Yes, baby," Taylor purred. "Fuck me with your tongue. You look beautiful between my legs."

But as she began to moan more loudly, Abby pulled her face away once again and glanced up at the senior, placing the tips of her two fingers against her dripping hole.

"Yes, Abby," Taylor panted, practically begging the girl to finger-fuck her. "Fuck me with your fingers while you suck my pussy. I need your lips on my clit so bad..."

But while Taylor looked down at her, watching her fingers sliding in and out of her dripping folds, Abby simply peered up her with an evil smile. As Taylor's mouth began to gape open in rising pleasure, she curled her fingers forward, pressing them against her G-spot.

"Yes, yes," Taylor grunted. "Stroke my G-spot. That feels so good. Suck my button. I want to come all over your face."

Abby grinned, remembering the special tricks Jade had taught her, and as she encircled Taylor's bead with her lips, she sucked it hard into her mouth, slurping on it like a lollipop. Taylor threw her head back and grasped the back of Abby's head with her hands, tightening her fingers into a fist around her soft curls. Abby could tell from the increasing pressure on her roots that she was moving closer toward orgasm, but she wanted to save the best for last.

She slowly released the suction pressure on her clit and began circling Taylor's nub with her tongue, flicking it from side to side while feeling it growing harder and larger in her mouth. By this point, Taylor was thrashing and moaning wildly in her chair while the other seniors groaned alongside her. Abby peered out of the corner of her eyes, noticing Willow's face buried between Reece's legs while the older girl clamped her head tightly between her thighs.

Realizing that many of the women were edging closer to orgasm, Abby began turning her tongue in figure-eight patterns over Taylor's pearl, pressing the tip of her tongue against the hood to stimulate the sensitive part at the tip of her gland.

"Oh God yes," Taylor grunted. "Right there. Don't stop. Make me come, Abby. You are so good–"

When Abby felt the inside of Taylor's vagina beginning to swell, she knew she was on the verge of coming and she sucked her clit harder into her mouth, stroking the underside of her G-spot with her fingers, feeling the outside of her buttocks quivering in anticipation. Suddenly, Taylor howled as she curled her fingers tightly into Abby's hair, almost pulling it out by the roots from the force of her grip.

"Nnn-gah!" Taylor grunted, holding Abby's head tightly between her thighs as she began convulsing. "I haven't come this hard in ages. Don't stop, I'm still cumming..."

While Taylor thrashed and moaned in rapture on her chair, Abby noticed the other seniors shaking and wailing alongside her in unison. Whether they'd been taken over the edge by the sight of Taylor going off first, or from the expert ministrations of their charges, she couldn't be sure. But while she listened to Reece growling in orgasmic delight as Willow shook her head between her quivering legs, one thing seemed certain.

This new class of pledges had passed their latest test with flying colors.

9

"Well, I have to admit," Taylor said after all the seniors recovered from their oral orgasms. "You guys sure seem to be quick learners."

Then she peered down at Abby's glistening face smiling back at her.

"And some of you already appear to be masters at the craft."

Taylor glanced at the group of remaining seniors sitting in their chairs with large wet stains in the crotches of their jeans.

"But we still have one set of sisters who haven't yet participated in the fun. In this last round, it's going to be the sophomores' turn to get in on the action. For your last test, you'll have a chance to prove what you're really made of in the open round."

"Open round?" Abby said, wrinkling her forehead.

"This time," Taylor smiled. "You get to do whatever you want with your partners. You'll be judged on your creativity and your ability to please your partner."

"How will we know who wins?" Willow said.

"Upon completion, each sophomore will rate her partner on a scale of one to ten. The one with the highest score will be guaranteed membership in the sorority."

"When will the round be considered over?" Abby asked.

"When the last sophomore reaches orgasm," Taylor said, motioning to the sisters. "Let's prepare the judging area."

The other seniors pulled four mattresses into a large rectangle in the center of the floor, then they took off their clothes, lying naked on the cushions.

"It looks like we have room for one more," Taylor said, counting off the number of sisters and pledges. "I suppose I'll just have to fill the gap to make sure everyone has a partner."

"What a surprise," Abby grinned, winking at Taylor.

"Each pledge can choose a partner and start at your leisure," Taylor said. "Unlike the previous stages, this is a two-way exercise, so feel free to enjoy yourselves while you engage with your partner."

As the new girls walked to a section of the mat to choose a partner, Taylor reached out to clasp Abby's hand.

"Except you," she smiled. "I want you all to myself."

"If you insist," Abby said, walking to an open corner of the mat.

The pledges lay down beside their partners, beginning to kiss them in a missionary position. But Abby pushed Taylor down onto her back, then she straddled her hips in a cowgirl position while she began to roll her pussy over the senior's bare mound and stomach.

"Mmm," Taylor purred, smiling up at Abby. "I was hoping you'd indulge me with some more of your beautiful pussy. I've been dying to feel you squirting over me ever since I fucked you from behind with the vibrating dildo."

"Well it looks like it's going to be my turn to be in the superior position this time," Abby grinned, placing her knees between Taylor's thighs and twisting her sideways as she pressed their pussies together.

"Fuck yes," Taylor hissed, staring up at Abby's firm, round breasts. "That feels a lot better than an artificial penis."

"Even a vibrating one?" Abby smiled.

"It's certainly a lot warmer and wetter."

"I'm just getting started," Abby said, rocking her moist pussy against Taylor's vulva.

"Yes," Taylor groaned. "Fuck me with your soft cunny. Your pussy feels so hot."

While Abby began to grind her snatch against Taylor's, she lifted Taylor's right leg, pressing it against her stomach. As the two women rocked their hips together, the sound of sloshing pussies began to fill the room. Abby glanced around her, noticing that most of the other pledges had taken her lead, scissoring their partners in one form or another. Willow was positioned in a reverse cowgirl position, bending forward to connect her clit with her partner's, while most of the others had chosen the traditional scissor position. Even Olivia was lying on top of her partner in a missionary position, grinding their mounds together while the two women moaned softly.

It looks like we'll be studying a few things other than our chosen majors, Abby smiled, watching the new girls becoming increasingly bold in experimenting with their partners.

"Mmm," Taylor groaned as Abby mashed their pussies together. "Fuck my cunt with your pussy. I want to watch you gush between my legs when you come."

"What about you?" Abby said, pausing for a moment. "I thought we were going to be rated on how well we pleased our partners?"

"Oh, you're pleasing me alright," Taylor panted, grabbing Abby's ass and pulling her closer. "If you keep doing that, you'll get me off in no time."

"Well, we can't have you coming too fast," Abby said, pulling away as Taylor began to moan loudly. "Besides, if you really want to watch me gushing between your legs, I can think of a better position for your viewing pleasure."

Abby grabbed the back of Taylor's knees and pulled her legs forward, tilting her hips up off the mattress. Then she squatted over Taylor's upturned ass, lowering her dripping pussy onto Taylor's flaring slit.

"Can you see me a little better now?" she smiled, pressing Taylor's thighs down over her chest.

"Yes," Taylor grunted, darting her eyes over Abby's body. "I can see every part of you."

"Well, you better watch closely then," Abby smiled. "Because I'm about to put on a show for you."

While Abby began to rock her hips forward and back over Taylor's upturned ass, her pussy rolled over Taylor's slit, providing a feast for the elder girl's bulging eyes. She leaned forward a few more inches, and when their clits touched, Taylor grunted.

"Oh my God," she gasped. "I can see your pearl rolling over mine. This is the best sex I've had in a long time."

"Surely you've had practice doing this sort of thing with your other sisters?" Abby taunted.

"Sometimes," Taylor grunted. "But none as pretty as you. You have the most magnificent body I've ever seen."

"Prettier than all the other pledges you've stripped down and sampled?"

"There's something about you," Taylor nodded. "It's not just your sexy, beautiful body. You know how to please a woman like no other. And you squirt harder than anyone I've known."

"You better get ready, then," Abby grunted, pressing her pussy harder over Taylor's sex. "Because I'm getting close. Are you ready to come with me?"

"Fuck, yes," Taylor panted. "I'm almost there. I won't be able to control myself once you start squirting–"

"Give me your hands," Abby said. "I'm going to need some extra support when I come."

Taylor raised her hands above her body and Abby interlocked their fingers, swaying their outstretched arms while she rocked harder over Taylor's ass. When she felt herself passing the point of no return, she pulled Taylor's arms forward until her hips were directly over her face. Suddenly, without warning, she started squirting hard streams of fluid all over Taylor's tits and blinking eyes while both women grunted in orgasmic pleasure, squeezing their hands tightly together. In the long interval it took for them to finish coming, Abby watched each of the other couples climaxing, until everybody lay in a heaving pile on the oversize mattress.

She peered down at Taylor, still holding her in a curled-up position with her hands and clamping thighs.

"How do you like it when I'm the one in charge?" she grinned, looking down at her.

"If this is any sign of your leadership abilities," Taylor panted. "It won't be long before you replace me as President of the sorority."

10

"Well, what do you think, ladies?" Taylor said after everybody recovered from their orgasms. "Do you think this new batch is worthy of inclusion into our club?"

Most of the sophomores nodded enthusiastically, smiling at their partners.

"Let's see who gets a free pass. It's time to score the candidates on their talent and creativity. We'll start with Jennifer and move clockwise around the circle. What do you think, Jennifer, how would you rate your partner?"

Jennifer peered at Olivia sitting next to her and nodded.

"Olivia certainly learns quickly," she said. "But she's a little shy about taking the initiative. I'd give her a score of seven."

"That's not too shabby," Taylor said. "Especially for a new girl."

Then she turned to the next couple.

"What about you, Amy? How much did you enjoy Naomi's attention?"

Amy turned toward Naomi and smiled.

"She's pretty hot, that's for sure. And she's a pretty good kisser, to boot. I'd give her an eight at least."

The group continued around the circle, with most of the sophomores giving their partners a rating of seven or eight. When it came time for Willow's turn, her partner Jennifer reached out her hand, stroking her belly softly.

"Willow definitely knows how to please her partner," Jennifer said. "Something tells me this isn't the first time she's been with another woman. I give her extra points for her unusual scissoring position and for giving me an unforgettable view. She's at least a nine."

There was a long pause, then everyone turned toward Taylor and Abby.

"What about you, Taylor?" Willow said. "Judging by the amount of noise you two were making, I'm guessing you were pretty pleased with Abby's performance."

Taylor glanced at Abby as she wiped the juices off her face.

"I have to say, I've never been fucked quite like that before," she smiled. "She had no hesitation assuming the dominant role, and besides her sexy figure, she has a special talent I've never experienced before. Let's just say I've never been so wet having sex with anyone before. She's a definite ten."

After everybody gave a round of applause to signal the end of the initiation ceremony, Taylor invited the new girls to a group dinner in the main dining hall. The pledges picked up their clothes and returned to their dorms to clean up, with Willow and Abby giggling as they headed toward their room. When they latched the door shut behind them, Willow pressed Abby against the wall.

"Holy fuck!" she said. "Can you believe what just happened? That was insane! I've never been so turned on my whole life!"

"So you didn't mind having sex with other girls?" Abby smiled, caressing her ass while they mashed their tits together.

"Mind?" Willow said, flaring her eyes. "That was the hottest sex

I've ever had. If this is any indication of what living in a sorority is like, sign me up!"

"Well, it looks like you're a sure bet to be accepted into the club. Both Jennifer and Reece seemed pretty impressed with what you're bringing to the table."

"Not as much as you," Willow said, sliding her finger into the crack of Abby's ass. "Taylor seems quite smitten with you, and she exercises considerable authority over the affairs of the club."

"Maybe," Abby said. "But I'm only interested in one kind of affair right now. I couldn't take my eyes off you the whole time we were together downstairs. I've wanted to fuck you from the moment I laid eyes on you."

"That makes two of us," Willow said, pulling Abby toward the lower bunk. "I've been looking forward to having a sample of that special talent Taylor was talking about."

Willow lay face up on the bed, and when Abby crawled on top of her, she pulled her hips up toward her head, burying her face in her crotch.

"Mmm," Willow purred, circling her engorged clit with her tongue. "You're still wet."

"And hard," Abby panted. "Suck my bean with your pretty lips. I want to watch you while you're eating me out."

"Like you did while I was going down on Reece?" Willow grinned.

"Yes," Abby nodded, rocking her hips harder against Willow's face. "I almost came watching you suck her pussy."

"Well don't stop now," Willow grunted, flicking Abby's nub with the side of her tongue. "I want to feel you gushing all over my face when you come."

"Are you sure?" Abby said, feeling the pressure starting to build inside her pelvis. "It can get pretty messy..."

"Yes," Willow nodded, clutching the sides of Abby's ass and pulling her harder against her face. "Fuck my face and mess me up. I want you to shower me with your love."

"Willow," Abby groaned, arcing her back. "I can't hold it any longer. Here it comes–"

As Abby clamped the sides of Willow's head tightly between her thighs, she curled her fingers over the headboard, feeling the contractions of her pussy jetting one powerful stream after another over Willow's face and neck.

"Gahhh!" she exhaled, savoring the sensation of Willow's lips surrounding her clit while she twitched and throbbed atop her face.

By the time she finished coming, Willow's face and hair were thoroughly drenched with her juices while she held her softly, exalting in the feeling of her warm pussy throbbing against her lips.

"God, I needed that," Abby said, climbing off Willow and lying down next to her.

"You mean more than the Magic Wand vibrator or the strap-on dildo or the feel of another woman's pussy?" Willow chuckled, kissing her softly.

"Nothing does the job like a pair of moist lips," Abby smiled. "And yours are the softest and sweetest I've felt in a long time."

"Not as soft or moist as yours," Willow said, caressing Abby's dripping pussy with the tips of her fingers.

"You didn't mind my drenching you as much as I did?"

"Are you kidding me?" Willow said. "I only wish I could learn that trick to enjoy my orgasms half as much as you."

"Actually, any woman can learn how to squirt," Abby said, propping her head up on her elbow. "It's really just a matter of getting over your fear of losing control and receiving stimulation to the right area."

"Losing control in what way?" Willow said.

"Most women think they're peeing when they squirt during orgasm. But it's actually coming from a special gland behind the G-spot that's the female equivalent of a man's prostate gland. It's a clear, odorless fluid that assists in the act of contraception. Women from Asian cultures have long recognized it as the source of their feminine essence."

"Can you teach me how to do it too?"

"Absolutely," Abby said. "But this time I want to position you a little differently. I want you to face in the opposite direction while I lick you, like you did with Jennifer in the last step of the initiation ceremony."

"Okay," Willow said, sitting up and turning around to position her pussy above Abby's head while facing the foot of the bed.

"The trick with learning to squirt," Abby said, caressing the sides of Willow's ass. "Is to relax your pelvic muscles when you feel ready to come. I'm going to stimulate your G-spot while I lick you, and I want you to let it go when you climax. Let your juices flow like they were naturally designed to do."

"I'll try," Willow said, lowering her ass onto Abby's face.

As Abby began to caress her clit, Willow rocked her hips gently over Abby's lips, growing increasingly excited about the idea of ejaculating on Abby's face. When she began moaning more loudly, Abby inserted two fingers into her opening, pressing them gently against the top inner third of her vagina.

"God, that feels good," Willow grunted, pressing her mound down harder over Abby's face.

"Remember to relax when you get close," Abby nodded, massaging her G-spot more firmly. "It's going to feel like you have to pee, but you won't actually be peeing."

"Yes," Willow grunted. "I can feel the pressure starting to build up now. Are you sure it's okay to let it go?"

"Yes, baby," Abby murmured, sucking Willow's clit harder into her mouth. "Let it go. It's a very freeing experience."

"Abby," Willow panted. "I can feel it. I can't stop, here it comes. Oh God..."

Suddenly, Willow's buttock muscles started quivering as her pussy contracted against Abby's fingers, jetting a waterfall of liquid over her face as she held Willow's jewel in her mouth. Willow howled loudly, thrashing and twisting atop Abby's face, unable to stop the powerful convulsions gripping her hips. When she finally stopped coming, she collapsed beside Abby, licking her dripping lips like a parched camel.

"Holy shit!" Willow panted. "Where did you learn to do that? That was the most powerful orgasm I've ever experienced!"

"I had a little help from a more experienced friend," Abby chuckled. "I'm just passing along the secret."

"Well, I don't think we should keep it a secret for very long. I'm sure our sisters would appreciate learning it just as much as I have."

"Maybe," Abby smiled, kissing Willow's lips softly. "But only after you've been fully accepted into the sorority. I might need to exercise a little leverage with my newfound friend if necessary."

11

After Abby and Willow cleaned up, they headed to the main dining hall, where Taylor formally invited the rest of the pledges to become full members of the sorority. When she returned to her room, she had a message waiting for her from her next-door neighbor, Jade.

Hi Abby, the text read. How are you enjoying your first week of college?

It's been a little crazier than I expected, Abby replied. These sorority girls are a lot more open-minded than I'm used to.

Oh? Jade said. Have you been expanding your sexual horizons?

Let's just say I've been putting some of the lessons you taught me to good use, Abby smiled.

I'm actually in your area for a business conference, Jade typed. Are you free for dinner?

I just had a big celebratory dinner with my sisters. But I'd love for you to stop by so we can get caught up. Would you like to have a tour of my new home?

That would be lovely. Drop me a pin for your location and I'll drop by in an hour or so.

After Abby sent Jade her address, she felt herself becoming

increasingly wet remembering all the wild sex they'd had while her parents vacationed in Europe. When Jade texted her to let her know she'd arrived, Abby ran outside to greet her.

"Jade," she said, giving her a big hug. "It's so nice to see you again. I've been thinking of you quite a lot these past few days."

"I would have thought you'd have plenty of other distractions during your first week at college," Jade chuckled, kissing her softly.

"Everything just seemed to pick up where we left off," Abby nodded, grabbing her hand. "Come, let me show you my new home."

Abby led Jade into the main entrance hall of the sorority house, where they bumped into Taylor.

"Oh, is this your Mom?" Taylor said, peering at the attractive older woman holding Abby's hand.

"Actually," Abby said. "This is my next-door neighbor from back home, Jade. She was in the area, so I thought I'd show her around."

"Glad you could stop by," Taylor said, peering at Jade's tight turtle-neck sweater and curvy ass in her skinny jeans. "Perhaps I'll see you again before you leave."

"I'll look forward to that," Jade said, clasping Taylor's hand tightly.

After Abby gave Jade a quick tour of the house, she led her to her dorm room, where Willow was working quietly at her desk. When she saw that Abby had a guest, she got up, placing her laptop under her arm.

"Oh, I didn't realize you had company," Willow said. "I'll leave you two alone to have some private time."

"There's no need," Abby smiled. "This is my friend Jade that I was telling you about."

Willow suddenly peered at Jade with bulging eyes.

"The one who–"

"Yes," Abby nodded. "The one who looked in on me this summer when my parents were away."

"I'm not sure looked in is the best way of describing it," Jade smiled. "Though we did share some stimulating glances through our bedroom windows."

"That wasn't the only thing we shared," Abby said, squeezing Jade's hand tightly. "Jade's the one who taught me how to make love to a woman and fully enjoy the pleasures of lesbian sex."

"Oh dear," Jade smiled. "Have you been sharing some of our intimate secrets?"

"Only the most exciting ones," Abby grinned, winking at Willow.

"Well, I hope you haven't been giving all of my secrets away," Jade said, staring at Willow's slender, sexy figure.

"I don't even think that's possible, with all the experience you've had with other women," Abby said.

"It sounds like you've had your own share of new experiences since you joined the sorority," Jade smiled.

"You have no idea," Willow said, shifting uncomfortably as her panties began to moisten remembering all the exciting encounters she had during the initiation ceremony.

"I'd love to hear about some of them if you're willing to share," Jade said.

Abby invited Jade to join her and Willow on her bunk while they shared their experience with their sisters, finishing with the impromptu squirting lesson in their private room.

"Wow," Jade said, pressing her heel against her throbbing pussy. "That sounds seriously hot. I'm only surprised there wasn't any three-way encounters, with such a large group of women getting together."

"Three-ways?" Willow said, wrinkling her forehead. "How is that even possible? I've heard of threesomes with one man and two women, but how does that work with three women?"

"Well, actually," Jade smiled. "I attended a special women's intimacy workshop recently where we learned many new interesting positions for tribbing between three women..."

By the time Jade finished describing the various positions she'd experienced at Laila's Tribadism workshop, Abby and Willow were squirming on the bed in excitement.

"That sounds crazy hot," Willow said. "I'd love to try some of those sometime."

"Well, if you guys are in the mood," Jade smiled. "I'd be happy to demonstrate one or two of them."

"With us?" Abby said, widening her eyes.

"I don't see any other women around to give it a try," Jade smiled, peering around the room teasingly.

"Yes, please," Willow said, beginning to take off her clothes.

"Which position would you like to try first?" Jade said.

"The Knit one, Pearl two one sounds exciting," Abby said. "I'm not sure there's enough room on this little bunk for some of the other ones."

"Mmm, that's one of my favorites," Jade said, pulling Abby's sweater over her head and unclasping her bra.

When all three women were naked, Jade lay down next to the girls, threading her legs between theirs in a three-way scissor arrangement. It took a bit of twisting and squeezing their bodies, but eventually they found a way to join their pussies together in a triangular-shaped, Swastika configuration.

"Oh my God," Willow grunted when she felt her pussy touching the other women's vulvas. "Just when I thought this couldn't get any better. This is even more exciting with two women!"

"The trick for gaining maximum traction between our pussies," Jade nodded. "Is to raise one knee toward your chest while you twist your body away from your partner. That way, we have the best chance for rubbing our clits together and enjoying the experience to the fullest."

Abby and Willow did as Jade instructed, and when they felt their lips meshing and their clits touching together, they groaned loudly.

"Fuck me," Willow squealed. "This feels incredible. You have got to visit us more often to share more of your tips. I've already learned more in one day than I have my entire previous life."

"There's lots more where this came from," Jade smiled, grabbing the two girls' asses and grinding their pussies together.

"Jesus," Abby panted. "I'm going to come soon if you keep rubbing me that way."

"I hope so," Jade said. "And I hope you remember how to gush like I taught you. It's even more fun when all three of us can come together."

"Yes," Abby grunted, peering at Willow opening her mouth in mounting pleasure. "And I'm not the only one who's learned how to ejaculate when she orgasms."

"Oh?" Jade said, feeling her pleasure about to spill over. "This should be fun. I'm almost there..."

"Oh God," Willow panted, feeling the pressure suddenly release inside her. "I'm coming, Jade! Squirt all over my pussy, Abby. This feels incredible."

"Yes, Willow," Abby wailed. "I feel it. Gush your juices all over my cunt. Fuck, I'm coming with you..."

Suddenly, juices began spraying in every direction all over the three women's bodies as they ground their pussies tightly together while they wailed in tandem, screaming and grunting in orgasmic unison. When they finally stopped climaxing, their dorm room door edged open, and Taylor stuck her head through the opening.

"Jesus, Abby," she said, bulging her eyes at the sight of the three naked women's dripping naked bodies joined together in a three-way scissor position. "You're waking up the whole house!"

"Sorry," Abby panted. "It's just that we've been learning some new techniques for sharing the lesbian love. Do you want to join us?"

Taylor paused as she peered at Jade, running her eyes over the older woman's taut, yoga-toned figure.

"Are you sure you don't mind?" she said. "Because I'm about to burst a gasket watching the three of you tied up together like that."

"I'm sure we can make room for one more," Jade smiled, kneeling over the two girls as she pulled her dripping pussy away from their crotches. "The more bursting gaskets, the better..."

BOOK 48

CARNY GAMES 1

1

W hen I received a new invitation from my friend Madison, I couldn't wait to open the message. She always hosted the sexiest parties, and with the cryptic heading Carny Games, I could already feel my panties moistening as I began to read the message.

Dear Jade,

    You are cordially invited to a party at my place this Saturday evening starting at 9 p.m.

    The theme of this event is Carnival Games, where everyone will participate in erotic contests simulating county fair games.

    From Ring Toss to Ping Pong Basketball, Whack-a-Mole, Hands-free Jenga, Bobbing for Peaches, and many more, these games will make you laugh and squeal in equal measure.

    But these contests aren't for the faint of heart, so be prepared to take your clothes off and let it all hang out. And remember to park your inhibitions at the door, because there's no telling who you'll be paired up with. From boy-on-girl to girl-on-girl to boy-on-boy to other surprise pairings, you can be sure to stretch your imagination in more ways than one.

*So come clean, come prepared, and come often. Because we're going to
have a ribald and riotous good time!*

RSVP before Thursday,

Maddy

*P.S.: Please bring a personal dick pic or pussy pic (twenty copies each),
fully erect and shaved if possible. This will be used for a special game of
the Pin the Tail on the Donkey.*

Holy fuck! I thought after reading her message. What has she
dreamed up this time? Ping Pong Basketball? Bobbing for Peaches?

I could guess what might be involved in the Ring Toss game and
Whack-a-Mole, but the other ones sounded vaguely female-centric. Of
course, Hands-free Jenga didn't leave much to the imagination. The idea
of watching a bunch of guys competing to see how long they could keep
a tower of bricks from falling over by poking out the blocks one at a time
with their hard dicks sounded erotic and hilarious at the same time.

But the Pin the Tail on the Donkey game had me stumped. What
was she going to do with the dick and pussy pictures? And what were
these 'other pairings' she alluded to in her message? Was it possible
that one or more of my favorite t-girls would also be invited to the
party? The combinations seemed almost endless.

As my mind began to wander about what she had planned, my
hand slipped under my panties, imagining who I'd be paired up with
doing what kind of depraved activities in front of the entire group.

Bring it on, Maddy, I thought, curling my fingers into my hole. I'll
be coming, alright. Sooner than you expect...

———

When I arrived at Madison's house on the night of the party,
she collected my pics then escorted me to the living room
where a group of twenty people lounged around, sipping wine. I
recognized some of the faces in the crowd, but there were quite a few
new people I hadn't seen before. With an even sprinkling of men and

women, I scanned the crowd while everybody made small talk introducing themselves.

In addition to my friends Lily, Bonnie, and Emma, there was the sexy neighbor couple from the last party, Brad and Laura, plus my old friends from work, Ryan, Neil, and Marco. But it was the new faces in the crowd that attracted most of my attention. With a mix of black, white, Asian, and Hispanic hotties, my pussy was already throbbing in anticipation of the coming pairings. Rounding out the group was my transgender friend Shae and the full-figured Christina Hendricks lookalike from my tribbing workshop, Paige.

As my eyes darted around the room, I suddenly became conscious of the growing wet spot in the crotch of my jeans. Sitting down on the sofa to take the last available spot, I nudged next to Shae, crossing my legs in embarrassment.

"I see you've already started planning your hookups," she smiled, glancing down at the stain in my crotch.

"I could fuck just about any one of these knockouts," I nodded, taking the large glass of chardonnay she handed me. "Although something tells me the decision is going to be out of my hands for most of the night."

After the last guest arrived, Madison carried the stack of photos into the kitchen, making short notations on the back of each one, then she carried the pile into the living room, distributing one dick pic to each woman and one pussy pick to each man. Shae peered at her picture, noticing a man's erect cock, and smiled.

"I guess I'll be playing the girl part for this game," she said.

"Lucky you," I nodded, glancing at the picture of a large, caramel-colored hard-on flapping up against the rippled abs of some unidentified stud whose face had been cut out of the picture. "You'll have dealer's choice for the rest of the night."

I peered at my photo showing a huge, dark-colored erection, then turned the picture over. Notated on the back next to a loop of sticky tape was the single letter 'H'.

"Any idea what the letters mean?" Shae said, pinching her eyebrows at the inscription on the back of her photo.

"No idea," I said, noticing Madison taking a seat at the head of the group. "But I have a feeling we're about to find out."

"Good evening, everybody," Madison smiled, peering around the room at the group squinting at their cards with an equal mix of curiosity and distraction. "Thank you all for coming and for bringing your intimate photos. First of all, let me assure you that these pictures will never leave this room and that they'll be safely disposed of after everyone leaves the party."

"Whew," Marco sighed. "I was having nightmares of my dick pic circulating on the internet while everyone speculated about who it belonged to."

The group chuckled, and Madison nodded with a knowing grin.

"Well, you're at least half right about your concerns," she said. "But we'll get to that part in a moment. First, let's take a few minutes to introduce ourselves, since not everyone knows each other. Tell us your name, where you're from, and what's your connection to the group. And to make it more interesting, I'd like every person to tell one truth and one lie about themselves. Later on, we'll try to guess which is which. Who'd like to go first?"

Never one to be shy, Shae raised her hand and Madison nodded in her direction.

"Hello," Shae said. "My name is Shae, and I'm originally from Missouri. I was introduced to members of this group by my good friend, Jade. Something you may not know about me is that I have an extra Y chromosome, which means I have both male and female reproductive organs. But even though I'm equipped to have sex with both genders, I've only ever been intimate with men."

"Hmm," Madison said after Shae finished introducing herself. "That's an interesting puzzle. We'll have to see which one of those statements is a lie and which one is the truth before the evening is over. Who'd like to go next?"

As each member of the group proceeded to introduce themselves, everyone listened to their brief profiles, chuckling softly at their self-effacing disclosures. By the time we finished with the handsome married couple Brad and Laura, we had a pretty good idea which of their joint declarations about each being their first and only sexual partner was a truth versus a lie.

"Alright then," Maddy said after everybody finished. "Now that we've scratched the surface of everyone's identity, let's see if we can begin to peel back some of the layers. I'm sure you're all eager to learn what we're going to do with the intimate pictures you've taken of yourselves. In our first game I like to call Shower versus Grower, we're going to ask the men to strip down naked and line up against the wall while the women examine their dick pics and try to match the erect penises with their flaccid ones."

Madison paused as she peered around the group, surveying the surprised expressions on the faces of the men.

"Who's ready to get this party started?"

2

"I assume because you've given me a dick pic instead of a pussy pic that you'd like me to be on the other side of the lineup for this game?" Shae said.

"With your unique sexual anatomy, it would be a little too easy to guess your identity," Madison nodded. "But don't worry, we'll get you involved in the other side of the action soon enough."

"And you expect us to remain soft the whole time these women are inspecting our dicks?" Brad said.

"That's half the fun," Maddy smiled. "There's a reason why we're naming this contest Shower versus Grower. We wouldn't want to spoil the mystery too fast."

Ryan grunted as he squirmed in his chair, adjusting his package uncomfortably.

"It might be kind of hard..." he said, clearing his throat at the obvious pun. "To keep from getting turned on while all these beautiful women are staring at our dicks," he said.

"I guess that's where we'll separate the men from the boys," Maddy said, glancing at his bulging crotch. "If you get too aroused during the inspection, you'll be automatically disqualified."

"Will there be a prize for the winner?" Marco asked. "At the county fair, we usually get a stuffed toy for winning each of the contests."

"Oh, there'll be a prize, alright," Madison grinned. "And it will be plenty soft and squishy. But this one will be infinitely more fun to nuzzle up next to."

I glanced at my photo and peered around the room, already beginning to narrow the list of likely matches.

"So, once we think we've identified the correct matching penis, how do we go about indicating our choice?" I said.

"Simply stick the back of your photo somewhere on your target's body," Maddy nodded. "Then I'll compare the identification symbols on the reverse side to see who guessed it right."

"Will this be a timed contest?" Bonnie said.

"I think it will have to be," Madison said. "With so many delicious penises on display, you ladies won't ever want to stop inspecting the goods. Plus, the longer it goes, the harder it'll be for the men to keep themselves composed."

"That's one way of putting it," Neil said as everybody in the room chuckled.

"Okay then," Madison said, turning on the living room TV and pairing her phone's electronic timer to the display. "You'll have exactly five minutes to match the flaccid penis with the erect one. Are you guys ready?"

"What if we're already half-erect?" Ryan said.

"Then you better start thinking about dead cats or your naked grandmother," Maddy laughed. "Because if you want to have a chance at putting that thing to better use, you'll have to maintain your composure a little longer."

Then she pointed to the opposite wall and nodded.

"Alright, you guys know the rules. Strip down naked and line up shoulder to shoulder on the far wall. When everybody has their clothes off, I'll start the timer."

The men peered at one another for a moment, then they slowly began to strip down, positioning themselves against the wall like a bunch of perps in a police lineup.

"Okay, ladies," Madison smiled, nodding at the row of naked studs standing awkwardly next to one another. "Have at it."

The women raised up out of their seats then queued up in single file to the left of the lineup, glancing at their photos and the flaccid penises of each of the candidates as they moved slowly down the line. Some of the men closed their eyes and scrunched up their faces, trying to distract themselves from the sight of ten beautiful women parading in front of their naked bodies, but for the most part they managed to keep themselves composed while their counterparts teased and cajoled them.

"Are you sure that thing is fully soft?" Shae teased Ryan, who was standing stiff as a brick with his hands resting tightly by his side like he was participating in a military inspection. "Because it already looks as big as some of the hard-ons I've seen."

"I guess that means I'm a shower," Ryan shrugged.

"That's too bad," Shae grinned. "I was kind of hoping to see it in its full glory."

While I walked down the line, I paused briefly beside each of the candidates, staring at their tools while I tried to imagine what they'd look like fully erect. But since there were only two black men in the lineup, my job was considerably easier, given the match in skin tones. When I stopped in front of the first black man who I remembered introducing himself as Linc, he tilted his head forward to peer at the photo in my hand, then he grinned.

"How hard can it be?" he said, turning his head to glance at the other African-American man three positions down the line. "There's only two of us."

"Well, you're kind of cheating," I said, glancing back and forth between the dick pic and his long, slightly curved dong. "The picture shows you shaved, but you're sporting a little stubble down there."

"Well, I didn't want to make it too easy for you," Linc smiled.

"I'll be back in a moment," I said. "Save that thought."

I took a quick glance at the TV screen, noticing that there was only two minutes remaining, then I scooted down the line toward the other African-American man, quickly comparing the dick pic to the real thing. Both men were circumcised and roughly the same size, but the second man's penis hung straight down, whereas my picture displayed a large curved erection, bending slightly to the side like a Japanese samurai sword. I jumped back into the now-chaotic swarm of shifting women, toward the first black man and smiled.

"You didn't disguise it that well," I said, grinning up at him. "You should have taken your picture from a different angle."

I turned his photo around, then slapped it against his hard pecs, watching his dick bounce excitedly once he realized I'd guessed him correctly.

"Okay ladies," Madison said, pointing toward the timer counting down on the TV screen. "You've got less than a minute remaining to make your decision. You better pin your pictures on your best guess, or you'll both miss your opportunity to participate in the next round."

Shae paused in front of the Hispanic newcomer named Diego, tilting her head up and down between the picture in her hands and the tan-colored organ dangling between his legs. Then she knelt down to take a closer look, blowing softly on his instrument, bobbing gently over his tightening balls as his blood coursed through his veins.

"Ahem," Madison said, shaking her head disapprovingly. "No touching and no teasing, Shae. You're cheating by helping him get an erection. You've got five seconds to make your decision."

"Fine," Shae said, standing up and slapping her photo against the handsome Latino's glistening chest. "I guess I'll just have to save the blowing part for later."

When the alarm finally sounded, the women stepped back from each of their chosen candidates, clapping and cheering loudly. None of them were sure they'd matched the penises correctly, but at this point it hardly mattered. For five glorious minutes, this had been the most fun any of them had had fully clothed.

3

"So, what happens now?" Shae said, peering at some of the men's penises beginning to rise and slowly hardening. "Do we get to play with the willies we correctly identified?"

"All in due time," Madison said, collecting the photos from each of the men's naked bodies and cross-referencing the letters on the back with a spreadsheet she held on a clipboard. She placed a check or an X beside each man's name, then she sat back down at the front of the group, smiling with a sly grin.

"We've got quite a few winners," she nodded. "But we'll have to wait until the results of the next contest to see who'll be moving on to the next stage."

There was a collective groan in the room, with both the men and the women disappointed they'd have to wait to do more than just look at their partners' sexy body parts. But I knew from previous experience that this was all part of Madison's plan to ramp up the sexual tension for the best part still to come.

"Now it's time to turn the tables and make the ladies squirm for a change," she smiled. "This time it will be the women's turn to let it all hang out while the men inspect their private parts in a game I like to call Matching the Curtains and the Carpet."

"But you told us to shave ourselves clean," Emma protested. "What if we don't have any fur down there to compare the upper half with?"

"I guess that will make it all the more interesting then," Madison nodded. "We can't make it too easy for the men to match your pussies. What would be the fun in that?"

Marco suddenly shifted on the sofa, straightening out his tool in his tightening pants.

"Will the women be completely naked like we were?" he asked hopefully.

"Of course," Madison grinned. "I'm an equal opportunity hostess."

"And will it be timed like the other contest?" Brad said.

"Like I said," Maddy nodded. "In this game, men and women are treated exactly the same."

"Will there be another squishy prize for the winner?" Shae said, glancing in the direction of Diego's still naked body.

"Absolutely," Madison said. "Though this one might not be so squishy by the time you finish with it."

"Mmm," Shae purred. "Do I get to be on the other side of the lineup this time?"

"Yes," Maddy smiled. "Though something tells me your partner will have a little less trouble than the rest of the men matching your body parts."

Everybody chuckled nervously, then the women stripped down and sat on the edge of the fireplace hearth, parting their legs slowly. After everybody got in position, the men ogled their naked bodies, darting their eyes up and down the row, soaking up the spectacle. When they saw Shae's big prick flapping over her glistening pussy, their eyes bulged, hardly believing their luck seeing a true hermaphrodite for the first time in the flesh.

"Is everyone ready to get started?" Madison said, pointing her phone toward the TV, preparing to restart the timer.

"I think some of the men are a little more ready than others," Shae said, noticing a few of the men's cocks standing at full attention while they gaped at the lineup of naked women.

"Fortunately, this game doesn't require the same degree of

restraint as the last one," Madison smiled. "Though the other rules still apply. You'll have to match the owner of the pussy in your picture only by looking at your partner."

"You better stand a few feet back then, Linc," I said to the handsome African-American, noticing his half-erect cock angling gently to the side while it levitated almost a full foot in front of his rippling abs.

"I'll try to demonstrate proper respect for your temple," he nodded, feeling a drop of precum forming on the crown of his cock.

"Alright then," Madison said, tapping her phone to start the timer. "Let the revelry begin."

The men wasted no time rushing up to the row of women, quickly moving opposite their suspected matches and examining their pictures while they carefully inspected the figures of their partners. I couldn't help chuckling when I saw a small crowd forming in front of Shae, knowing there could only be one person holding a picture of her unique genitalia.

I guess everyone's somewhere on the continuum after all, I thought to myself, remembering the old saying that every individual harbors some degree of physical attraction to both sexes.

While I watched the women sitting on the edge of the bench with their legs spread apart, I glanced at the shaved pussies of the two women sitting next to me. Each of them had a unique shape and texture to the contours of their vulva, with some having straight, symmetrical labia, while others had curved and flappy folds. Just like individual snowflakes, everyone had a unique shape and tone, and I seemed almost as fascinated as the men were appraising the lineup of glistening, pink flowers.

After a few minutes, Linc finally stopped in front of me, standing between my parted legs with his enormous, tanned poker pointing toward my left breast.

"Looks like I guessed you correct," I smiled, licking my lips. "That thing is even more impressive when it's angry."

"Sorry," he said, glancing down at his hard-on dangling a string of precum six inches below his flaring helmet. "It's kind of hard to remain relaxed when I'm staring at a bunch of naked women."

"Don't apologize on my behalf," I smiled, feeling the juices beginning to dribble out of my pussy and down the insides of my thighs. "I'm enjoying the show just as much as you are."

"I'm not sure about this one," he said, pulling his photo closer to my snatch as he squatted between my legs, comparing the two images. "Can you give me any hints?"

I leaned forward a few inches to peer at his photo, then I glanced up at him with a smile, recognizing the familiar picture. When he saw my pupils dilating in recognition, his penis flapped excitedly, emitting another long string of precum down onto the floor.

"You better be careful there, big fella," I grinned. "Somebody could slip and fall on that puddle you're leaving on the floor."

"Good," Lincoln said, meeting my gaze with a brilliant white smile. "I can use every advantage I can get to keep you all for myself."

4

After the previous two contests, all the group members were pretty worked up, not only because everyone was still naked and staring at each other's genitals, but also because they were already anticipating the next hookup. But I knew Madison had carefully planned everything to ramp up the sexual excitement to make the final connections all the more satisfying. While the men shifted uneasily, trying to conceal their throbbing hard-ons, Maddy peered around the room, grinning like a Cheshire Cat.

"I'm happy to see most of the guys are still aroused waiting for the next contest," she said. "Because those cocks are going to need to be rock-hard to make it to the end of this one."

"Are we going to do more than just look at each other's genitals this time?" Neil asked impatiently.

"As a matter of fact, yes," Maddy smiled. "This one will be a very tactile event, indeed."

She reached behind the sofa and carefully lifted a tall stack of interconnected wood blocks resting on a platter, placing it in the middle of the coffee table between the two sofas.

"In this game we'll call Joystick Jenga, you'll be putting your stiffie to good use trying to beat your fellow contestants."

"Ugh," Neil groaned. "I was kind of hoping we'd have a chance to connect with each other a little more...intimately."

"Well, in this event you will," Maddy grinned. "The winner will be sucked off by the loser."

"But it's only going to be played with men?" Neil said, furrowing his brow in disappointment.

"And your point?" Maddy said.

"What if some of us aren't gay?"

"We told you to park your inhibitions at the door," Madison nodded. "I warned you in the invitation that there'd be multiple-gender pairings. If you're going to play the game, you have to agree to play by the rules."

Brad suddenly shifted uneasily in his chair, peering at his wife with a lopsided frown.

"How will we decide who's the winner and who's the loser?" he said, worried about stretching the boundaries of their admittedly open marriage.

"It's pretty simple," Madison smiled. "The loser is the one who topples the tower."

"Then who'll be the winner if there's nine of us still standing after it topples?"

"That will be the one the loser chooses to perform fellatio on," Maddy said matter-of-factly.

"You mean we actually get to choose?" Ryan suddenly perked up, licking his lips as he swiveled his head among the group of bobbing dicks awaiting the start of the game.

"Of course," Maddy said. "That makes it all the more interesting."

"In that case, I'd hardly call the one who topples the tower the loser," the gay man grinned while gaping at Lincoln's huge, slightly curved dick.

"I told you we were going to stretch more than your imaginations in this game," Madison smiled. "I guess we're about to see just how fluid everyone's sexual persuasions really are. Are you guys ready to get started?"

Neil squirmed uncomfortably in his seat, crossing his legs to conceal his hidden organ.

"What if we're not hard yet?" he said.

"Well, you better get working on that pretty fast," Maddy smiled. "Because it will be a hell of a lot harder to push the blocks out of the stack with a soft penis."

While the men slowly crowded around the edge of the coffee table, Neil began rubbing his flaccid dick, trying to make it rise for the occasion. As I peered at the rest of the men, I found it interesting that virtually everybody else was already ramrod hard, their phalluses bouncing proudly over their bellies while little drops of precum began forming on their glistening crowns.

Fluid indeed, I smiled, knowing most of the men officially identified as being straight. Whether they were turned on by the idea of the women watching them strut their manhood or by the realization that one of them would soon to be sucked off, I couldn't be sure. Either way, all of the women leaned in closer on the edge of our chairs, eager to watch the action.

"Okay," Madison said, placing a spinning game dial on the table and flicking the pointer. After it stopped spinning, it pointed toward the handsome Latino, Diego. "It looks like you'll be going first, Diego. Then we'll proceed clockwise around the table until someone topples the stack."

Diego paused for a moment while he squinted at the tower, trying to plan out his strategy.

"So we simply poke out any random block using our penis only?" he said.

"Exactly," Madison nodded. "No touching allowed with any other body parts."

Linc suddenly cleared his throat, bending over to examine the size of the blocks more carefully.

"What if, um, our dicks are too large to fit through the holes?" he said.

"That's why I had this set specially constructed by our in-house carpenter, Brad," Maddy smiled. "I anticipated this eventuality, and with each block roughly twice the size of a regular set, I think even you'll have enough room to poke the bear, metaphorically speaking."

"Humpf," Linc huffed, shaking his head doubtfully.

"Okay, Diego," Madison said, nodding toward the group. "Let's get the party started. The ladies are just as impatient as the men to see who's going to win this game."

"Alright," Diego said, moving his flapping johnson closer to the stack of blocks. "Here goes nothing–"

"I'd hardly call that nothing," Shae chuckled at the handsome Latino she'd picked out of the lineup earlier. "I just hope I'll be the first one to suck that beautiful flute before anyone else has a chance to."

5

Diego bent his knees slightly and flexed his buttocks, touching the tip of his dick against a block in the middle of the stack. As he gently prodded the loose dowel, it slowly began to poke out the opposite side, until it finally fell with a loud plop onto the glass surface of the table.

"Woo hoo!" the women cheered as Diego carefully withdrew his throbbing organ from the hole in the stack.

"Hold that thought, Diego," Shae teased. "Because I've got something a whole lot wetter and tighter for you to insert that thing into when you finish up there."

Diego glanced over at Shae, his face flushing in excitement at the thought of fucking the hot transgender girl.

"Don't get me more distracted than I already am," he chuckled. "This is hard enough without imagining screwing someone as pretty as you."

"Okay, Ryan," Madison nodded toward the man standing next to Diego. "You're up next."

"Oh, I'm up for it, alright," the gay man smiled, peering over at Diego's beautiful instrument. "With any luck, I'll have a chance to beat Shae to the punch having my way with that beautiful cock."

He placed one knee on the side of the coffee table, then he angled his hips forward, tapping the end of a block a few inches above the hole that Diego had left. As he prodded the block softly, feigning an exaggerated humping action, the other end of the brick edged out the other side until it teetered on an angle, hanging by a thread. Ryan withdrew his penis from the hole, then he leaned over, rubbing his ass against the side of Diego's thigh while he blew softly into the hole.

"Hmm," he said. "This reminds me of another crevasse I'd like to insert my dick into. It's too bad this one's made of wood, because my stiffie could use something a little tighter than this stack of bricks to get off."

"If you play your cards right," I chuckled, watching the brick topple out of the other side. "You'll have your choice of ready candidates soon enough."

"Speaking of," Madison said, turning toward the next man standing clockwise in the circle. "It's your turn to go next, Neil."

I glanced at Neil's organ and noticed it was now standing at full attention, bobbing excitedly over his shaved balls while he stared at the other men's upturned erections.

This was absolute genius, I thought to myself, making eye contact with Maddy. Gay, straight, or bi, there was no denying this game had a bit of something for everyone. The gay and bi guys got to indulge their fantasies of watching a bunch of turned-on dudes displaying their manhood in all their glory, while the straight men got to show off for the women. All while the women got to indulge their own fantasies of watching two hot guys hooking up at the end of the game. I had no idea what she had planned for the women in the next round, but I was already as wet as a four-stroke engine.

Neil paused for a moment while he studied the stack of bricks, planning his best strategy. While the two previous men had chosen to remove blocks from the center of the tower, he seemed more interested in examining the edge of the stack where the bricks could be wedged out more easily from the side than from the middle. After a few seconds, he pointed the tip of his dick toward one near the bottom of the stack, surmising that the weight of the blocks above would provide more stability to his prodding of the delicate tower.

As he gently poked the block with his purple glans, I noticed a drop of dew on the wooden piece from his slippery tip. I wasn't sure if he was getting excited by the sight of all the women intently watching him using his joystick to move the block, or if he was beginning to look forward to the possibility of being sucked off by one of the men looking on from the other sides of the table.

While the block see-sawed from side to side, the women ooed and awed loudly, adding to the drama of the scene. When it finally slipped out of the stack and the tower leaned to one side, teetering precariously on the edge of toppling, the women's eyes suddenly flared, eagerly anticipating the straight guy receiving his first gay blowjob. But after a few seconds, the tower stopped swaying, leaning over like some kind of twenty-first century modernist apartment block.

"Now it's beginning to get interesting," Madison smiled, glancing at the tower and the next man in the line, Lincoln.

"You're up next Linc," she said. "But you better be careful. I don't think the tower can withstand much more stress at this point. I hope you've studied engineering or architecture, because there's no telling where the weak point is now."

"Unfortunately not," Linc sighed. "And I'm pretty sure my finance degree isn't going to offer much help. Except insofar as the way compound interest increases the value of a future payout. Because my interest has definitely been growing with every game you've introduced, and I don't know how much longer I'll be able to hold out."

He peered down at the dripping string of precum hanging off the end of his cock and frowned.

"Although I suppose a little lubrication will only help reduce the friction in this instance..."

He glanced at the hole in the side of the stack where Ryan had removed the last piece, then he knelt down on the floor, pointing his long erection toward a center block lower on the stack. As he began to prod the piece slowly out the other side, the stack gently tilted from side to side while the women stared with wide eyes at his enormous organ. But after the piece edged halfway through the stack, Linc's curved erection began rubbing against the inside of the hole, causing the tower to sway even more precariously.

He paused when he realized his predicament, knowing that if he prodded any further, the combined friction of his thickly curved tool in the confined space would push the tower over before he had a chance to poke it out the other side.

"Can I change my target halfway through?" he said, peering over at Madison.

"I don't see why not," Maddy smiled. "We didn't mention anything about that in the rules. As long as you eventually remove one block from the stack without toppling it, you're still in contention."

"Okay," Linc said, glancing at the gap Ryan had left in the side of the tower with his previous turn. "It's time to start thinking like an engineer instead of a finance major."

He pulled his dripping tool out of the middle of the stack and pointed the glistening tip toward the block immediately adjacent Ryan's missing piece on the opposite side. But as he tried to push it off to the side as Ryan had, his slippery cum made it hard to gain traction against the block, and he paused once again, shaking his head in frustration.

"Mmm," Ryan interrupted, flaring his eyes at Lincoln's dripping dagger. "Why don't you save some of that for me? I'll be happy to lick you clean if you drop the tower. I'm looking forward to impaling my face on that weapon."

"I'm afraid I don't lean that way," Lincoln frowned, swiping the end of his dripping dick against some of the other blocks to dry the tip. Then he pressed the new block more firmly with his tool, slowly edging it from side to side until it toppled a few inches beside the base of the tower. The stack swayed for a few moments, then eventually righted itself with only two narrow blocks remaining on the lower row to hold the rest of the tower up.

"Hmm," Madison nodded, appraising Lincoln's handiwork. "That was pretty ingenious. But something tells me you've just made the job that much harder for the next contestant."

She peered over at Brad, who was studying the tower carefully, and smiled.

"Looks like you're up next, Brad. Do you think you can survive one extra round?"

Brad glanced at his wife Laura who was grinning at him with an enormous smile, and cocked his head.

"I'll give it my best shot, babe," he said. "But I'm in unfamiliar territory."

"Something tells me you're about to be in some other unfamiliar territory pretty soon," she grinned.

6

Brad paused for a moment, trying to figure out his best plan of attack, then he swiveled his hips toward the side of the tower, pointing his hard-on a few inches above the two holes left by Ryan and Linc.

"It looks like the side pieces are a little easier to slip out than the middle ones," he said, prodding the end of one block tentatively with his flapping erection.

"You better be careful, dear," Laura teased. "You don't want to knock it over with your bouncing dick before you have a chance to push the block out."

"That's the problem," Brad frowned. "It seems to have a mind of its own right now."

"Typical man," I chuckled. "Always thinking with his little head instead of the big one."

While the rest of the women laughed out loud, he tilted his head in my direction, sneering in mock amusement.

Then he slowly resumed tapping the block with his penis, trying to edge it out of its space. But with each tap, the tower began to wobble further and further, and by the third knock, it had begun to build an unstoppable momentum over the narrow support beneath it, and he could only watch helplessly as it toppled in a loud crash onto the surface of the coffee table.

"Ohhhh!" the women groaned, unhappy the game was over so fast. But their attention soon shifted when they realized the best part was about to come, when the married straight man would have to perform head on one of the remaining contestants.

"So what happens now?" Brad said, feigning ignorance.

"You'll have to perform fellatio on one of the men," Madison smiled.

Brad peered around the circle at the collection of throbbing penises standing proudly erect, shaking his head in dismay.

"I wouldn't know where to begin..." he said.

"Oh, come now," Madison grinned. "It's not so hard. It's just like sucking a popsicle."

"A very warm one, filled with cream," Brad frowned.

"Nobody said you had to swallow it," Maddy chuckled. "Though the least you can do is let your partner cum in your mouth. That's what every man has expected of us since the beginning of time, right ladies?"

"Damn right," Shae nodded. "What's good for the goose is good for the gander. And believe me, I should know."

Brad turned to his wife and shrugged his shoulders as if seeking for her permission to proceed.

"What do you say, dear?" he said. "Do you have anyone in particular you'd like to watch me giving head to?"

Laura glanced around the circle, pausing when she noticed Lincoln's long, dripping tool.

"As much as I'd love to watch you suck Lincoln's giant python, I'm not sure you'd be able to get your mouth around that thing. Why don't we see if we can find someone who's endowed with a size more similar to your own, so you can appreciate what it feels like for me to suck your dick..."

She darted her eyes around the circle, pausing when she noticed Diego's handsome, caramel-colored erection. Then she glanced up at the Latino's chiseled face and smiled.

"What do you say, Diego?" she said. "Are you up for a little boy-on-boy action?"

"It's been a while since I tried it in college," Diego smiled. "But if I remember correctly, it feels pretty much the same once I close my eyes."

"You heard the man," Laura grinned, turning toward her husband, then tilting her head, instructing him to get on his knees.

When Brad glanced at Diego, his dick flapped unconsciously, betraying his excitement at the idea of participating in his first homosexual encounter.

"How do you want me to do this exactly?" he said to Diego.

"It's pretty straight-forward," Diego said, smiling in the direction of Laura. "I suppose if I stand, your wife will be able to watch everything more easily."

Brad paused for a moment, temporarily taken aback by the Latino's provocation, then he glanced toward Laura, and she nodded with a big grin.

"It's okay dear," she said. "I'll be with you in mind and spirit. Maybe you'll pick up a few pointers that you can pass along to me. Everybody says men are better at giving head than women. It shouldn't be so bad."

Brad took a deep breath, then he kneeled down in front of Diego's bobbing organ, gripping it tentatively with the tips of his fingers and edging his mouth closer toward the flaring tip. When he opened his lips and encircled the glans, he hesitated for a moment, then he closed his eyes and lowered his head, engulfing Diego's circumcised crown in his mouth. As he began to bob his head over the tip of his cock, Diego moaned softly, titling his head down to watch the straight man blowing him uncomfortably.

"Don't just bounce on it like some kind of bobbing head," Laura chided, watching the pair intently. "You have to use your tongue to make it interesting. Imagine you're sucking on my clit while you roll your tongue over my nub to turn me on. Just under the edge, that's where you men like it best."

Brad paused for a moment, listening to his wife's instructions, then I noticed the side of his cheek moving as he began to swirl his tongue around Diego's corona, edging his head slightly lower.

"Nnngh," Diego moaned, grabbing hold of Brad's head and pushing his dick further into his mouth.

"Yeah, baby," Laura said, egging her husband on. "Just like that. Suck his tip like a lollipop. Suck it like you want to get to the gummy center."

"Mmm," Brad began to moan along with Diego, getting into the rhythm as he thrust his own hips forward, dry-humping the air.

"Do you like that, baby?" Laura said, lowering her hand toward her pussy while she separated her legs, watching the two men rocking their bodies together. "Would you like to be on the other end of one of those blowjobs some time?"

"Mmm," Brad nodded, dropping his hand onto the tip of his dick, becoming increasingly aroused by his first time touching a man intimately.

"Focus, sweetheart," Laura said. "This is about your partner, not you. Cup his balls with your hand and tease him underneath his sack. It feels three times as good when you stimulate his other erogenous zones when you suck his cock. There'll be plenty of time for you later."

Brad nodded his head, then he raised his right hand, cupping Diego's tightening balls while he sucked his corona more vigorously. When Diego tilted his hips upward, Brad's mouth slid further down his shaft, engulfing half of his organ, and he suddenly choked.

"It's okay, baby," Laura interjected, continuing to guide her husband. "Try to relax your throat so you don't gag. You breathe through an entirely different channel. Concentrate on breathing through your nose while you slowly take him deeper."

Brad slowed his sucking action as he concentrated on his breathing, then he slowly took more and more of Diego's organ into his mouth while the Latino pressed more firmly on the back of his head, encouraging him to go deeper. Within a few minutes, he'd impaled Diego's entire pole in his mouth with his lips flaring around the base of his balls while the Latino humped his face with increasing urgency.

"Fuck, yes," Diego hissed. "Suck my balls. Don't stop–that feels so good."

"Jesus, baby," Laura grunted, slipping three fingers into her sopping pussy. "You're a natural at this. We're going to have to incorporate this into our love life more often. I had no idea what we'd been missing all this time."

"It's always better when you can do it two ways," Shae nodded along with Laura as she sank two fingers into her dripping slit while jerking her hard-on with her other hand. "He's only beginning to scratch the surface of the possibilities."

"Mmm, yes," Laura said, turning her attention between Shae's erotic display and that of her husband moaning atop Diego's buried organ. "Tickle the area behind Diego's balls with your other hand. I can see that he's getting close. I want to watch him dump his load down your throat."

When Brad threaded his other hand behind Diego's balls and began stimulating the area between his testicles and his anus, Diego placed both of his palms behind Brad's head, pounding his dick harder against his face.

"Oh God," he grunted. "I can't hold it any longer. I'm going to come. Don't stop, here it comes..."

Suddenly, the Latino grunted loudly as he buried his dick deep into Brad's throat while gripping his hair tightly, emptying his seed down his partner's gullet while he bent over in heaving spasms. It seemed to take Diego almost a full minute to stop cumming as his buttocks flexed and his hips shook in delirious pleasure. When he finally stopped shaking, he withdrew his dripping organ from Brad's mouth, while his partner stared at his engorged organ with bulging eyes.

As I marveled at how quickly a straight man could be turned, I peered at the rest of the men still standing around the coffee table, noticing each of them flapping their hard dicks until they came together in a Bellagio-style fountain onto the glass table, over the pile of tumbled bricks.

How fast the castle crumbles, I thought, rubbing my pussy along with the rest of the women looking on in rapt attention, feeling my own orgasm rapidly approaching...

7

"Well," Madison said, surveying the sticky mess on the coffee table. "It looks like everybody enjoyed that game even more than I expected. Why don't we take a little break while I clean up and prepare for the next round? You'll find some refreshments in the kitchen, and the powder room is down the hall to the left."

"Should we get dressed while we wait?" Neil asked.

"You can if you want," Madison said. "But we're going to be alternating back and forth between boy games and girl games, and based on the last contest, I expect everyone will enjoy them more fully naked."

While everybody shuffled off to the kitchen to enjoy some hors d'oeuvres, Madison swept the sticky Jenga bricks into a bucket then wiped the coffee table down with Windex and some paper towels. When the group returned to the living room, they noticed a row of yoga mats lying on the floor and a raised curtain hanging over the fireplace with a series of cut-out holes spaced about a foot apart.

"What's all this?" Shae said, squinting at the strange setup.

"This time it's the ladies' turn to have some fun," Maddy smiled. "In this game I call Ping Pong Basketball, each of the women will be given five ping pong balls which they'll have to fling through the holes."

"When you say fling," Shae chuckled. "I'm assuming you don't mean with our hands?"

"What would be the fun in that?" Madison grinned. "The men had to play their game hands-free, so I think it's only fair the women do the same in this contest."

I glanced toward Madison, bulging my eyes.

"You want us to fire the ping pong balls through the holes with our pussies?" I said.

"Why not?" she said. "Strippers have been doing it for ages. Plus, it's good exercise for your Kegel muscles. It's a good way to tighten up your pussy and learn more control during sex."

"How will we choose the winner?" Laura said, walking up to inspect the setup more closely.

"Simple," Maddy said. "The winner will be the one who gets the most balls through the hole."

"And what's the prize this time?" Shae said.

"The winner will get her choice of which contestant she wants to go down on her."

"I'm assuming I get to play the girl part this time?" Shae smiled.

"Yes," Maddy nodded, peering down at her bifurcated genitals. "Although you'll have your choice of which role you wish to play if you happen to win the contest."

"Mmm, I like the sound of that," Shae grinned.

"Okay, ladies," Madison said. "Are you ready to do this?"

"How do you want us to prepare?" Laura said, still somewhat confused about the game rules.

"Each woman will lie down next to one another on a separate yoga mat, facing the curtain. There's a bucket behind each hole that will collect the balls you manage to toss through the panel."

"Will this game be timed, like the first two contests?" the cute straight girl, Lily, asked.

"No, just like with the men in Joystick Jenga, there's a bit of a learning curve involved. You can take all the time you need to finish the contest. Are you all ready to give it a try?"

"I guess..." Lily said, peering at the other women with a worried expression.

"Alright," Madison said, placing a cup with five ping pong balls beside each yoga mat. "Assume the position."

The men moved in closer to the mats to watch the action, then Marco suddenly peered up at Madison with a lopsided smile.

"Can we stand behind the curtain to watch it more closely?" he said. "Maybe it will be easier for them to fling the balls at our open mouths."

"I'm afraid that will be a little too distracting," Maddy chuckled. "But don't worry, you'll have your chance to get behind the curtain soon enough. This is an all-girl contest, so you'll just have to enjoy the show from the sidelines."

The women lay down face-up on the yoga mats then they spread their knees apart, peering at the adjacent holes in the curtain roughly five feet away.

"How do we do this exactly?" Laura said, lifting a ball out of her cup. "That looks like a long way to fling a ball using only my pussy."

"It's a little bit like childbirth," Maddy nodded. "You need to relax and contract some of the same muscles, just faster and with a lighter weight. After you insert the ball inside your slit, flex your abdominal muscles and exhale quickly while simultaneously trying to relax your pelvic floor muscles."

"Okay," Laura said, smiling in the direction of her husband. "Are you watching this, honey? Maybe we can use this technique to practice for our next baby."

"I'm game if you are," Brad laughed.

Laura slipped the ball into her opening, then she tilted her hips upward, exhaling rapidly. The ball spilled out of her slit, landing a foot in front of her hips, bouncing softly to the base of the curtain.

"Hmm," she said. "I see what you mean about a learning curve. It looks like this will take a bit of practice."

"That's why I gave each of you five balls," Maddy nodded. "Why don't you try it next, Lily?"

The cute blonde glanced at the other women lying next to her on the mats, then she shyly slipped a ball between her parted thighs and grunted heavily. The ball flung out of her pussy with a loud fart sound, bouncing off the curtain a few inches beside her targeted hole.

"Did you just fart?" Shae said, turning her head toward Lily.

"I'm not sure if it was a pussy-fart or a fart-fart," Lily giggled, turning a deep shade of crimson. "But it seemed to work. I almost got the ball through the hole. Now it's just a matter of perfecting my aim."

"You heard the woman, ladies," Madison nodded. "Saddle up and load your weapons. It's not as hard as it looks."

Each of the women proceeded to insert a ball into their pussies, then they grunted and exhaled as Madison instructed, sending a volley of white orbs toward the curtain. Some of them passed through the holes and some of them bounced back off the curtain onto the floor. With each volley of rounds, the room erupted in a cacophony of grunts and fart sounds, until the women dissolved in a jumble of hysterical laughter. By the time they finished, nobody knew who'd fired the most balls through the hole, but they hadn't had so much fun playing with their pussies since they were teenagers.

8

"Well, you guys enjoyed that even more than I expected," Madison said, rising off the sofa to count the balls in the buckets.

"Who knew pussies could be used for such novel entertainment?" Shae chuckled. "I might have to incorporate this into my cabaret act. I don't think I've made a room full of strangers laugh this hard in ages."

"It certainly was entertaining," Madison nodded, pulling back the curtain to count the number of balls that had landed in each of the buckets. As she began counting off the number of successful shots for each contestant, the group cheered and clapped at the results.

"Laura ended up with two," she said, pulling the balls out of the bucket one at a time. "Not too shabby for a first-time effort."

"Hear that, sweetie?" Laura said, peering over at Brad. "I only landed two balls with my pussy. Story of my life."

"Don't worry," Brad said, winking toward Diego. "I have a feeling we'll be introducing a few more into our love life soon enough."

Everybody laughed, and Madison resumed counting the balls in each bucket.

"And Lily," Madison continued, reaching into the bucket in front of Lily's mat. "You managed to get three balls successfully through the hoop."

"Woo-hoo!" Lilly clapped excitedly. "I guess all that pussy-farting pays off once in a while."

"Let's see how Jade did," Madison chuckled, reaching into the next bucket. "Also, three. Are you sure you guys haven't practiced this before?"

"Not unless you count the endless hours practicing with my Ben-Wa balls," I smiled.

Madison continued down the line, counting each woman's bucket collection until she reached Shae at the end of the row. When she reached into the pail, she lifted five balls cupped in her two hands.

"It looks like Shae had a perfect score," she smiled. "As the winner, you get to choose which of the women you'd like to share your reward with."

"Mmm," Shae purred, sitting up to inspect the lineup of sexy women sitting next to her on the mats. "There's a lot of worthy candidates, to be sure..."

Then she noticed Laura darting her eyes between Brad and herself, nodding excitedly at the prospect of having sex with her first transgender girl.

"But I think it's only fair that I give Laura a chance to return the favor from the last round. That is, if she's game for a little ladyboy action?"

"Oh, I'm game, alright," Laura grinned, shifting her hips over the wet spot rapidly forming on her mat. "But how do you want me to do this? Madison said the loser had to go down on the winner. I'm not sure which part you want me to play with, the boy part or the girl part?"

"Why not both?" Shae smiled, raising an eyebrow toward Madison. "You said you've never had sex with anyone other than her husband before today. Here's your chance to stretch your boundaries while putting some of those newfound skills your husband just demonstrated to good use."

"Works for me," Madison nodded. "Assuming that is, that Brad's on board with the idea."

"Fuck, yes," Brad grunted, his semi-flaccid dick already beginning to rise at the prospect of watching his wife go down on the sexy t-girl.

"Okay then," Madison said, motioning for Laura and Shae to move over to the leather sofa. "Why don't you two make yourselves more comfortable? I think it will be easier for you to service Shae while she's resting on the sofa."

"Yes," Shae smiled, strolling over to the couch and spreading her legs far apart as her erect dick flapped excitedly over her dripping pussy. "I believe it will."

Laura gawked for a moment at her bi-sexual genitalia, then knelt down in front of her, peering up at her thin waist and plump breasts. Even though Shae had a fully-functioning male penis, in all other respects she looked, sounded, and behaved like a voluptuous, sexy woman.

"Jesus," Laura murmured. "I hardly know where to start..."

"Why don't you start with the familiar part, then work your way down?" Shae smiled. "I don't see any timer, so you can take your time exploring my body. Maybe your husband can give you some tips along the way."

"Mmm," Laura smiled, grabbing hold of Shae's throbbing hard-on with two hands and beginning to stroke it up and down. "You're a little bigger than he is, so I might have to use both of my hands in this case."

"I think you're going to need more than two hands to manage all of that," Brad chuckled, darting his eyes between Shae's dripping pussy and her bobbing hard-on.

While Laura continued to stroke Shae's instrument as she moaned softly, the rest of the group inched closer, fascinated watching the true hermaphrodite display her glistening genitalia for the whole room to see. The men, in particular, seemed fascinated by the brazen display of the futa girl, stroking their own cocks unconsciously while they gaped at her like she was some kind of circus attraction.

"That feels good, Laura," Shae grunted, watching her phallus sliding in and out of Laura's tight fists. "But I'd love to feel your mouth, too. I could use a little extra lubrication to enjoy this fully."

"Mmm," Laura grinned, licking her lips. "I thought you'd never ask."

Without hesitating, Laura took Shae's big organ into her mouth, eagerly sucking and licking the head in the same way she'd instructed her husband earlier.

"Yes," Shae groaned, nodding her head approvingly. "It's not so different from your husband, is it?"

"This part, no," Laura said, raising her head for a moment to smile at Shae. "But the rest of you, that's a different story."

Shae paused as she glanced up at Diego, who was watching intently from the other side of the circle, cupping his balls with one hand while he stroked his dick with his other.

"It's kind of nice to have my lower parts stimulated at the same time," Shae said. "Like your husband did earlier with Diego. Touch me like you touch yourself when you're alone sometimes. I want to feel your fingers in my pussy."

Laura peered up at Shae with wide eyes, then she lowered her head over her throbbing tool as she slipped two fingers into the front of her slit, fucking her softly while she circled her tongue over her crown.

"Yes," Shae groaned. "Just like that. Caress my G-spot while you suck my dick. That feels so good."

"Holy fuck," Brad hissed from a few meters away, watching his wife go down on the sexy ladyboy. "This is the hottest thing I've ever seen."

"Even more than watching porn?" Shae grinned, watching him fapping his dick rapidly.

"I've never seen anything like this on PornHub," he huffed, gaping his mouth open in excitement. "Nothing with someone as beautiful as you, having both male and female body parts."

"Well, if your wife continues to perform like this, you two are welcome to borrow me whenever you please. Because these parts can be used to satisfy either one or you, or even both of you at the same time."

Brad's eyes suddenly widened imagining the possibilities, then he spurted into his hand, unable to control himself. As he hunched over, shaking in pleasure, Shae chuckled, grabbing hold of Laura's head.

"I'm going to come soon too if you keep touching me like that," she said. "Do you want me to come in your mouth, or would you rather watch?"

Laura paused for a second, lifting her head temporarily off Shae's dripping organ.

"I'd be happy to have you come in my mouth," she said. "But something tells me the rest of the group would prefer a clear line of sight. Can I suck your pussy and stroke your dick instead?"

"Absolutely," Shae nodded. "But I have to warn you. I squirt almost as hard out of my pussy when I come, as I do from my cock. You might want to prepare yourself."

"Oh, I'm prepared alright," Laura grinned. "I haven't had this much fun playing with a pussy since, well, the last exercise we just participated in."

"Yeah, well, I'm about to blow soon, so get ready to stand back."

"Mmm," Laura said, pressing her face hard against Shae's sopping pussy while she buried her tongue deep inside her slit, glancing up while she massaged Shae's bulging cock with her slippery hands.

"Yes, baby," Shae grunted, rocking her hips more rapidly on the sofa while she watched Laura eating her cunt. "Fuck me with your tongue. I'm gonna come any minute. Oh God, I'm going to come so hard. Fuckkkkk...."

Suddenly, she lifted her hips off the sofa and her big prick exploded in a shower of strings jetting up toward the ceiling while her pussy began spraying juices out from the side of Laura's face. When Laura realized her partner was coming from both orifices, she pulled her head back as the whole room peered on in fascination, watching her squirt and spray her juices in every direction.

It didn't take long for every man and half the women in the room to orgasm soon after, while they pounded their dicks and dripping pussies with their balled-up fists, unable to control their overflowing pleasure taking in the erotic spectacle.

9

"Well, that was a lot of fun," Madison smiled after everybody recovered from their orgasms. "I hope you boys have still got some fuel left in the tank, because our next game will need you to be hard and fast in a different way. Can I ask each of you to clean up the mess you made on the floor while I reset the stage? We wouldn't want any of you slipping during the active contest that follows."

While the rest of the group dutifully cleaned up the wet spots on the hardwood floor, Madison rearranged the curtain in front of the fireplace, then she disappeared into an adjacent room to collect the materials for the next game. When she returned, she carried another bucket with a collection of nerf baseball bats resting upside down.

"What are you going to have us do now?" the full-figured girl, Paige, chuckled. "Play a game of nude softball?"

"You'll be hitting some balls alright," Madison grinned, pulling one of the bats out of the pail with a dripping blue tip. "But not the kind you're imagining. In this erotic version of the popular carnival game Whack-a-Mole, you'll be trying to club a darting penis instead of a poking woodchuck."

"That sounds painful," Lincoln said, crossing his legs uncon-sciously.

"It's not as bad as it sounds," Madison laughed, squeezing the end of the soft bat with her fist. "These clubs are made out of foam, so it shouldn't hurt if you manage to get struck with one."

"What's the blue stuff on the end?" Laura said, peering at the drip-ping bat.

"It's non-toxic body paint, easy to wash off. We'll need some way of verifying when you make contact. Something tells me after I reveal the prize for the winner that the men will want to hide the truth."

"And what's that?" Linc said, glancing in my direction. "Another sexual favor from our choice of contestants?"

"Yes and no," Maddy said. "You'll receive a sexual favor, but this time you won't know who's performing it. The winner will stay behind the curtain while I choose who'll stimulate you from the other side."

"Oooo!" the ladies whistled, teasing the men about the surprise twist.

"So how are we going to do this exactly?" Diego said, peering toward the tall curtain with the row of waist-high cut-outs.

"Each man will stand one-at-a-time behind the curtain, randomly choosing which hole to thrust his penis through while one woman on the other side will try to strike it with her bat before he withdraws it back through the hole. You must poke your dick through one of the holes at least five times to qualify for the prize. The winner will be the one who completes the contest with an unsoiled crotch."

"Do we have to be hard for this contest?" Neil said.

"It'll certainly be more fun that way," Madison chuckled. "For the participants on both sides of the curtain."

Ryan suddenly shifted uneasily, peering at the group of women rubbing their hands together in anticipation.

"So, this is a boy-girl contest this time?" he said. "What if we don't swing that way?"

"Like Diego said earlier," Madison smiled. "You won't be able to tell who's sucking your dick on the other side if you can't see them. It'll feel pretty much the same way no matter who's doing it."

"I like the sound of this," Laura grinned, rubbing her hands together. "We get to take out our frustrations on our men's cocks, then watch them get sucked off by somebody else for their reward."

"That's one way of looking at it," Madison laughed. "But it's all in good fun. Kind of like cracking open a piñata to get to the prize inside."

"Except in this case, the prize will be nice and creamy," Laura smiled.

"Exactly," Madison nodded, turning toward the men. "Who'd like to go first?"

The guys peered at one another for a moment, unsure who wanted be the first contestant, then Laura reached into the pail, pulling out one of bats.

"It looks like my husband is a little more ready than the rest of the group, judging by the angle of his erection," she smiled. "Can I have the first crack at turning his balls blue?"

"I don't see why not," Madison said, glancing at Brad's bobbing erection. "You know the drill, Brad. Get behind the curtain and let's see if you can tease your wife in a different kind of way."

Brad paused as he grinned at Laura, then he ducked behind the curtain while Laura gripped her bat tightly with two hands, tensing it over her shoulder. After a few seconds, his cock darted through the hole on the left side of the curtain and Laura lurched to the side, swinging her bat at the prodding penis, missing it by inches before it disappeared back behind the panel.

"Oooo," the women hooted, laughing at the novelty of the game.

"That's pretty fast, sweetheart," Laura said to her husband from the other side of the curtain. "But it's not always good to be fast when using your penis. Let me paint that pretty dick with my brush and I promise to clean it off later with my tongue."

"Nice try, baby," Brad chuckled. "If I manage to evade your strikes, I've got a good chance at getting sucked off by somebody else. You already had your turn with one of the ladies, isn't it only fair that I get my turn now?"

"We'll have to see about that," Laura taunted. "Let's see who's the more adept one when it comes to swinging. Poke that pecker through another hole and let me have another swipe at it."

Brad hesitated for a moment then his dick suddenly poked out the other side of the curtain, before Laura had a chance to adjust her position.

"Ha, I'm on to you now," she smiled, moving closer to the center of the curtain and spreading her legs apart, preparing to strike again.

This time, Brad stuck his cock through the same hole, and Laura quickly slapped her bat down on it, splattering the tip with blue paint.

"Ouch!" Brad squealed from the behind the curtain, clutching his cock with two hands. "That hurt!"

"Oh, come on," Laura chided. "It can't be that bad. Why don't you come out while I'll kiss it better? It's somebody else's turn to run the gauntlet now."

When he stepped out gingerly from behind the curtain, the women cheered loudly, and he slapped the side of Laura's ass with his stained dick, smearing her with the paint.

"Alright," Madison nodded, happy to see everyone getting into the swing of things. "Who'd like to go next?"

One by one, each of the men took a turn behind the curtain, darting their erect cocks through the holes, eventually getting smeared by their partner on the other side, emerging with only their dignity hurt. The last man to go up was Linc, and as he retreated behind the panel, Madison peered toward the lineup of women, raising an eyebrow to see who wanted to take her turn this time. I raised my hand and nodded my head excitedly, and Madison motioned for me to approach the curtain.

"Do I at least get to know who'll be batting for me on the other side?" Lincoln said, watching the shifting shadow through the narrow holes.

"No way," Madison smiled. "This is a blind contest for the men. You're just going to have to suck it up for the next few minutes."

"That's okay by me," Lincoln laughed. "As long as my partner is prepared to suck it up from the other side when we're finished."

"I suppose that'll be up to you," Madison grinned. "Depending on how deftly you can wield that sword of yours."

10

I smiled at Madison, then spread my legs apart on the floor, holding my bat tightly with two hands, preparing to strike the first object that poked through the curtain. Knowing Linc had the largest cock in the room, I expected to make short work of him, easily tagging his oversize organ before he had a chance to pull it back through the panel.

But he was far faster than I expected thrusting it in and out of the holes, and as he moved from side to side with the agility of a linebacker, I barely missed him each time. By the time he successfully pushed his cock through the fifth hole, the entire room erupted in applause at his athletic accomplishment.

"Damn," I huffed in frustration. "That was harder than I expected."

"It was hard alright," Madison grinned. "But something tells me it's getting even harder while he awaits his prize behind the curtain. Who wants to be the one to finish him off?"

The women peered at one another for a moment, each of them eager to take a turn playing with Lincoln's huge, curved pole. I tilted my head and put on my best puppy-dog face, begging to be the one chosen after my initial contact with Linc in the first game.

"Shouldn't it be one of the ladies who tagged their partners earlier?" Paige said. "I mean, technically, Jade lost this contest with Linc. Shouldn't we be sharing the spoils with the rest of the women?"

I glanced at Paige dumbfounded for a moment, tilting my head and mouthing the word 'bitch'.

The rest of the women laughed then Madison peered toward at me, shaking her head.

"Sorry, Jade, but I'm afraid she has a point." She nodded her head, motioning for Paige to approach the curtain where Lincoln already had his flapping hard-on poking out of one of the holes, awaiting his prize.

"Mmm," Paige purred, kneeling in front of his undulating organ. "Can I use any part I choose to stimulate him?"

"I don't see why not," Madison smiled. "That is, if you're okay with the idea, Linc?"

"Absolutely," Lincoln grunted from the other side of the curtain. "I like these kinds of surprises."

"Well then, first..." Paige smiled, leaning over toward to his arcing organ. "I just want to touch this beautiful erection. I've never seen a penis as big as this one before."

She clamped her two hands around Lincoln's throbbing tool, her fingers only reaching halfway around his shaft, with two hand-widths still separating her fists.

"Are you sure you don't need a little extra help with that?" I said, feeling my juices beginning to drip down the insides of my thighs while I watched her stroking Linc's enormous pole.

"I think I've got the matter well in hand," Paige smiled, noticing his glans emitting a drop of precum while she stroked him harder.

"What does it feel like?" Laura said, gaping at his magnificent tool with bulging eyes. "Why don't you share your experience with the rest of us so we can at least enjoy it vicariously?"

"It's warm," Paige nodded. "Very warm, like a fresh-baked loaf of French bread coming out of the oven. And throbbing as hard as a fire hose."

"Oh my God," Emma groaned. "What I'd do to have my hands or my mouth impaled over that dagger."

"Fuck that," Laura said. "I want that thing deep up inside my pussy. Though I'm not sure how far he could get it in. I can't imagine I'd be able to take more than half his length."

"I'd be happy to find a way," Shae chuckled. "I've never seen anything like that. And believe me, I've seen a lot of dicks in my day."

"You guys are getting me all worked up talking like that," Paige murmured from the other side of the room. "You're making me wet just thinking about it."

"What are you waiting for then?" I said. "The least you can do is give him a proper fucking since you denied the rest of us the opportunity."

"Don't mind if I do," Paige smiled, hesitating as she contemplated how she wanted to take him.

She peered at the lineup of women salivating while they gawked at Linc's pulsating organ and she slowly stood up, turning around with her back to the curtain. Then she reached between her legs to grasp the tip of his glistening rod, bending her knees slightly to press it slowly inside her spreading slit.

"Oh God," Emma grunted again, slipping her fingers inside her dripping pussy. "This is almost as good as having the real thing. Put on a show for us, Paige. I want to imagine it's me riding on top of that horse."

"Like this, you mean?" Paige grinned, swiveling her hips slowly like she was performing an erotic dance, sinking Lincoln's organ deeper inside her with each shift of her hips. He began to moan behind the curtain and she smiled, raising her hands to her huge tits, squeezing them tightly while she pumped his veiny cock with her plump ass.

Somehow the combination of her beautiful, rotund figure rocking overtop of his huge phallus simply added to the excitement of the spectacle. We could only imagine how Lincoln was reacting behind the curtain, but the sound of his increasing moans told us everything we needed to know. While Paige slowly worked his long pole deeper and deeper into her pink pussy, each of the women rubbed their clits furiously, imagining it was them fucking his thick spear instead of her.

"Holy fuck," one of the men hissed behind us, and I peered over my shoulder to see Neil gripping his hard-on tightly with two hands while he spread his mouth open, twitching in delirious pleasure. Before long, everybody else in the room began stimulating themselves while they watched the beautiful redhead pumping her hips up and down over Lincoln's hard piston, while he grunted ever louder behind the curtain.

"Fuck, yes," Laura panted, watching Paige lower her pussy all the way down over his thick balls. "Fuck that beanstalk. I want to watch him blow his load inside you."

Unghh," Paige moaned, her cheeks growing redder while she tightened the muscles in her face. "I'm almost there. Are you about ready to pop off, Linc?"

"Absolutely," Linc grunted. "Can I come inside you?"

"I'm on the pill, so no worries," Paige huffed, squeezing her tits harder.

"Fuck, yes," Linc groaned from behind the curtain. "This feels insane. I haven't had anyone who's been able to take my whole length before."

"Let it go, baby," Paige panted, her sex flush beginning to roll down over her bouncing tits. "I'm going to come with you."

"Yes," Linc grunted, shaking the curtain rapidly behind Paige's rocking body. "Here it comes. I can feel your pussy clamping down on me."

Suddenly, Paige thrust her two hands over the front of her slit while she jilled her clit furiously, gaping her mouth open in ecstasy. When her orgasm finally washed over her like a ton of bricks, she hunched over, heaving her body up and down while we watched Linc's thick organ pulsing strongly as he emptied his load inside her. But the sound of their moans was soon drowned out by the collective groan emanating from all around the room while everybody orgasmed in tandem with the sexy couple. As I convulsed over my dripping fingers deeply embedded in my pussy, I glanced over at

Madison, noticing her hand thrust down the front of her jeans while a deep flush rolled over her cheeks.

I guess we're not the only ones enjoying this little county fair, I smiled to myself. She must have been wetting her pants anticipating how much fun this was going to be for every one of us even before we arrived.

11

"Whew!" Madison said after everyone recovered from their orgasms. "I don't know about you guys, but that was a lot more fun than any county fair I've ever been to!"

"I think you're on to something here," I nodded. "Maybe you should start your own public fair with your own set of games. Something tells me it would be sold out in hours."

"Hmm," Madison grinned. "I'm not sure it would be legal, with the current state of public indecency laws. But I have thought more than once about starting up my own sex club."

"Go for it," Laura said. "We'll be happy to spread the word. Your parties are the best ever!"

"Thanks," Maddy smiled. "But I've still got quite a few activities planned for this event. Maybe you guys can be my guinea pigs and tell me which ones are the most fun."

"Absolutely!" Emma said. "What's next on the agenda? Isn't it the ladies' turn this time?"

"Right you are, Emma," Maddy said. "But this time we're going to mix it up a little bit. What kind of a country fair would it be without a few rides?"

"What kind of rides?" Shae said, pinching her eyebrows. "It's not like you can fit a roller coaster in your living room."

"Perhaps not," Maddy smiled, flipping over a cover to reveal a miniature pommel horse sitting next to the fireplace. "But we can fit a few solo rides in here. In this next event I like to call Ride-em Cowgirl, we're going to test your stamina."

I peered at the familiar sex machine from a slumber party I hosted where I invited the manager of the local adult store to demonstrate her offerings.

"Is that a Sybian machine?" I said, widening my eyes.

"Indeed it is," Madison nodded. "Have you had some experience using one before?"

"Maybe once or twice," I grinned.

"Then I guess you'll have a bit of a leg up, in a manner of speaking, competing in this contest. Because the winner will be the one who can last the longest without coming."

"What's the prize this time?" Laura said, wrinkling her forehead. "If we come on the machine, won't it be a little anticlimactic for the winner to have sex with the loser?"

"Not if the winner gets to take it home with her afterwards to enjoy many more orgasms on her own," Madison smiled.

"What?" Paige said, suddenly flaring her eyes. "The winner gets to keep the machine?"

"For a little while," Maddy nodded. "At least until I open my own club, where I could use a little help setting up shop."

"How does it work, exactly?" Emma said, strolling closer to the machine to squint at the diamond-shaped plastic dildo propped up in the middle of the seat.

"It's pretty simple, really," Madison said, walking over to demonstrate the device. "You simply sit on the dildo while I adjust the controls to increase the vibrations."

"So, it's really just some type of glorified vibrator?" Emma said, rubbing her hand over the strangely shaped dildo.

"Well, yes," Maddy smiled. "But I think you'll find it's like nothing you've ever tried before. In addition to the vibration embedded in the unusually shaped dildo, the seat of the machine also vibrates. It's quite a stimulating experience, if I do say so myself."

"Now I see why you call it Ride-em Cowgirl," Shae nodded. "It kind of looks like riding a horse."

"Yes," Madison grinned. "A very sexy and hung horse."

"So, who'd like to be the first to give it a try?" Madison said, glancing around the group of women. "What about you, Emma? You seem particularly fascinated with the shape of the device."

"Okay," the pretty blonde said. "But why is the dildo shaped like a diamond?"

"You'll just have to see for yourself," Maddy smiled. "You know what they say–a diamond is a girl's best friend."

"We'll have to see about that," Emma nodded, straddling the saddle and turning her head toward Madison. "Is there a proper way to sit on it?"

"You can position yourself in either direction," Madison said. "But I think if you face the front of the room, the rest of the group will be able to enjoy it almost as much as you."

"Okay," Emma said, squatting down over the dildo and flaring her eyes when the knob slipped inside her pussy.

"It's a little smaller than some of the other cocks I've sampled," she smiled, twisting her hips seductively on the seat.

"Maybe so," Maddy said, lifting the electronic controller attached to the device and beginning to turn the dial. "But can the other cocks do this?"

She twisted the dial slowly, and the machine began to hum with the plastic plate holding the dildo to the frame flapping softly in front of her slit.

"Oh!" Emma squeaked, raising her eyebrows. "That's a little different..."

"Different good?" Madison grinned.

"Yes," Emma grunted, rolling her hips gently over the apparatus. "Very good."

"It gets even better," Madison smiled, twisting the dial a little further clockwise.

"Oh my God," Emma groaned, placing the palms of her hands on the front of the machine to support her quivering body. "That feels incredible."

"Better than your usual vibrators?"

"Yes," Emma purred. "There's something about sitting on top of it and being able to ride it like a–"

"Horse?" Madison grinned.

"Something like that," Emma grunted.

"Well hold onto your britches, because this horse is about to start galloping..."

Madison twisted the dial all the way to the maximum setting, and Emma suddenly threw her head back, spreading her legs wide apart while her tits bounced excitedly on her chest.

"Holy shit," she panted, gaping her mouth open in pleasure while the whole group watched her shaking atop the vibrating device. "This is crazy. I can't hold it much longer..."

"Just let it go, baby," Madison said, smiling while she watched the flush on Emma's chest spreading up her neck toward her twisted face.

"Ngah!" Emma suddenly cried out, slumping over the front of the machine as her whole body convulsed in a powerful orgasm.

12

"Not too bad," Madison said, turning down the vibration as Emma began to stop shaking. Then she peered at her stopwatch and nodded. "Ninety seconds. That's longer than I lasted when I first tried the machine."

"Maybe I had a little stage fright holding me back," Emma smiled, lifting herself gingerly off the dripping dildo. "It was a bit more difficult trying to concentrate while everybody was watching me."

"Some people get off even faster on that," Maddy nodded. "Who'd like to try it next? What about you, Laura? This is your chance to try out a different kind of cock. Though this one mightn't be quite as warm and juicy as Shae's."

"True," Laura said, smiling toward the sexy transgender girl. "But she denied me the chance to sit on her pretty cock earlier. I've been wanting a hard dick up my cunny ever since the first Shower versus Grower game."

"Give me a moment to clean the machine and get it ready for you," Madison said, wiping off the glistening dildo and the surrounding area with a moist cloth.

"Alright," she said when she finished. "Your chariot awaits."

"Don't get too comfortable on that thing, sweetheart" Brad teased as she straddled the apparatus and slowly lowered herself over the upturned dildo. "I'm not sure I'll be able to compete with an automated dick machine."

"Maybe not in terms of recovery time," Laura grinned as she inserted the hard plug into her hole. "But you're certainly a lot prettier than this machine."

"All set to begin?" Madison said, placing the controller in one hand and her stopwatch in the other.

"As ready as I'll ever be," Laura grinned, winking toward her husband.

Madison turned the dial partway to the way to the right, and when the machine started humming, Laura's eyes flew open, surprised at the intensity of the device.

"Okay," she nodded. "That's definitely not like any other dildo I've tried before."

"How does it feel different?" Brad said, his dick already starting to rise while he watched his wife ride the vibrating machine.

"It's hard to describe," Laura grunted. "It's more of a full-body experience, like when I'm riding on top of you. Just more–"

"Intense?" Brad said, wrinkling his forehead.

"Well, your dick doesn't exactly vibrate when you're inside me," Laura chuckled, rolling her hips over the undulating platform.

"Or change speed automatically," Madison smiled, twisting the dial further to the right.

"Unghh," Laura panted, placing her hands overtop of her thighs to support herself while she rocked on the shaking machine. "This feels so good. Maybe you should try it sometime, honey. Gay guys say the anus has as many nerve endings as a woman's pussy."

"Well, I'm not gay," Brad grinned, watching his wife becoming more turned on with each passing moment. "But I can think of some other ways we might enjoy that machine together."

"I'd like that," Laura grunted, locking eyes with him while she squeezed her shaking tits. "You could press your dick against me while you hold me, and we could enjoy the vibrations together."

"Yes, baby," Brad said, stroking his cock while he imagined the two of them riding the machine together. "But I don't know how long I'd be able to last with you looking so hot on that thing."

"I'm going to come soon," Laura hissed. "Watch me while I come for you. Oh baby..."

As she tilted her head back in escalating ecstasy, Madison turned the wheel to the maximum setting, and suddenly Laura's body began jerking while her thighs slapped against the side of the frame. Both she and Brad gaped their mouths open in pleasure while the rest of the group looked on in rapt attention, feeling their own erogenous zones pulsing in unison with the happy couple.

When Laura finally stopped coming, Madison turned off the machine and peered at her watch.

"Two minutes, ten seconds," she nodded, making a notation on the clipboard beside her. "A little better than Emma, but I think you had a little help from your husband."

After Laura got off the machine and Madison wiped it down, each of the women took a turn on the device, lasting anywhere from one to three minutes before climaxing in uncontrollable pleasure. Nobody seemed prepared for the unusual combination of the vibrating platform shaking under their ass and the pulsating dildo purring inside their pussies. With Madison expertly controlling the progression in pleasure, none of them had a chance holding out for more than a few minutes.

When it finally became my turn to ride the machine, I hesitated overtop of the diamond-shaped dildo, trying to slow my pulse and my breathing. When I lowered my pussy over the plug, I closed my eyes, trying to shut out the distractions from the rest of the room, knowing that watching my friends playing with themselves while I squirmed over the hotseat would only add to my excitement.

While Madison slowly ramped up the speed of the undulating dildo, I tried to think about work and other boring topics, but the sensation of the vibrating horse and the shaking dildo eventually turned my attention to the escalating pleasure emanating from my midsection. As much as I tried to resist the rising crescendo, after a few minutes, my body succumbed to the pressure, unconsciously rocking in symbiosis with the machine.

As my orgasm slowly began to spread across my pelvis, I contorted my face, trying to hold it off as long as I could. But when Madison turned the dial all the way to the max, I let out a high-pitched squeal, pulling my thighs hard against the side of the machine and spraying out my juices in every direction while I shook uncontrollably in undeniable pleasure. When I finally stopped shaking, Madison turned off the machine and peered at her watch with a lopsided grin.

"Wow," she said. "Maybe I should try closing my eyes more often when I have sex. You managed to hold out for an impressive four and a half minutes during that ride. That puts you in first place, with only one contestant to go."

13

Madison glanced in Shae's direction and the t-girl peered back at her with a surprised expression.

"You mean I get to participate with the women again?" she said excitedly.

"Of course," Maddy smiled. "You've got an innie like the rest of us, don't you?"

"Well, yes," Shae grinned. "I've got both an innie and an outtie. I seem to have an unfair advantage being able to play on both sides of the table."

"Well, it looks like the rest of the group doesn't seem to mind," Madison said, noticing everyone inching closer to the machine to watch the sexy transgender girl ride the device. "It seems that they're just as excited as I am to see if you'll experience twice the pleasure with twice the equipment."

"We'll have to see about that," Shae nodded. "I normally have multiple partners to stimulate me when I have sex. This time it'll be only my girl part that has a chance to get stimulated."

"I suppose that answers the question about which part of your introduction was a truth versus a lie," Madison chuckled. "Something tells me you'll have no shortage of willing partners after we finish this first phase of the party."

"You mean there's more to come after this?" Shae said, widening her eyes in surprise.

"We're just getting started," Madison nodded. "We're only about a third of the way through the planned events. I hope you guys will still be able to get it up after getting your rocks off so many times. Because the remaining events won't work very well with a soft dick."

Shae chuckled while she glanced down at her bobbing hard-on, already beginning to get excited about the prospect of riding the sex machine in front of the rest of the group.

"Oh, I'm up for it alright," she smiled. "Like Jade said earlier, this thing has a mind of its own."

"Have a seat then," Madison said, motioning for Shae to sit on the device. "I think her time will be pretty hard to beat."

"She always sets the bar high," Shae nodded, peering over in my direction. "Ever since we compared cucumbers at the grocery store, I knew she had a unique talent."

While Shae lowered her pussy over the plastic dildo, everyone crept in a little closer, watching her big dick pointing up over the base of the machine like the tall horn of a saddle. Everybody knew this was going to be a special show, and the men were already stroking their dicks, excited to watch the sideshow distraction.

"Are you ready?" Madison said, holding the controller in her hand.

"Not as ready as everybody else seems to be," Shae chuckled, peering at the circle of men gawking at her with wide eyes.

"Here goes nothing, then," Madison said, twisting the knob slowly.

"Uhnn," Shae groaned as she felt the vibrating dildo shaking inside her pussy. "That feels exquisite. I've never had a vibrator stimu-lating my pussy and the base of my cock at the same time."

"Take your time and enjoy it, sweetie," Madison purred, twisting the dial a little slower than with the others. "I know the rest of us surely will."

Shae glanced down, noticing her cock emitting a drop of precum, and smiled.

"Do you mind if I touch myself while you stimulate me?" she said. "I'd kind of like to jerk off with the rest of the guys to enjoy this experience fully."

"No problem on my end," Madison grinned. "But I don't know how much that will help you hold out longer to win the game."

"I don't care about winning," Shae said, gripping her hard-on tightly with two hands. "I've already hit the jackpot watching this group of hot men and women staring at me while I get off."

"Suit yourself, babe," Madison said, turning the dial further to the right.

"Mmmh," Shae grunted, rocking her prick in and out of her hands while she squirmed her hips over the seat of the machine. "Bring it on. Give me everything you've got."

Madison grinned while she watched the rest of the group rubbing their crotches as they gazed at the sexy t-girl stroking her dripping dick. She knew Shae wouldn't be able to last much longer and while she watched her squirming over the machine, she lost track of time, rocking her hips in synchronicity with Shae. She didn't even have to touch herself, feeling her pleasure rising in lockstep, lost in the passion of the moment.

When she noticed Shae's mouth beginning to gape open on the brink of climax, she began to feel her own pleasure approaching the tipping point. She turned the speed dial all the way to the right, and they both climaxed together, shaking powerfully in their respective chairs. While Shae shuddered atop the machine, jetting long arcs of spunk toward the gallery, the entire room groaned in simultaneous pleasure taking in the erotic scene.

After Madison indicated that her time was second to my own, I hard cared. All I could think about was how much I wanted to use the machine in tandem with Shae, sitting atop her pretty cock while we both came together over the shaking horse.

BOOK 49

CARNY GAMES 2

A SEX PARTY

VICTORIA RUSH

1

After the last game where we watched Shae spurting while she rode the Sybian machine to orgasm, I was excited to discover what the next contest would be. Madison had alternated the focus of each game between the men and the women, and watching the guys' still-bobbing dicks dripping strings of cum from their flaring heads was getting me even more worked up thinking about it.

"That was crazy-hot," I said. "But from the look of things, I think the boys are eager to see what's in store for them in the next round."

"Funny you should ask," Maddy smiled, reaching behind her to reach into her game kit behind the sofa. "Because I've been looking forward to this next contest ever since I came up with the idea for this party."

She lifted her hand, clutching a cluster of pink plastic rings.

"In this next version of the classic carnival game *Ring Toss*, the ladies will be aiming at something a little more interesting than Coke bottles. That is, if the boys can stay hard long enough to let the women claim their prize."

"I dunno," Brad's wife Laura said, glancing at her husband's flagging erection. "After that last exhibition, I'm not sure how much more energy the guys have left. Some of them have come three times already."

"I suppose that depends on what the *prize* is," Brad grinned, grabbing his dripping tool and trying to bring his hard-on back to life.

"Just like with the previous contests," Madison nodded. "Each winner will have a chance to hook up with their partner."

"How do we decide who's the *winner*?" the sexy redhead, Paige, said.

"Each of the ladies will be given five plastic rings," Madison continued. "While the men line up side-by-side, the women will toss their rings toward their opposing partner. The one who lands the most rings on their partner's penis, wins."

Lincoln furrowed his brow, squinting at the narrow hoops in Madison's hand.

"Are you sure those rings are *large* enough?" he said. "Because it seems to me that those of us who are, er, a little better endowed, are at a distinct disadvantage in this game."

Madison peered at Linc's thick pole and raised herself up off the sofa with a devilish grin on her face.

"Why don't we *test* it to make sure?"

She slipped one of the rings over the tip of his hard-on, sliding it slowly up and down his long shaft.

"Seems to fit well enough," she said. "What you may be losing in wider girth should be more than counterbalanced by your longer length. You'll be that much closer to your partner while she aims for your dick."

Shae shuffled her feet impatiently while she watched Madison place a line of masking tape on the floor a few feet in front of the fireplace.

"Which side of the line do you want *me* to be on this time?" she said. "I seem to qualify on both sides."

"I'll leave that up to you," Madison smiled.

"Frankly, I could use a bit of a rest," Shae said, licking her lips while she appraised the lineup of rising dicks as the men took positions in front of the fireplace. "Besides, I'm kind of hungry for a *different* kind of treat this time."

"Alright then, ladies," Madison said, watching the men standing cheek-to-cheek with their hard-ons bobbing in front of their stomachs. "Choose a partner and assume your position. Each of you will be given five rings, which you'll toss directly toward your opposing player. Anyone who steps over the line will be immediately disqualified."

The women scrambled to the front of the line, bumping against one another as they fought to claim their preferred position. Madison grinned when she saw that Laura had chosen to lineup opposite the handsome Latino, Diego, instead of her husband, also noticing that Shae had quickly positioned herself in front of Linc. While the rest of the women smiled at their chosen partners, she handed out the rings to each of the contestants, then she moved to the side of the line to act as referee.

"Is everybody ready?" she said.

"It looks like it didn't take long for the guys to recover their stamina," I chuckled, glancing at Brad's erection tapping against the front of his stomach while he peered back at me.

"What's good for the goose is good for the gander," he grinned, winking at his wife, who was staring at Diego as she licked her lips.

"Alright then," Madison nodded. "Gentlemen, start your engines."

Each of the women leaned forward as far as they could without stepping over the line, then they tossed their rings toward their partners' erections, bouncing off their dicks and onto the floor.

"No fair!" Laura protested, watching the rings bouncing on the floor. "This contest is rigged, just like the one at the county fair. The rings are too small to fit over the targets!"

"It doesn't appear to be a problem for *Lincoln and Shae*," Maddy smiled, nodding toward the couple at the far end of the line.

Laura turned to peer in their direction and frowned when she saw Shae's first ring resting on Linc's big cock half way down his shaft.

"It's obviously not a *size* issue," Madison said. "It looks to be more a matter of technique."

"Hmm," Laura said, glowering at Diego while his dick flapped in front of his stomach. "Stop *moving* while I try to lasso that bobbing prick."

"It's not as easy as it looks," Diego replied. "This thing has a mind of its own."

Everybody laughed, then the women leaned forward again, pausing as they took aim at the men's fluttering penises. This time a few more rings landed on their targets while the other women groaned watching their rings fall onto the floor.

"You're not leaving me much room to snare your dick," I said, peering at Brad's erection pressed up against his stomach.

"I can't help it," he said. "It's *always* like this when I'm this turned on."

I glanced to the end of the line where Shae stood grinning while she stared at Linc's purple prick, standing proudly at attention with two pink rings encircling his shaft.

"Well, *somebody* seems to have found the secret to landing these things. Just do whatever Lincoln's doing. Otherwise, those two are going to be having all the fun once again when this contest is over."

"Okay," Brad said, bending forward a few degrees, trying to present an easier target.

This time, some of the women tilted their heads toward Lincoln and Shae before they threw their next ring, noticing Linc jutting his hips forward and gripping the base of his pole to angle it in Shae's direction.

"They're cheating!" Bonnie said, flaring her eyes at Madison. "He's using his *hand* to help capture the ring!"

"Nobody said you couldn't use other parts of your anatomy," Maddy grinned. "As long as you don't move your feet, you're welcome to do whatever you can to win the contest. You wouldn't hold still while someone tried to throw a piece of *popcorn* into your mouth, would you?"

"*Now* you tell us," I huffed, peering toward Brad.

He grasped his shaft and bent it down a few inches, and this time my ring landed on the tip of his pole, sliding off the slippery crown and bouncing onto the floor.

"Wipe your pre-cum off the tip of your cock," I scolded him. "That extra lubrication isn't helping things."

Laura suddenly leaned over, glancing at her husband's glistening tool.

"Are you getting *excited* about the prospect of fucking another contestant, sweetheart?" she teased.

"After my *last* hookup, I'm ready to take my chances with somebody of the opposite sex," Brad smiled.

"So am I," Laura said, grinning at Diego, who nodded excitedly as he peered down at her last ring encircling his pole.

For the next couple of rounds, each of the couples paused to line up their targets while the men used their hands to angle their pricks in the direction of the rings, but after the final disk had been tossed, the winner was plain to see. When Madison stepped forward to inspect the men's penises, Lincoln's huge penis had four rings attached to it while Diego and Marco had two, and most of the others only had one.

"It looks like size *does* matter in this instance," Madison grinned, flapping Lincoln's cock to the side as the rings jostled loudly on his flaring dick. "It seems that you two are going to be the center of attention once again while the rest of the contestants stand back and watch."

2

"Have you thought about how you'd like to engage with your partner this time, Shae?" Madison said.

"Are you kidding me?" Shae smiled. "I've been dreaming about what I'd like to do with this python ever since I saw it unsheathed in the first round."

"It looks like you've got a few more options than most," Maddy chuckled, peering down at her engorged penis and dripping pussy.

"Can I use *all* of them?" Shae said.

Madison paused for a moment, then shook her head.

"In the interest of sharing the spoils, I think it's only fair that you use one part at a time. I'm pretty sure there are a few *other* guests that would like to take a turn with you. Besides, the party isn't even half over, and the clock's ticking for our next contest. Why don't you two put on a little show while the rest of us fantasize about what's coming next?"

Shae smiled and took a step toward Linc, slapping the side of her cock against his like she was sword fighting.

"Well, if it's a *show* they want," she said. "Maybe we should let it all hang out this time. Are you up for a little *cock play*, Lincoln? I know you said you don't swing that way, but if you're doing it with somebody with *tits*, it's not really gay, is it?"

Lincoln hesitated while he peered down at Shae's throbbing hard-on, slowly sliding his gaze up her body, pausing at her bouncing tits and rosebud lips.

"With you, I'm prepared to do just about *anything*," he smiled.

"Sit down on the floor and spread your legs then," Shae said while she rubbed her fingers over the tip of his dripping crown. "Because it's about to get interesting."

Lincoln sat down on the floor and bent his knees, propping his arms behind his back while his long erection bobbed between his legs. Shae sat down in a similar manner, facing him as she slowly pulled the plastic rings off his glistening dick one at a time.

"Mmm," she purred, gazing into his eyes while she paused near the tip of his prick, twisting each ring around the sensitive flesh under the frenulum. "Maybe I'll get a chance to slide something *else* over this beautiful tool before this night is over. It's a shame to leave so much of this organ to waste."

"Just say the word and I'll be happy to dip it into your pool," Lincoln said, meeting Shae's gaze with a pearly smile.

"It's tempting," she smiled back at him. "But right now, I want to feel your manhood pounding against *another* part of my anatomy."

After she lifted the last of the rings off his cock, she shimmied her hips forward, pressing the underside of her hard-on against Linc's upturned pole, gripping both of their instruments with two hands.

"Fuck, yes," Shae groaned. "That's what I'm talking about. Do you like the feeling of our cocks pressed together?"

"Yes," Linc panted. "It feels so–*warm*."

"And *slippery*," Shae smiled. "You're dripping like a fountain over your monument."

"So are you," Linc said, peering between their legs at the puddle of fluid accumulating between Shae's legs.

"That's the advantage of being a *real* ladyboy," Shae grinned. "I get to fuck you with my outer part while I lubricate us with my inner part."

"Yes," Lincoln groaned. "Rub my dick with your pretty girl-cock. I want to watch you spray your cum all over my chest."

"That makes two of us," Shae said, leaning forward to kiss Lincoln while she slid her cock against his, gripping their dicks tightly in her hands.

"Mfft," Linc grunted as he felt Shae's tits sliding against his muscular chest.

He wrapped his arms around her back and pulled her closer to him, thrusting his hips more rapidly in her hands. The sensation of his dick sliding against her burning organ while his balls rubbed against her dripping pussy only added to the excitement of his first-time encounter with a transgender partner.

While the rest of us looked on from the edge of the sofa, we rubbed our own dripping genitals as we stared silently at the erotic scene unfolding before us. While Lincoln and Shae amped up the intensity of their muffled humping and moaning, each of us began to feel our own orgasms building toward an inexorable climax.

"Fuck, yes," Lincoln groaned into Shae's mouth. "Grip my dick harder with your hands. I want to feel you pulsing against me when you come. I'm getting closer..."

"Yes, baby," Shae hummed. "Let it go. Squirt all over my tits while you come in my hands. Your cock feels so hot..."

"Yes, yes, yes," Lincoln huffed as the tips of his fingers dug into Shae's back. "That feels so good. Oh God, here it comes–"

Suddenly, he lifted Shae's body off the floor as he tilted her pussy onto the base of his dick while he thrust his hips hard into her hands one last time, jetting a long string of ropes onto her belly and tits while he thrashed and groaned on the floor, moaning into her mouth. When Shae's cock began squirting soon after, the entire room erupted in a cacophony of squeals and moans, with the rest of us unable to resist our own overflowing pleasure any longer.

While I squirted my own juices over Madison's leather sofa, I glanced over at her, noticing she'd removed the last of her clothing, with the fingers of two hands deeply embedded in her pussy, shaking uncontrollably along with the rest of us.

We're going to have to find another way to get her involved in the action, I thought to myself, catching her eye as we convulsed together in mutual ecstasy.

3

"Whew!" Madison said after everybody came down from their powerful climaxes. "Why don't we take a break so everyone can clean up and recharge with a little nourishment? There's plenty of wine and beer in the fridge and some hors d'oeuvres on the kitchen table."

"What's up next?" Lily asked. "Isn't it the *girls'* turn for some fun in the next round?"

"Right you are, Lily," Madison nodded. "But I'd rather keep it a surprise until everyone regroups. All I can say is I guarantee you'll be dripping *wet* by the time we finish the next round."

Everybody retired to the kitchen and milled around the large island while we noshed on cheese tarts and pita with tzatziki. By now, we'd all lost any reservations about prancing around naked, having already been exposed in the most intimate settings. When Lincoln and Shae entered the room after cleaning up, everybody grinned at them, clapping loudly.

"That was fucking hot," I said to Shae as she nudged in next to me, helping herself to a generous serving of tzatziki.

"Tell me about it," Shae nodded. "I think Lincoln sprayed more jizz on me than this whole bowl of tzatziki."

"I wouldn't doubt it," I laughed. "With that giant poker and cannon balls, I'm sure he's storing more than his fair share."

"So what do you think Madison's planning next?" she said. "Each game seems to be getting wilder and crazier than the one before."

"I don't know, but based on how hard she came watching you and Linc go at, she must be almost as eager as the rest of us to resume the festivities."

"It's too bad we can't get her more involved in the action," Shae nodded. "It doesn't seem fair for her to stand back as a spectator for each of the contests."

"We'll have to see if we can switch roles somewhere along the way," I said. "Not every game needs a referee, and I'm sure she'd love to be on the receiving end of some of the games."

"Or the *giving* end," Shae smiled.

"Let's see what this next contest involves," I nodded. "With the focus returning to the girls, there should be plenty of opportunity for her to get more involved."

W hen we returned to the living room, I noticed the furniture had been rearranged with the sofa set back a further distance from the fireplace and set perpendicular to the opposing wall. Madison had draped a waterproof tarp over the edge of the hearth, and in her hand she held a clutch of brightly colored panties.

"What's all this?" I said. "It looks like you're getting ready for some kind of *flood*."

"Well, there'll be water involved," Maddy grinned. "But with any luck, it'll be concentrated in a small area so as not to make too much of a mess."

"What's with the colorful panties?" Shae said. "Just when we were beginning to get comfortable running around naked."

Madison raised one of the panties and spread it apart, revealing a patch of concentric circles woven into the crotch.

"In this next contest I'll call *Bullseye*, the boys are going to be taking their turn shooting water pistols at your pussies. Kind of like in the carnival game where you shoot pellets at a paper target, the challenge will be to soak the targeted area in the allotted time."

"Do we have to soak the *entire* bullseye?" Ryan said, peering at the large red circles on the front of the garment.

"Yes," Madison nodded. "I'll be inspecting each set of panties upon completion to see if the full outer ring is darkened."

"How much time will we have?" Diego said.

"Three minutes."

"And we'll be firing from the edge of the sofa?" Brad said.

"Exactly."

"That doesn't sound so hard," Marco huffed.

"It *will* be, when you're using a small water pistol with limited water storage," Madison said.

She grabbed a bucket of water and placed it in front of the sofa, then reached into her game kit to hand each of the men a plastic pistol.

"Where do you want me to sit this time?" Shae said.

"Why don't you take a turn with the *boys* for a change?" Madison smiled. "Your pecker might be a bit of an unnecessary distraction for your opposing partner."

"That's too bad," Shae laughed. "I was kind of hoping I could act as referee this round so we could get *you* more involved in the action."

"You might be able to twist my arm for the contest coming up in a couple of rounds," Madison said. "This one's pretty simple, but it will still require a discerning eye."

"What's the prize for the winner?" Lincoln said.

"Same as always," Maddy nodded. "Another hook-up with your opposing partner."

"Will there be any limitations on what we're allowed to do with each other this time?" Lincoln asked.

"You can do whatever your partner wants. Although she'll likely be pretty worked up by the time you finish the contest. You better be ready to dive in as soon as we announce the winner."

"Oh, I'll be ready to *dive in*, alright," Lincoln grinned, peering at the women's glistening pussies while Madison handed out the panties. "I'm ready to sink my sword to the *hilt* this time."

"I wouldn't get your hopes up too high," Madison nodded, glancing at his rising organ. "This time it's going to be a pretty level playing field."

4

After each of the women pulled on their bullseye panties and took up positions on the edge of the hearth, the men sat down side-by-side on the sofa, dipping their water pistols into the bucket to fill their reservoirs and lining up their partner's pussies through the gun sights.

Laura flapped her knees apart while she grinned at her husband, who'd chosen to line up directly opposite her position on the hearth.

"It shouldn't be so hard for you to find the magic spot this time," she teased, peering down at the bullseye between her legs.

"Maybe we should wear these more often," Lily nodded, adjusting the center of the bullseye over the base of her mound. "It's pretty hard to miss the clit with these bright red circles pointing directly to the target."

All the women chuckled, then they slowly spread their legs apart, revealing the titillating target of five pulsating pussies daring the men to soak their snatches. I was happy to have the handsome Hispanic hunk, Diego, as my counterpart this time, and I winked at him while he raised his pistol, awaiting Maddy's start signal. As she raised her arm and prepared to start the timer, I could already feel my panties dampening anticipating his teasing of my private parts.

When she lowered her arm and signaled for everyone to start, a
volley of water jets squirted in our direction, spraying each of us all
over our bodies. While we blinked our eyes and spat out the water
splattering over our tits and faces, we laughed out loud at the men's
clumsiness.

"Come on, boys," Paige teased, wiping the drops off her melon-
sized tits. "Surely you can do better than that. Even my high-school
boyfriend got to second base faster than that."

"It's not for want of trying," Marco huffed, shaking his head as he
took aim again. "These pistols have crappy aim. It's going to take a
little practice to adjust our targets."

"That's what they all say," Bonnie chuckled.

The men refocused their aim, holding their pistols with two
hands while they lined up their partner's bullseyes, and this time
most of the volleys landed closer to the women's hips. I felt Diego's
next shot land just below my belly button, and I tilted my hips
upward, feeling the trickle dribble down over my clit. As crazy as this
concept was, I found it highly stimulating to have my partner
shooting water jets at my pussy, and before long, my own lubrication
began to dampen the cloth between my legs as much as Diego's
increasingly accurate shots.

After a few more volleys, some of the men's pistols ran out of
water, and they hastily dipped them back into the bucket to refill
them, desperately trying to finish soaking their partner's bullseye
before time ran out. I peered down at my crotch and noticed the
outer rings had begun to darken from Diego's sure aim, but the inner
circle still remained clean and dry.

"Shoot a little higher," I encouraged Diego. "Aim for my clit, and
I'll help do the rest."

"One minute left!" Madison called out, glancing at the timer
counting down on her phone screen. "You guys better speed up the
pace, or we might not have *any* winner this round."

Diego nodded when he heard my coaching, and I lifted my hips a
few inches off the hearth, feeling my pussy beginning to buzz in
excitement. When his next two volleys caught me square on my

button, I moaned in pleasure, feeling a sense of urgency building up inside me.

"Yes, Diego," I panted, noticing my wet spot beginning to spread in my panties. "Keep hitting me right there. That feels so good. You're going to make me come soon if you keep doing it like that."

"Mmm," Diego nodded, his cock starting to rise between his legs when he realized the effect he was having on me. "Who cares about *winning* when the process of getting there is so exciting? I haven't had this much fun since I spied on my middle-grade classmates through the girls' locker room window."

"If you finish the job, I'll give you more than just a *peek* at my pussy," I grinned, feeling my pleasure growing stronger with each pulse of his water pistol upon my gland. "I'm getting close..."

Just as Madison called the time and signaled for everyone to stop, Diego's last volley jetted hard against my clit, and I suddenly shuddered, feeling my juices gushing out of my pussy, soaking the entire crotch of my panties. While Madison began to walk down the line inspecting each of the women's panties, I shook silently, enjoying my quiet orgasm while Diego nodded at me knowingly. By now, his cock was standing at full attention as he caressed the glistening tip, watching me staring back at him with my mouth half-agape.

When Madison reached my position at the end of the line, she peered down at my panties and smiled.

"It appears that we have a winner," she nodded. "Though from the look of things, I think Diego may have had a little help from the opposite side of the range. Jade's panties are soaked all the way through. Somebody seemed to enjoy that more than the many of us expected."

Then she peered back at Diego and smiled.

"Are you ready to claim your prize, Diego?"

"Damn straight," Diego said, standing up and displaying his rock-hard erection angled up over his tight balls. "How would you like me to do this?" he said, approaching me with a sexy flush on his face.

"Just *take* me," I panted. "I've already come. I just want to feel you inside me."

"You don't have to ask twice," Diego said, kneeling down in front of me and pushing my legs apart while he tore off the patch in front of my crotch.

When he saw my dripping vulva exposed in the hole of my panties, he grabbed the sides of my ass and pulled me close to him, inserting his tool deep into my crevice. I grunted when I felt him penetrate me, then I wrapped my arms and legs around his body as he pounded me against the fireplace with everybody staring at his flexing buttocks while he fucked me shamelessly. It barely took a minute for both of us to climax together while we shook in each other's arms with everybody nodding appreciatively.

While Madison stood on from a distance away, caressing her breasts softly with two hands, I glanced down at her parted legs, noticing a trickle of lubrication dripping down the inside of her thighs.

Damn girl, I thought. *This carnival game concept is fucking genius. It's almost as much fun watching the action as participating in it.*

Almost, I grinned. *Next time, it's your turn.*

5

"Mmm," Madison said, emerging from the kitchen carrying a large bowl after Diego and I recovered from our orgasms. "That was positively *delicious!*"

The bowl was filled with some kind of fluffy pink material that looked like spun cotton.

"Speaking of delicious," she said, lifting a wooden ladle out of the bowl, covered in cotton candy. "What county fair is complete without a *candy floss* treat?"

"Okay..." Shae said, squinting her eyes at the fluffy concoction. "Is this another one of your special *hors d'oeuvres?*"

"I guess you could look at it that way," Madison smiled. "But I had something a little more titillating in mind for its use. It's the boys' turn to be on the receiving end of the action this time, and I thought it would be a little more exciting if you licked it off their *penises* instead of just a cardboard stick."

Everybody's eyes widened, then Ryan shifted uncomfortably.

"Won't that be a little *messy?*" he said.

"Yes, I suppose so," Madison grinned. "But isn't that what makes these carnival games all the more interesting? The more mess we make, the more fun we all seem to have."

"Is this going to be another *contest* of some kind?" Lincoln said.

"Yes," Madison said, glancing at his oversized organ. "But this time I think you'll find your special endowments are more of a liability than an advantage. Because the winner will be the one who can lick all the candy floss off their partner's dick in the least time."

Laura suddenly laughed, shaking her head.

"Where do you come up with these ideas?" she said. "I mean, if the regular county fair had even *half* of these games, they'd sell out overnight."

"What can I say?" Madison grinned. "Sometimes I've got nothing better to do on lonely nights than dream up kinky sex games."

"It's pretty *kinky*, alright," Brad chuckled. "It's a good thing you told us to shave our private parts before we came to this party. Otherwise, we might have a hell of a time getting that stuff out of our pubic hair."

"Just another reason to stay clean and smooth," Madison nodded, noticing the men's dicks beginning to rise again at the thought of the women licking their tools.

"Can we choose our partners this time?" Ryan said, darting his eyes in Shae's direction.

"I don't see why not," Madison said.

"Can I choose *Shae* then, assuming she'll be on the women's side?"

"It's fine with me, as long as that works for Shae," Maddy nodded, glancing over at Shae.

"Absolutely," Shae smiled, peering at Ryan's hardening tool. "I can swing *both* ways, as it appears *Ryan* can too."

"Alright then," Madison said, motioning for the men to line up in front of the fireplace. "Let's get this party started."

"Do we have to be fully *hard* to do this?" Marco said, looking around self-consciously at some of the men's thickening cocks. "I mean, the less the women have to work with, the quicker they can complete the task."

"That may be true," Madison said. "But something tells me it'll be a helluva more fun for *both* of you if you're fully erect.

"And besides," she said, lifting the ladle out of the bowl and slathering a thick coating of sticky candy over Marco's tool. "By the time everyone's dicks are covered in cotton candy, it'll be hard to notice the difference."

By the time each of the women lined up in front of the men and Neil's penis had been coated in floss at the end of the line, I noticed all of the men's instruments standing proudly at attention. Even Marco's cock was jutting straight up now, as his partner Paige licked her lips, grinning up at him while she rested on her knees.

"Are you girls ready?" Madison said, holding her smartphone in her hand, ready to tap the timer.

"Not half as ready as the *men* seem to be," Laura chuckled, staring at Diego's candy-coated instrument flapping excitedly in front of her face.

"Alright then," Maddy smiled, preparing to tap the screen. "You'll have exactly three minutes to remove all traces of the candy from your partner's genitals. If there happens to be some *other* kind of residue left on their cocks by the time you're finished, we'll just consider that a bonus."

I peered down the line toward Laura, who'd chosen to line up opposite Lincoln.

"You better be careful cleaning that thing," I grinned. "If you're not careful, he'll poke your eye out."

"No worries," she winked, glancing up at Brad, whose erect penis was flapping hard against his belly, directly in front of me. "You just take care with my husband. Because from the look of things, he could pop off any second."

"Mmm," I said, licking my lips. "That will only make this treat all the more delicious."

When Madison signaled for everyone to start, the women began bobbing their heads and moving their faces from side to side as they hurried to remove the sticky cotton candy from their partners' genitals. While they sucked and licked with increasing urgency, the men moaned in rising unison, watching the women licking their tongues along the underside of their shafts and listening to the popping sound of their mouths plopping off their heads.

While I tried to grasp Brad's springy dick to gain better access to his top side, I glanced out the corner of my eye at Shae, who was sucking Ryan's cock like a porn star. She'd already removed most of the floss from around his shaft, and as she bobbed her head over his flaring crown, she rolled her hands around his balls, trying to remove the last vestiges of fluff. By the time I caught onto her technique and grabbed Brad's tool with both hands while I flicked his head with my tongue, Madison announced the end of the contest.

When the men groaned in disappointment at the early completion of the game, the women glanced down the line to compare their handiwork. The men's penises were still glistening and bouncing in excitement from their partner's attention, but each of them had traces of pink candy still encircling the base of their shafts and around their balls. Only Ryan's proud phallus shined clean and bright, his tight balls pulled up to the base of his flaring dick as he stared back at Shae's flushed face, still panting heavily. Madison walked down the line inspecting each man's junk, but it was obvious to everybody who had won the contest.

"I think you chose your partner wisely," Madison nodded when she reached the unlikely pair. "It seems that only someone who *owns* a cock knows how to properly suck another cock. It looks like Shae gave your balls just as much attention as your knob during that exercise."

"As every man should," Ryan smiled.

"Except I'm not a *man*," Shae huffed. "I might have a cock, but I'm just as much a woman as all the other ladies sitting here on their knees."

"I think we'd have to concur with that," Madison nodded. "It looks like you'll have your choice as to which side of the coin you'd like to avail yourself of in this case, Ryan. Have you thought about how you'd like to *finish* with your partner?"

"Mmm," Ryan hummed, staring down at Shae's big prick bobbing up between her legs. "As much as I enjoyed her expert *oral* attention, I've been wanting to feel that girl-cock inside me ever since I saw her rubbing dicks with Linc."

6

"Okay," Madison said, noticing a dribble of pre-cum leaking out of the tip of Shae's cock. "I'm sure everybody would love to have a bird's-eye view of the action, if you guys up for it. How can you position yourselves so we can enjoy the experience as much as the two of you?"

Shae paused for a moment peering up at Ryan, then she glanced at the fireplace, spreading a wide smile over her face.

"Why don't I rest on the hearth while you sit on my cock, facing away?" Shae said. "That way, you'll have maximum freedom of movement while I play with your cock from behind your back."

"Mmm," Ryan nodded. "And that will also be the perfect viewing position for the *rest* of the group."

"Works for me," I chuckled, imagining the sight of the two lovers fucking on the edge of the fireplace like two squatting frogs.

"Jeesuz," Paige said, flapping her hand in front of her face to signal how excited she was becoming. "Is it getting *hot* in here all of a sudden?"

"Not nearly as hot as it's *about* to be," Laura said, grabbing her husband's still bobbing cock and leading him over to the sofa for a prime viewing spot of the action.

"Why doesn't everybody line up boy-girl, boy-girl on the sofa so we can *all* enjoy the action equally?" Madison said, noticing both the men and the women squirming in anticipation of the show. "I'm sure the *rest* of the men are just as eager to get off as Ryan is after we ended the contest prematurely."

"Screw that," Bonnie chuckled. "I think the women are even *more* excited to watch this show. You guys might enjoy watching two women having sex, but we get just as turned on watching two guys go at it."

"Or in *this* case," I smiled, clarifying the terms of engagement. "A ladyboy and a gay boy."

"You heard the lady," Shae said to Ryan, sitting on the edge of the fireplace with her cock pointing straight up. "Sit on my dick, Ryan. Let's give these straight people a show they'll never forget."

Ryan paused for a moment, then he peered over at Madison.

"I don't suppose you've got any *lube* handy?" he said.

"Way ahead of you," Madison nodded, reaching into her game kit and tossing him a small purple bottle.

He peered at the label then squirted a dollop of jelly into his hands, rubbing it sensuously up and down Shae's throbbing hard-on.

"I'm not sure how much of this we actually need," he said, flaring his eyes at her dripping cock. "The combination of this lube mixed with Shae's jizz feels utterly sublime."

"Not as much as it will when I'm *inside* you," Shae groaned.

"Fuck, yes," Ryan said, spinning around and squatting over Shae's hips while she guided his pucker toward her hard-on.

When he felt the tip of her dick enter his sphincter, they both groaned while the rest of the gallery gasped watching her organ disappear inside his ass.

"Holy *fuck*," Laura hissed, watching their bodies rock together while she stroked Brad's sticky cock absent-mindedly beside her. "That's quite possibly the sexiest thing I've ever seen. Are you enjoying this as much as me, sweetheart?"

"I'm enjoying it, alright," Brad grunted, rocking his hips back and forth in his wife's hand. "But it would feel even better with a bit of extra lube."

Ryan glanced at the rest of the men sitting on the sofa next to their partners while they received their own hand jobs, then he reached down for the bottle of lube on the floor, tossing it gently toward Brad. He squirted a drop onto the top of his dick, then he passed it down the line while the rest of the men followed his lead. Within a few minutes, virtually everybody in the room was moaning and panting as they touched themselves and their partners while they watched the erotic scene unfolding only a few feet away.

Shae peered around the side of Ryan's stomach, and when she saw the rest of the women stroking their partner's cocks on the sofa, she reached around his hips and began stroking his erection while she squeezed his balls with her other hand.

"Fuck, that feels good," Ryan grunted, tensing his leg muscles as he bobbed up and down on Shae's flexing shaft.

"I bet you never knew it could be this much fun to fuck a *girl*, did you?" Shae joked, moaning in tandem with him.

The sight of her shiny dick sliding in and out of Ryan's ass while she pumped his darkening tool from behind was one of the sexiest things I'd ever witnessed. As they began to moan louder and louder in mutual pleasure, I stroked Neil's dick with my left hand while I jilled myself hard with my other hand. After a while, I noticed Madison standing slightly to my side near the edge of the sofa, quietly circling her clit while she watched the couple making out on the hearth, and I motioned for her to join me on the sofa. When she sat down next to me, I moved my right hand overtop of her pussy and slid my fingers into her slit, rolling my thumb over her hard clit. She placed her left hand over my pussy, and before long, everyone in the room was lost in the moment, enjoying the erotic show while they rubbed themselves closer to climax.

When Ryan began groaning with increased urgency and he lowered his ass all the way over Shae's glistening dick, we all watched with amazement while his hard-on erupted in a never-ending series of long squirts while Shae held him tightly with two hands. When his powerful spurts landed inches away from the base of the sofa, I listened to the rest of the group moaning along with Ryan and Shae, lost in the sweet symphony of the band of friends enjoying the shared experience of open-minded love.

7

"Wow," Madison said after everybody recovered from their powerful orgasms. "I don't know about the *rest* of you girls, but am I the *only* one who's feeling a twinge of penis envy?"

"That was pretty fucking hot," Paige nodded. "I wouldn't mind trying one of those on for a couple of days. There's something about the act of penetration that's kind of alluring..."

"That's why we *gay men* like to make use of every available orifice," Ryan smiled, raising up off Shae's dripping cock and wiping himself down with a nearby towel.

"And why we *hermaphrodites* are doubly blessed," Shae nodded, wiping down the insides of her thighs from her leaking pussy. "We get to experience it both ways."

"I *hate* you," I said, staring at Shae with a devilish grin.

"You can strap one on any time Jade, if you want to fuck me from behind," Shae chuckled.

"Speaking of cocks and fucking from behind," Madison interrupted. "I think our next contest might satisfy *everyone's* desire for penetration. In this variation of the game Pin the Tail on the Donkey, we're going to try to pin our partner's ass with a something a little more interesting than just a floppy tail."

"You mean...?" Brad said, widening his eyes in excitement.

"That's right," Maddy nodded. "In this game, each of the men are going to try to complete the exercise by connecting their *cock* with their partner's ass."

"Blindfolded?" Lincoln said.

"Of course," Madison said. "Otherwise, it wouldn't be half as much fun."

"Who'll be the lucky girl on the receiving end?" I said. "If the men are all going to take a shot at the same target, doesn't that mean that only *one* woman will be involved this time?"

"So it would seem," Madison nodded. "Shall we draw lots to see who'll go first?"

Each of the women peered at one another for a moment, then we all turned together, staring at Madison.

"I think *Maddy* deserves a chance to participate in the game this time," I said. "Don't you agree, ladies?"

"Absolutely," Laura nodded. "She's obviously gotten just as turned on as the rest of us watching the action. It's only fair for her to have a turn."

"Plus, it doesn't look like there needs to be a *referee* to monitor the activity," Shae grinned. "It's going to be pretty obvious who'll be the winner."

"What do you say, Maddy?" I said, turning toward my friend. "Are you up for it?"

"You're twisting my arm," Madison chuckled. "Do you guys know how to play the game?"

"It's pretty simple, isn't it?" I said. "Each of the guys gets blind-folded one at a time, then we spin them around to disorient them a little, then they have to find their way to the target while we tell them if they're getting warmer or colder."

"Sounds about right," Madison nodded. "But to make it a little more challenging, you might place a few obstacles in their way to make it harder to find me."

"Like a chair or a footstool?" Emma said.

"Or maybe even another *person*," Maddy smiled. "Nothing works as well as a distraction like another person's naked body."

"Mmm," Paige nodded. "This is getting more interesting by the second."

"How long will each of us have to find you?" Marco said.

"I think about three minutes should be about right, given the size of the room," Madison grinned. "I'm not sure I can take six dicks up my ass if *everybody* wins."

"Is *that* where you want it if we win?" Lincoln said.

"I dunno," Madison said, looking at Linc's thick tool. "After that last demonstration with Ryan and Shae, I'm kind of intrigued to try it out. I'll leave it up to the winner to decide how he wants to connect with me. But in *your* case, Linc, you'd rip me apart if you tried going in the back door."

"You could be right about that," Lincoln chuckled. "I guess we'll just have to make it a surprise."

"Mmm," Maddy purred. "I like surprises."

"I suppose it's only fair that we blindfold *Madison* too, then," Shae said. "It's not like she's made it any easier for any of *us* so far."

"Works for me," Maddy nodded.

"Who'll be in charge of the timer?" Paige said.

"That depends on whether Shae wants to join the boys or the girls this time," Maddy smiled.

"I could use a bit of breather, to be honest," Shae sighed. "After coming three times already, I need a couple of rounds to recover."

"Alright, then," Maddy said. "It looks like we're all set to go. Who's going to be our first candidate?"

"There doesn't seem to be an advantage going first or last in this case," Shae said, peering over at the men's swelling organs. "But based on who's got the hardest *tool* at this point, I'd have to give the nod to Brad."

Laura glanced at her husband's erect cock flapping up against his stomach and chuckled.

"I haven't seen you recover this fast from an orgasm in *ages*," she teased.

"What can I say?" Brad joked. "They say variety is the key to keeping your love life interesting. With so many willing partners at my disposal, this thing has a life of its own."

8

After everyone agreed on the rules of the game, Shae reached into Madison's game bag and tied a thick blindfold around Brad's eyes, spinning him around three times to disrupt his sense of direction. Then Madison tip-toed toward the kitchen, placing her hands over the edge of the island and bending over to reveal her shiny ass.

"Fucking eh," I sighed. "Maybe I'll strap on a dildo and give it a whirl too, if none of the guys manage to capture their prize. That's far too tempting a target to go to waste."

"You heard the lady," Shae said, tapping her smartphone to start the timer. "You've got exactly three minutes before the prize passes to someone else."

Brad raised his arms and began stepping gingerly in the opposite direction of Madison, and after a few seconds the viewing gallery began to hiss in unison.

"What does that mean?" he said. "Am I getting warmer or colder?"

"Colder," Emma said. "At this rate, Madison's pussy will *freeze over* before you reach her."

Brad stopped and turned around a hundred and eighty degrees, then he retracted his steps, heading toward the kitchen. When Laura saw that he was heading in the right direction, she jumped to her feet and scampered a few feet in front of him, standing rigidly like a statue. When he bumped into her, he groped her tits and ass, then his mouth widened with a lopsided smile.

"This figure feels familiar," he grinned. "And I'm pretty sure it's not Madison. Besides, she's not bending over like a *donkey*."

"Well, we can't make it *too* easy for you," Laura said, standing her ground. "You know how I always like to make you work for it. I'm afraid you won't come *back* to me if you sample too many of the goods tonight."

"Never fear, dear," Brad smiled. "My *cock* might be divining another source of opportunity, but my *heart* will always be true to you."

"Uh, huh," Laura huffed as he stepped around her and continued creeping toward the kitchen. She rushed back a few extra feet, pulling a large ottoman in his path, and Brad stumbled over it, falling onto the soft padding.

"You *really* don't want me fucking Maddy tonight, do you?" he grunted.

"I'm just trying to save your energy for the *next* contest," Laura grinned. "Madison always alternates the games between the boys and the girls, and I just want to make sure you'll be up for next opportunity."

"Don't worry, sweetheart," Brad said, picking himself up and beginning to walk toward the powder room. "I haven't felt this energized since I was a *teenager*. I'm pretty sure I'll be up for whatever Madison decides to throw at us."

He continued heading in the direction of the powder room until he bumped his head against the door frame, lifting his hand to his forehead.

"You guys aren't going to make it any easier for me, are you?" he said, turning around and heading off in the direction of the dining room.

"*Ssss...*" the group hissed again, signaling that he was moving in the wrong direction.

He stopped and turned his head, trying to sense where Madison was hiding, but just as he began to head in the right direction, Shae announced that time was up.

"Shoot!" Brad said, tearing off his blindfold and watching Madison bending over the kitchen island teasingly, shaking her ass at him. "This is harder than it looks."

"Especially when your wife is *cock-blocking* you at every turn," Paige joked.

"Well, hopefully I'll have a chance to return the favor before the night is over," Brad said, returning to the sofa to sit beside the rest of the men, whose peckers were eagerly standing at attention, begging to be called next.

"Okay," Shae said, appraising the lineup of waving willies. "Who'd like to go next?"

"Shouldn't we blindfold Madison first, if we're going to keep it a secret?" I said, dipping into her kit bag and pulling out another bandana to place it around her head.

Shae paused to make sure she couldn't see anything, then she pointed toward Diego to go next. I led Madison by the arm into the adjacent living room, then hid her behind the big eight-person table before slapping her gently on the ass.

"Don't worry, babe," I said. "We'll get you properly hooked up before this contest is over."

"Can you try to give *Lincoln* a little head start?" she whispered to me. "I'd really like to feel his thumper up my ass if there's any way you can arrange it."

"I'll see what I can do," I chuckled, before returning quietly to the main group.

Each of the men tried their turn finding Madison in different areas of the lower level, but in each case, they bumped into various sundry obstacles, tripping and losing valuable time. When it finally became Lincoln's turn, he shook his head, doubting he'd ever capture the prize in time.

"I thought you girls said you wanted Madison to get her share of the spoils in this game?" he protested. "From the look of things, you're determined to deny her every chance."

"Have faith, Linc," I grinned. "Being last, you must have a pretty good sense of where the fixed objects are by now. Just follow your nose, and you'll get there eventually."

"Or your big *poker*," Shae laughed, wrapping the blindfold around his eyes. As she spun him around, she stood teasingly close to his body, flapping his long hard-on from side-to-side while it slapped against her hips.

When she let him go, he crouched down a few inches, holding his hands out in front of him to locate the position of the surrounding furniture while the women gently coached him in the direction of Madison, who'd returned to her original location beside the kitchen island. As he twisted and turned closer and closer to her position, the women called out the words 'colder' or 'hotter', until he bumped up against her bent-over ass.

"Mmm," he said, holding out his hands to caress her buttocks. "This feels familiar. Although it's a lot softer and smoother than a *donkey*. Could this be the lovely hostess who's been tormenting us from one contest to another, making us jump through hoops and firing assorted objects at one another's private parts?"

"Possibly," Madison purred, reaching behind her to stroke his throbbing dagger. "Is this the hunk with a prick the size of a *horse*?"

"Possibly," Lincoln smiled, pressing the tip of his cock between her cheeks. "Do you have a preference for where you'd like me to connect my prize?"

"I think you'll find the *front* side a little more accommodating," Madison panted. "Not to mention wetter and warmer. I've been dripping like a *faucet* waiting for you to find me."

"Mmm," Lincoln said, grabbing the sides of Madison's ass and lifting her feet off the floor.

He tilted his dick up to her flaring hole, easing the tip of his thick organ into her glistening slit. When he pressed his hips forward and Madison felt his instrument spreading her apart, she groaned loudly, clutching the edge of the island for support. While he bucked her softly against the side of the table, sliding her tits over the smooth granite surface, we watched his muscular buttocks flexing as he pounded her pussy.

It didn't take long for the rest of the group's hands to wander between their legs while they jerked and jilled themselves, moaning in tandem with the sexy couple bent over the kitchen island. As I listened to Madison's escalating moans and gasps, I smiled, knowing she'd captured the ultimate prize.

Maybe that's the way she planned it all along, I thought, slipping three fingers into my dripping pussy, imagining what it would be like to be fucked by Lincoln's baseball-bat-thick firehose. *Two can play that game*, I grunted, determined to get my *own* piece of his organ before the night was over.

9

After Madison and Lincoln collected themselves, everybody retired to the kitchen to enjoy some refreshments while they milled around the island, wondering what the next contest would involve. The boys were eager to get back in the game, having been denied a chance to complete the last exercise, but Madison was being elusive about providing any details. Instead, she gorged herself on hors d'oeuvres, licking the tzatziki off her snacks while she stared at Lincoln's dripping instrument with flushed cheeks.

"Don't you think you've had *enough* of him after that last round?" I said, watching her drooling over his buff body.

"I'm not sure you can *ever* have enough of that thing," she grinned, gazing at his big dick. "He never *did* manage to get it all inside of me."

"Yeah, well, you might save a little bit for the *rest* of us girls," I huffed. "There's still six more of us who wouldn't mind having a shot at him."

She paused as she glanced around the table, noticing the other women staring at her enviously.

"Well, at least everybody will have an equal opportunity in the upcoming round. Because in the next contest, it will be the women who are wearing the blindfolds."

"Oh?" Brad said, squeezing in next to us, overhearing the conversation. "Are you going to make the ladies run the gauntlet this time trying to find our waiting cocks?"

"It shouldn't be hard *finding* them," Madison grinned. "The hard part will be determining whose dick belongs to whom."

"With the usual prize for the winner?" Shae said, edging in closer.

"Yes," Maddy nodded. "But in this case, there should be more than one winner. It's starting to getting late, and I don't know how much more stimulation the boys can handle before their dicks begin to fall off. With any luck, *everybody* will have a chance to get off in our grande finale."

"Finale?" Diego said, his ears perking up. "Just when I was starting to get comfortable playing these exotic games. Don't most county fairs close down later than this?"

"Maybe," Madison chuckled. "But never fear, I've got enough ideas for a whole *new* edition of carnival games. I just want to make sure you guys have enough time to recharge your batteries. Because at my *next* party, you're going to need even more strength and stamina to make it through the challenges."

"Mmm, I can't wait," Paige said, joining the group. "Can you at least give us a *hint* about what we can look forward to next time?"

Madison paused when she saw the rest of the group squeezing in around the island, eager to hear about her plans.

"Well, I don't want to give *too* much away," she smiled, darting her eyes around the participants. "But maybe the names I've given some of the contests will give you a bit of an idea. *Firing Range, Kissing Booth, Paint by Numbers, Bobbing for Peaches, and House of Mirrors* are just a few of the games that I've got planned."

"Wow," Lily laughed. "You really *do* stay up late on lonely nights dreaming this stuff up."

"Yes," Madison smiled, intertwining her arms with the others around the table. "Except it's not so lonely when all my friends come over to participate in another round of sexy games."

"So what's this big finale you've got planned?" Marco said, his penis already beginning to flutter at the knowledge it would be the boys' turn to go next.

"Well, since you boys were blindfolded in the last round," Maddy said. "I think it's only fair that we make the *women* work a little harder for the prize this time."

"By being blindfolded, you mean?" Emma said.

"Yes," Madison nodded. "It'll be a bit like our second contest, where the women had to match the flaccid penises with pictures of the men's hard ones. Except in this game that I'm calling Milk the Bull, you'll be doing it purely by *feel*."

Lincoln suddenly cocked his head, widening his eyes.

"You want us to remain *flaccid* while the women are caressing our cocks?" he said.

"God, no," Maddy laughed. "What would be the fun in that? The harder you are, the easier it will be for your partners to guess whose cock it is. Plus, they've had the whole evening to stare at your erect penises while you've participated in each of the exercises. My guess is that it will be a lot easier and quicker for the women to match the erections to the owners when you're fully *aroused*."

"Do we get to choose our partners again?" Laura said, eyeing up Lincoln's lengthening tool with greedy eyes.

"In the interests of fairness, I think the matchups should be by random selection this time. That's the advantage of being blindfolded. Like Brad said earlier, the more variety, the more fun it is."

"Which side of the table will I be sitting on this time?" Shae asked. "Since the ladies will be doing the fondling, I seem to be the odd one out."

"Hmm," Madison said, pinching her eyebrows together as she pondered the predicament. "You're right, with officially six women and six men in the group, being a *transgender* woman, you're kind of the wildcard. It looks like I'll just have to join in the contest once again to even the numbers."

"Then who'll do the *officiating*?" Brad said.

"We'll have to put you on your honor this time," Madison said. "If the women guess you correctly, all you have to do is confirm it verbally."

"Is any other talking allowed?" Diego said.

"I think that would make it too easy to match the men's voices," Madison grinned. "But that shouldn't stop you from *grunting and moaning* all you want."

"How many guesses will each of the women be permitted?" Emma said.

"*Three* should about do it," Madison said. "That will give you at least a fifty-fifty chance of guessing your partner right."

"I think the odds will be a little higher for *some* of the contestants," Bonnie grinned, nodding toward Lincoln's long snake.

"Perhaps so," Maddy nodded. "But the purpose of this contest isn't so much about *winning* as giving everybody a chance for a happy ending."

"And by happy ending," Paige said. "You mean *finishing* our handies?"

"Or however *else* you'd like to satisfy your partner," Madison grinned.

"Including using certain other body parts, if we so desire?" Laura said.

"Absolutely," Maddy smiled. "We did say *everybody*."

10

After Madison finished explaining the contest rules, the men wrapped blindfolds around the women's eyes then they all sat down a few inches apart on the long sectional sofa. When Marco said that the men were ready, the women turned around and groped their way to different areas of the sofa, kneeling in front of their randomly selected partners. By now, the men's flagstaffs were standing straight up awaiting their partner's attention, and the women hummed in excitement after they felt their erect shafts.

When I felt my partner's hard-on, it wasn't immediately apparent who I was touching, since his erection seemed to be of roughly average size with no obvious distinguishing characteristics. But with his crown fully exposed, that narrowed it down to five, remembering that Marco's and Neil's cocks were uncircumcised. And it obviously didn't belong to Lincoln, with his huge, slightly curved cock, or Shae, with her pussy in place of the usual balls. So that only left Brad, Ryan, and Diego.

I rolled my fingers around the tip of my partner's dripping head, and he groaned with a familiar timbre to his voice.

"Mmm," I smiled. "I think I've heard that moan before. Is this *Diego's* pretty cock I've got in my hands?"

"Mmft," my partner grunted, trying to suppress his growing pleasure as I stroked his dick softly with two hands.

"No?" I said, widening my smile while I narrowed the possibilities.

"Maybe *this* might help," I said, cupping his balls with my left hand as I caressed his shaft.

"Uhnn," he groaned, obviously enjoying my two-pronged stimulation of his genitals.

Then I recalled the unique squealing sound that Ryan made when Shae had gripped him from behind while she skewered him with her cock.

"Hmm," I nodded, pulling the tip of his dick down toward my face and releasing it while I listened to it slapping up against his stomach. "I remember this springy dick. Only *Brad's* cock tilts up against his belly like a little boy's. It looks like you've still got plenty of juice left in your batteries."

"You have an unfair advantage," Brad grunted while I fondled his balls and stroked his dick gently. "You've already *felt* my balls and cock during the candy floss contest."

"Yes, but that was mostly with my *mouth*," I grinned, rolling my tongue around the sides of my lips.

"There's no one stopping you from using that to full advantage now," he panted. "Madison said you could use any part of your body to stimulate us after you identified your partner."

"True," I grinned, squeezing his dick harder in my hands. "But I think I'll make you wait a little longer until we see how many of the other contestants guess their partners."

Suddenly, I heard the woman next to me chuckle as she nudged her hips softly against me.

"I guess that rules my *husband* out," Laura said while her partner groaned and huffed a few feet over her head. "As if I needed any help figuring *that* one out. So, using Jade's reasoning, that means this is either Diego or Ryan, since I can tell you're obviously cut."

She paused for a moment while I heard her shift position between her partner's legs as he moaned softly above her.

"But I remember Ryan makes a unique sound when his balls are squeezed. Is that *you*, Ryan?"

Her partner huffed and grunted, trying to suppress his pleasure while Laura teased his balls, then she leaned back, nodding triumphantly.

"Mmm, I *thought* it might be you, Diego," she purred. "Your cock is so smooth and straight. It's *burning* in my hands."

"Yes," he panted. "Stroke me with both hands. I want to watch my cock pumping in and out of your fists."

"Fuck, yes," Laura hissed, raising her voice to make her husband more jealous, who was huffing along with Diego while I stroked him in kind.

One by one, the women sitting opposite their partners narrowed down the field of candidates as they listened to the others reveal their identities, until there were only two contestants left. Lincoln was the first to be identified by Paige, who was kneeling on my opposite side, then Shae was quickly tagged by her partner Madison, who immediately recognized the transgender girl when she felt her dripping pussy under her flaring cock. That left only Marco and Neil, but with three guesses each, their partners quickly narrowed down the choices to the correct owners after pulling on their tight foreskins.

I smiled when I realized how Madison had formulated this contest to be easily won by all of the candidates, and as I listened to the men moaning in unison while their partners jerked their cocks between their legs, I flipped off my bandana and glanced down the line. It was a beautiful sight watching the look of pleasure on the men's faces while they stared at the women stroking their hard-ons with single-minded purpose, but I was eager to finish up this contest with a flourish.

"Screw this *jerking off* business," I said out loud. "I'm taking matters into my own hands before we turn the lights out for the night. What do you say, ladies? Madison said we could finish this contest any way we wanted. I don't know about you girls, but I plan on finishing with my *own* a happy ending along with the rest of the guys. Let's ditch these bandanas and enjoy this last game as a united group!"

"You took the words right out of my mouth, Jade," Madison said, ripping off her bandana and staring at Shae's throbbing hard-on and dripping pussy with wide eyes. Let's give our partners something truly memorable to take away with them before they leave the party. Let's see who can come the hardest and the quickest!"

"Damn straight," I nodded, standing up and flipping around to lower my pussy over Brad's bobbing organ. "That is, if you don't mind my availing myself of your husband's perky penis, Laura."

"Of course not," Laura said, following my lead and squatting down over Diego's erection, facing away. "Why do you think we came to this party anyway? To keep having boring sex only with our *own* partners?"

"I wouldn't exactly call it bor–" Brad protested before being drowned out by Paige's loud moan as she planted her thick butt over Lincoln's tall tool.

Within seconds, all of the women had impaled themselves over their partner's dicks, bouncing happily up and down while they peered at one another with glassy eyes and gaping mouths, groaning in delirious pleasure. While they played with their tits with one hand and squeezed their partners' balls with their other, I glanced to the other end of the sofa watching Madison's face beginning to flush as she thrust three fingers into Shae's gaping hole while she bounced her hips over her flexing hard-on.

It didn't take long for everybody to begin screaming and howling in mutual ecstasy while the women rode their partners' cocks together in the reverse cowgirl position, whooping and hollering like a band of drunken schoolgirls.

Country fair, indeed, I smiled as I felt my climax wash over me with the rest of the group. *Except in this one, everyone's a winner.*

BOOK 50

CARNY GAMES 3

1

Two weeks after her first carnival-themed sex party, I received another email message from Madison, inviting me to her next event. The subject heading read *Carny Games 2*, and I almost tripped over my office chair rushing to open the message on my computer.

Dear Jade,

You are cordially invited to another party at my place this Saturday evening starting at 9 p.m.

The theme once again will be carnival games, where everyone will participate in more erotic contests simulating county fair games.

With names like Firing Range, Paint by Numbers, Bobbing for Peaches, and Orgasm Face, these games will make you laugh and squeal in equal measure.

But these contests aren't for the faint of heart, so be prepared to take your clothes off and let it all hang out. And remember to park your inhibitions at the door, because there's no telling who you'll be paired up with. From boy-on-girl to girl-on-girl to boy-on-boy to other surprise pairings, you can be sure to stretch your imagination in more ways than one.

*So come clean, come prepared, and come often. Because we're going to
have a ribald and riotous good time!*

RSVP before Thursday,

Maddy

*P.S.: Please bring an ink blot of your pussy to be used for a special
game of Guess the Rorschach. The easiest way to do this is to spread food
coloring on your vulva then sit with your legs apart on a clean sheet of
paper under your ass.*

WTF? I thought, after reading her message. *Guess the Rorschach?
Paint by Numbers? Orgasm Face? This girl really does have too much time
on her hands.*

Nonetheless, the idea of participating in another one of her kinky
parties with some of my friends and a few new strangers was getting
me incredibly turned on. I slipped my hand under my panties and
thrust two fingers into my pussy, caressing myself while I imagined
what she'd dreamed up this time.

W hen I arrived at Madison's house on the night of the party,
she collected my pussy pictures, then escorted me to the
living room where I saw many of my friends from her last party
lounging around, sipping wine. But there were also a few *new* faces in
the crowd, and as I scanned the tight figures of the participants, my
panties began to moisten.

Brad and Laura had returned, plus there was a *new* married
couple, Toby and Elle, looking like movie stars straight out of the
pages of People Magazine. I nodded toward my friends Lily, Bonnie,
and Emma from my last camping trip, and smiled at my friends from
work, Ryan, Marco, and Neil. I was happy to see the cute Hispanic
hunk Diego was back, as was the hung African-American dreamboat,
Lincoln. And of course, no sex party would be complete without the
participation of my sexy transgendered friend, Shae.

But I was surprised to see two familiar participants from my Fountain of Venus squirting workshop, the pretty African-American goddess Trinity, and the cute redhead, Piper. While my eyes darted around the room and I began to mingle with the group, I suddenly became conscious of the growing wet spot in the crotch of my jeans. After a few minutes, Trinity brushed up beside me and grinned, caressing the back of my ass.

"I see you haven't lost your special talent developed at our last workshop," she said, slipping her finger between my cheeks.

"And I haven't even *come* yet," I grunted, squirming in response to her touch. "But if you keep doing that, I'm *really* going to make a mess of myself."

"Mmm," she smiled. "I can't wait. What's this party all about? When I saw Madison's invitation, I was perplexed by the names of the games."

"That makes *two* of us," I said, twisting my hips away from her probing hand. "If it's anything like the last one, I won't be the *only* one squirting before long. She always comes up with the wildest party ideas."

"Did you bring your pussy blots?"

"Yes," I nodded. "It was kind of weird making them, but when I saw the final result, I thought it looked quite interesting. Mine reminds me of a lotus flower, how about yours?"

"Mine looks more like a bat with flapping wings," Trinity chuckled. "I'm not quite sure what she intends to do with these pictures, but my pussy is already throbbing watching some of these hot party guests."

"You have no idea," I smiled, nodding toward Lincoln and Shae. "Lincoln's hung like a horse, and that pretty girl has got a prick you wouldn't believe."

"She's a *tranny*?" Trinity said, flaring her eyes while she stared at Shae. "I never would have guessed."

"Technically, she's a hermaphrodite," I said. "A rare individual with both male and female sex organs. She's quite versatile and enjoys mixing it up with *women* as much as men. But don't call her a tranny, she prefers to be referred to as a ladyboy. Would you like me to introduce you?"

"Yes, please," Trinity said, licking her lips.

But just as the two women began chatting, Madison called the meeting to order, and a hush fell over the room, with everybody excited to begin the festivities.

2

"Has everybody helped themselves to some wine and refreshments in the kitchen?" she said, nodding toward the gleaming island bedecked with cheese tarts, cucumber canapés, and crab cakes.

When everybody nodded and raised their glasses filled with Rioja and Chardonnay, she smiled, moving in front of the fireplace to address the group.

"I see a lot of familiar faces as well as a few new ones. For those of you not familiar with the theme of this party, everybody will be participating in a series of contests patterned after carnival games."

"Will there be prizes for the winners, like in the county fair?" Trinity said.

"There'll be prizes alright," Maddy grinned. "But they're going to be a little warmer and softer than the ones you might be used to."

"And *wetter*," Laura joked.

"Or *harder*, depending on which side of the contest wins," her husband Brad said.

"Yes," Madison nodded. "The carnival games in this party are going to be a little more risqué and provocative than the ones at your typical county fair."

The new married couple shifted their weight uneasily, gripping each other's hands tightly.

"Will we be performing these fully *clothed*?" Elle said, glancing at her husband nervously.

"I suppose you could perform *some* of them that way," Maddy chuckled. "But I think you'll find most are a lot more fun experienced naked."

"And we'll be performing most of these games in *pairs*?" Elle's husband said.

"Most of them, yes," Madison said. "Though the couplings will be fairly random, so I hope you came prepared to mix it up. Variety is the spice of life, and this venue will offer plenty of opportunity for mixed-gender hookups."

Toby and Elle peered at one another for a long moment, then they nodded softly.

"So, what's our *first* challenge?" Shae said, stepping forward a few paces. "I wasn't sure if you wanted a picture of *my* pussy too, since I've got a bit of an unusual arrangement down there."

"Absolutely," Maddy smiled, pulling the prints of the women's pussies out of a folder and taping them up against the fireplace mantel. "Anyone with a vulva is free to participate in this game. In fact, I think we should all take a moment to celebrate the magnificent diversity of this female feature. Take a look at these pictures, and revel in the sublime beauty of our sexual organs."

Everybody stepped forward a few feet, taking turns peering at the lineup of colorful imprints, each outlined in a different shape like a panel of expressionist paintings.

"Wow," Piper said, leaning in to examine some of the prints. "And here I was so self-conscious of my own flappy folds. Each of these vulvas is quite unique and different, like the flowers of an English garden."

"Exactly," Madison nodded. "I think Georgia O'Keeffe captured it perfectly with her exotic renderings of sensuous blossoms. Each one so soft and delicate, like the women they belong to."

"Are these what we're going to be using for the *Guess the Rorschach* contest?" Laura said.

"Yes," Maddy said. "Each of the men will be given a random ink blot, then they'll have to guess which woman it belongs to."

"By lining up next to one another *naked*?" Elle said, widening her eyes.

"Like I said," Madison grinned. "It's a lot more fun playing these games naked."

"Talk about *variety*," Toby said, squinting at the colorful inkblots one at a time. "If Rorschach was right about our interpretations of these paintings reflecting our inner thoughts, we could have a *field day* comparing the pictures."

"This one looks like a chimpanzee riding a bicycle, Brad laughed, pressing his face close to one of the pictures. "What does that say about me?"

"That you're a pervert who likes to stare at women's pussies?" his wife Laura frowned.

"Well, pretty soon he's going to have a chance to get even closer than he imagined," Madison chuckled. "Because in this next game, the women will be lining up to display their *real* vulvas while the men attempt to match the pictures to the artists."

"What will be the prize for the winner?" Diego said.

"As with my previous party, the men who match the correct paintings to their owners will get the opportunity to examine their pussies with more than just their *eyes*. Subject to their partner's approval, of course."

"And each of the pairings will be randomly assigned?" Neil said.

"Of course," Madison grinned. "It's a *party* after all. Isn't the purpose of every party to mingle and have fun getting to know one another?"

"Not in the *biblical* sense," Bonnie joked.

"Nobody's forcing anyone to hook up with anybody they don't want to," Madison said. "But if this unfolds in any way similar to the last time, it won't take long for everybody to lose their inhibitions. Are you ready to get started?"

The party guests peered at one another, then each of them nodded slowly. I glanced around the room, noticing some of the men's crotches bulging in anticipation, with an equal number of the women's jeans darkening between their thighs. Apparently, more of them were excited about getting started with the contest than they were letting on.

Madison pulled the pictures down from the fireplace and handed one copy to each of the men, then she instructed the women to take off their clothes and relax on the sectional sofa, sitting side-by-side.

"Do you want us to take *everything* off?" Piper asked.

"Technically," Madison said. "You only need your *lower half* exposed. But if you feel comfortable, feel free to let it all hang out. I expect everybody will be getting fully naked soon enough, so you might as well get used to it at your first opportunity."

"What about the *men*?" Diego smiled.

"There's not much advantage in *your* being naked at this point," Madison laughed. "But don't worry–your turn will come soon enough in the next round I'm calling *Firing Range*."

"I can't wait to see what *that* involves," Ryan laughed, glancing at the image he'd been given and peering toward Shae with a familiar grin.

"Do we just hand our pictures to our counterparts once we've made a decision?" Lincoln asked.

"That'll work," Maddy nodded. "Once everyone's finished, I'll match the codes on the back with the correct owners."

"Then the fun will *really* begin," Brad smiled.

"Just try to keep your dick in your pants until we're *finished*," Laura huffed. "At least leave some of the spoils for the rest of the group."

"It's going to be difficult," Brad grinned, rearranging his hardening tool. "This thing has a mind of its own."

3

After the women removed their clothes and sat on the sofa, each of the men lined up single file, crawling on their hands and knees to compare the picture they'd been given with each of the women's vulvas. While the women spread their legs and proudly displayed their pussies, the men glanced back and forth, squinting their eyes as they shook their heads uncertainly. Some of them took longer than others to examine the women's crotches, and when Brad paused for a long moment to stare at Trinity's pussy, Laura glanced up at Madison with an annoyed expression.

"Isn't there a *timer* on this game?" she said. Because if we let my husband have his way, this contest will *never* be over!"

"I didn't think it would be necessary," Madison chuckled. "But now that you mention it, why don't we limit each man to ten seconds per participant. I thought you boys were eager to get to the fun part?"

"This *is* the fun part," Brad grinned, straightening out his erection. "Talk about foreplay. I haven't been this turned on since I peeked at my first Penthouse magazine."

"If you don't move along smartly, you'll have to pull out your old collection when we get home," Laura huffed. "Because that's the only pussy you'll be seeing for a while if you deny the rest of the men a chance to finish this contest."

As the men continued down the line, I became more and more excited watching them staring at my throbbing pussy while my juices dripped down my legs. When Lincoln finally pulled up next to me, I glanced at the picture in his hand and nodded softly.

"We never got a chance to hook up at Madison's last party," I smiled. "But I would have thought you've seen enough of my pussy by now to recognize the familiar signs."

"Mmm," he nodded, peering back and forth between me and the blot of my pussy, before handing me the image gently. "I'm looking forward to pollinating your flower when everybody finishes this exercise. Save that thought, and I'll be back soon enough."

After all the men finished inspecting the women's vulvas and handed their pictures to their chosen candidates, Madison walked down the line, turning over each of the women's pictures to cross-reference the codes on the back with the notes she'd made on her clipboard.

"That was harder than it looked," Marco sighed. "Some of those Rorschach blots are just as mysterious as the owners they belong to."

"That's the idea," Maddy said, placing an X or a check mark on the back of each picture before handing them back to the women. "We wouldn't want to make it too easy for you. Just like at the country fair, you've got to *work* to win your prize."

"I actually found the images highly *erotic*," Ryan said, winking at Shae with a lopsided grin. "The impressions of their *anuses* were almost as vivid as those of their vulvas."

"Not to mention their *clitorises*," Diego nodded. "Are you sure we can't take some of these pictures back with us as a memento of our participation in the event?"

"I suppose that'll be up to your *partners*," Madison smiled. "Depending on how well you do in the next phase of this contest. Ladies, are you ready to reveal your scores?"

The women turned over their prints and glanced at Maddy's notes, then some of us peered up with broad smiles on our faces.

"It looks like Lincoln guessed *me* right," I said, flipping my page around to show Madison's check mark.

Then Shae turned her image around, glancing in the direction of Ryan.

"And Ryan guessed me also," she nodded. "Although I think he had a bit of an unfair advantage with my hard *cock* in place of the usual clitoris."

Suddenly, Elle shifted uncomfortably on the sofa, darting her eyes nervously in her husband's direction.

"And *Diego* guessed me right too," she said, turning her picture around slowly.

"So what happens now?" Toby said, crossing his arms over his chest.

"That depends on the women," Madison nodded. "We said the winners would have a chance to hook up with their partners. How they choose to do that exactly depends on how their counterparts wish to engage."

"Well, I don't know about *you* girls," I grinned, staring at Lincoln's python snaking down the leg of his pants. "But I've been looking forward to riding Lincoln's beanstalk ever since the last party."

Elle paused while she slowly ran her eyes up and down Diego's taut body.

"I'm not quite ready to jump into full-on coupling right out of the gate," she said. "Maybe we could ease into this a little more slowly..."

"You seemed to enjoy having my face close to your vulva while I was examining you," Diego smiled. "Perhaps I can pay homage to your pretty pussy with a *different* part of my anatomy?"

Then he glanced over in Toby's direction.

"Assuming you two are willing to share the spoils?"

Toby hesitated for a moment, then he nodded slowly.

"We didn't come to this party to be prudes," he said. "We knew what we were getting ourselves into when we accepted the invitation. I'm game if my wife is."

Diego peered back at Elle, and she nodded softly as her mouth curled slowly upward.

"Speaking of different *parts*," Ryan said, glancing between Shae's legs at her upturned erection. "I'd love to lick you somewhere *else* if you're up for it. We gay men have learned that the anus can be just as sensitive as the other parts of the perineum. I'd love to jerk your pretty pole while I caress your *pucker*, if you're willing."

"Oh, I'm willing, alright," Shae grinned, dripping a drop of pre-cum over her flaring glans while she imagined the treat she was about to receive.

4

The three men knelt in front of their partners then they one by one lowered their heads between the women's legs, humming softly while they teased and sucked their folds. Shae was the first one to gasp out loud when she felt Ryan's tongue on her sphincter, grabbing her throbbing cock with two hands while he teased her rosebud. Elle was the next one to utter a groan, as she closed her eyes and surrendered to Diego's expert manipulation of her hardening clit with his flickering tongue.

While I stared at Lincoln's bobbing head between my knees, becoming increasingly turned on by his gentle caressing of my labia, I was tempted to lift his head off my pussy and pull him closer to my dripping hole, eager to feel his thick organ inside me. As I reveled in the sight of the other women moaning and sighing beside me, I felt my pleasure slowly building while he teased and caressed me.

"Jesus," I grunted, watching his face eating my pussy. "Who knew you were as good with your *tongue* as your big prick? If you keep doing that to me, you're going to make me come even before I feel you inside me."

"I'm not sure about the *rules*," Lincoln smiled, lifting his head to peer at me with dripping lips. "But if we're only allowed one orgasm per partner, we better get busy before we run out of time. How would you like me to give it to you?"

"If you're referring to what *position*," I grinned. "I'll take it any way I can get it. But I kind of like you on your knees. Why don't you fuck me from the front while I watch your beautiful instrument going in and out of me?"

"Mmm," Lincoln nodded. "I like the sound of that. Plus, you'll be able to control how much of me you take inside. In certain other positions, I'm liable to hurt you."

When he leaned back, I noticed his English-cucumber-sized dick flapping up in front of him.

"Just go slow while I savor every inch of you," I smiled, feeling my pussy beginning to leak like a faucet.

He pressed his hips forward, and I grasped the head of his instrument, pointing it toward my hole. When he slipped it inside my slit, I gasped feeling him spreading me apart, then I pushed my hips forward a few inches to take more of him inside me.

"God, yes," I grunted, watching his thick pole disappearing inside my pussy while he rocked his hips forward and back. "What a beautiful sight this is. I just want to *watch* you while you fuck me."

"Your *pussy* is beautiful, too," he moaned, watching my lips flaring around his shaft while my nub slid along the top of his veiny shaft. "I knew it was yours as soon as I saw you."

"You mean you didn't need my help matching the picture after all?"

"No," he grinned. "I've had the image of your pussy seared into my memory ever since the *Matching the Curtains with the Carpet* contest from our first party."

"I had no idea," I grunted, placing my hands on his hard pecs and drifting them down over his washboard stomach. "All this time I thought you barely *noticed* me while you were busy fucking the other women."

"I noticed, alright," he huffed, a soft flush beginning to form on his chest and beginning to spread up his neck. "I was just biding my time, waiting for a chance to win one of the games with you."

"Well, it was worth the wait," I panted, lowering my fingers onto his throbbing cock and gripping it with both hands while he pounded me with the upper half. "This is the most magnificent tool I've ever seen. I'm just afraid you'll blow me apart when you climax. I remember how much you shoot when you come."

"Almost as much as *you* do if I remember correctly," Lincoln grinned, grabbing the sides of my ass and pulling me harder over his flexing organ. "I think we're a good match in more ways than one."

"Yes," I growled. "I want to feel you explode inside me while I watch you pulsing in my hands. This is the sexiest thing I've done in ages."

"I got the impression you preferred *women* from our last experience?" Lincoln rasped, growing closer to the tipping point.

"Sometimes," I nodded, squeezing his dick harder in my hands. "But I haven't had a dildo as big and hard as *this* one to play with for quite some time now."

"You're going to make me come if you keep squeezing me like that," he hissed.

"Oh yeah?" I grinned. "Do you like that? Open the taps on this firehose. I can feel you pulsing already."

"Yes," Lincoln moaned, his pupils rapidly dilating while he stared into my eyes. "I'm going to come, babe. Feel me when I come, oh God–"

Suddenly, he growled like a wild animal as I felt his thick tool pulsing in my hands. Normally, I didn't feel it when a man came inside me, but in this case the jetting of his hard squirts against my cervix only added to my excitement, and when I saw him climaxing, I quickly lost control over my own pleasure, and as he spasmed against my rolling hips, I began squirting hard over his balls.

"Oh *fuckkk*," he groaned, peering down to watch me spurting along with him while I held his cock tightly, daring him to try pulling out of me.

While our simultaneous orgasm seemed to go on forever, I peered over at Elle and Shae, who soon after also started climaxing as Diego and Ryan sucked their pussies. While the three of us shuddered in mutual ecstasy, I glanced at the rest of the group, who were looking on with their mouths agape and crotches dripping. Even Elle's husband was rubbing his bulging hard-on as he gazed into his wife's glassy eyes.

I don't imagine they'll be keeping their clothes on much longer, I grinned. *If I know Maddy, she's already planning the next event to raise the bar even higher.*

5

After the three of us recovered from our orgasms, the men seemed particularly eager to get started with the next contest, remembering how Madison usually alternated between the boys and the girls. Ryan and Diego seemed especially excited, with their erect penises clearly visible in the outline of their pants.

"Mmm," Maddy grinned, glancing toward our still-dripping pussies. "Are you guys hungry for a little more?"

"More *pussy*?" Brad said, turning toward Madison with raised eyebrows. "I thought it was the *boys'* turn for a little excitement this time?"

"Right you are, Brad," Madison smiled. "In our next game I'm calling *Paint by Numbers*, you're going to have a chance to dip your quill in a slightly different manner. After all, you could use some practice using your dicks to stimulate us in some manner other than pounding it in and out of our pussies, am I right, ladies?"

"Damn straight, Maddy," Laura nodded.

"Well, in this *next* contest, they're going to have a chance to use their instruments more creatively, by painting a picture for each of us."

"With our *penises*?" Marco said, bulging his eyes.

"Of course," Maddy said. "What fun would it be if you did it the usual way?"

"What will we be using for pigment?" Neil said.

Madison reached into her party kit and pulled out eight bowls of colorful cream, placing each bowl on separate tables scattered around the room.

"This paint is actually a type of food dye that I've created specially for the occasion," Maddy smiled. "It's body-safe and non-allergenic, and feels quite sensuous to the touch, not unlike certain types of lube."

"It looks like it'll be the *boys'* turn to smear food coloring all over their genitals this time," Emma grinned, nodding at the other women.

"Exactly," Madison said. "Except in this case, it will be a slightly more *active* exercise."

"What will we be using as our canvas?" Lincoln said. "Unless you want us to smear the paint on the walls like children?"

"It's going to be a big enough clean-up operation as it is," Madison chuckled, reaching behind the sectional sofa to lift a stack of small cardboard easels. "Can you ladies help me set these up next to each of the bowls? You'll see the instructions on the back of each panel."

Shae paused for a moment while she counted the bowls, then she peered back at Madison.

"I'm assuming because there's eight bowls and only seven guys that you'd like me to join the *men's* side this time?" she said.

"Absolutely," Maddy smiled. "Anyone equipped with a penis is eligible to participate in this contest. That is, assuming you're able to still get it up after your rimming by Ryan in the last contest. It'll be a little difficult to perform this exercise with a floppy dick."

"I think I can manage that," Shae nodded, caressing her thickening organ with her right hand.

Toby squinted at the bowls of paint then he peered toward Madison with a raised eyebrow.

"Is there a reason why we're using *food dye* instead of the usual body paint?" he said.

"I'm glad you asked, Toby," Madison said. "Because the winner of this contest will have a randomly selected participant *lick* it off their dicks when they're finished."

Toby glanced toward his wife, and she cocked her head with a lopsided smile.

"Looks like it might be *your* turn to mix it up this time, baby," she said.

"With any luck," Toby grinned.

"How will we decide who's the winner of the contest?" Diego asked.

"The women will be asked to vote on the most interesting composition."

"Will we be judged on *creativity or accuracy*?" Lincoln said.

"Both," Maddy smiled. "You've heard the expression that a good dancer is also a good lover? Let's see if the same can be said about *painters.*"

"Don't worry, Linc," I said. "I'll let you paint on *my* canvas any time you want."

"Will this be a *timed* contest?" Ryan asked.

"As much as I don't want to rush you guys learning how to use your instruments more creatively, I'm afraid we're going to have to," Madison nodded. "We still have quite a few games to follow after this, and you're going to need to conserve your energy for some of the more difficult ones. Ten minutes should be more than enough time."

"I can't imagine what could be more difficult than painting a picture with our *dicks*," Lincoln chuckled.

"Don't worry, I've got some good ones lined up," Madison said, peering down at the men's bulging trousers. "Are you guys ready to get started? Because it's going to be pretty hard to perform this game with your *pants* on."

When the men took off their trousers, their hard-ons quickly sprung to life, revealing how excited they were at the idea of the women watching them paint with their cocks.

"Mmm," Laura grinned, licking her lips. "That's the most delicious sight I've seen in a long time. I'm ready to lick those dicks even before they get started."

"At least you can wait until everyone's seated at the table," Brad joked, echoing her comment from the last round. "Try to save a little bit for the *rest* of the women."

6

———

Each of the men took a position in front of one of the bowls, then they dipped their erections in the colorful cream and began swiping the tips across the paper easels. I found it interesting that Madison had made a different food color for each bowl, and as the men began to slap their dicks awkwardly against the easels, their meandering patterns started off looking more like toddlers' random finger painting than any kind of recognizable portrait. But after a couple of minutes, some of their illustrations began to take shape, reflecting familiar patterns and symbols.

Marco started off creating a simple smiley face with two dots and a curved line for the mouth, but after the women chided him for his lack of creativity, he tried to embellish his figure with a wavy stick figure.

"Come on, Marco," Lily laughed. "You're going to have to do better than that if you expect one of us to put a happy face on *you* when this contest is over. I hope your lovemaking isn't as one-dimensional as your draughtsmanship."

"It's a lot harder than it looks," he huffed, swiveling his hips from side to side as he tried to control the direction of his blue-paint-coated penis over the paper. "I'm not used to using my penis this way."

"Well, you better get *used* to it," Bonnie chuckled. "Because nobody likes a lover who does it the same boring way every time."

"At least *Neil* chose a more inspiring subject," Emma nodded, turning toward the next easel.

He'd chosen to paint a heart with his red food color, with three radiating outlines symbolizing a beating organ.

"True," I nodded. "But it's not exactly a *Rembrandt.* "Can't you guys try to paint something a little more three-dimensional?"

"It's pretty obvious where *Ryan's* mind is going," Laura nodded, glancing at Ryan's rendering of a woman's ass with a set of balls nestled under her cheeks.

"What can I say?" Ryan grinned, tilting his orange-hued dick higher up the easel to outline his subject's back with two breasts peeking out the sides. "I seem to be developing an affinity for *ladyboys.*"

"Unlike *Brad*," Trinity chuckled, peering at Brad's easel. "He seems to have a one-track mind."

He'd chosen to paint a crude rendition of the trucker's mudflap girl, showing a yellow silhouette of a naked women sitting with her arms outstretched behind her.

"Seriously?" Laura huffed, glaring at Brad. "Is that the only way you think of women? Like sexualized *bimbos*?"

"Well, it's not like Madison's *helping* anything with this erotic-themed party," Brad grunted. "With everyone taking off their clothes and getting freaky in increasingly kinky games, it's pretty hard to think of anything else."

"At least *Diego's* chosen to represent his appreciation for women in a more subtle way," Laura said, turning her head toward Diego's canvas.

His painting showed a flower with soft pink petals and a protruding pistil, echoing the image of a woman's vulva and clitoris.

"Does that remind you of anyone in *particular*?" I said, smiling in Elle's direction.

"Maybe," Diego nodded. "But *every* woman's flower is a work of art."

"Ohhh," Elle sighed, glancing at the other girls with swooning eyes. "That's the nicest thing anyone's ever said to me."

"Did you hear that, Toby?" Laura said, turning her head toward Elle's husband's easel. "It looks like you've got a little catching up to do with the front-runner."

"I'm trying my best," Toby said, twisting his hips while he painted an elaborate landscape scene on his easel.

When everybody turned to glance at his drawing, they gasped in surprise when they saw what he'd produced. His illustration showed a leafy tree at the side of lake with two green butterflies dancing next to one another.

"Holy cow," Piper said. "I think you may have missed your calling, Toby. If you're as adept with that brush in the *bedroom* as you are in front of an easel, your wife must be one lucky girl."

"I might have to watch him do this more often," Elle nodded, rubbing her thighs together while she gazed at her husband's dripping phallus. "This is the best foreplay I've ever had."

"That leaves only two more candidates to consider," Trinity nodded, twisting her head to the last couple of easels.

Everybody turned toward *Shae's* easel, where she'd drawn a gender pictogram combining both the male and female symbols.

"I like it," Piper said. "They say everyone's sexual preference is somewhere on the continuum. I think we should *all* adopt this symbol to reflect our orientation."

Then everyone's eyes turned toward Lincoln, whose buttocks were flexing rapidly while he attempted to etch something on his board. We twisted our bodies to see what he was drawing, and our eyes widened when we saw what he'd produced. In near-perfect italic script, he'd written the words *love is the answer*.

"Oh my God," Emma gasped, flaring her eyes at the composition. "How can anyone write that clearly with their *penis*? I haven't been able to write in cursive since elementary school."

"It's pretty impressive," I nodded. "Especially considering the *thickness* of his brush."

"One minute left," Madison announced, glancing at her timer.

"You guys will have to put the finishing touches on your masterpieces before time runs out."

"If I try to embellish my picture any *more*," Marco groaned, trying to flesh out his smiley figure with a few more curves and shadows. "I'm going to cum on my paper. All this stimulation with the creamy food dye on the tip of my cock feels pretty good."

"Not as good as it's going to feel if one of us has a chance to *lick it off*," Emma grinned.

7

"Alright," Madison announced. "Brushes down, time's up. It's time to inspect your compositions and choose a winner." The men stepped away from their paintings and turned around, revealing their bobbing erections coated with creamy paint.

"Are we talking about their drawings or their pretty *penises*?" Elle smiled.

"I think we should focus on their creations," Maddy said. "After all, the whole point of this exercise was to demonstrate that it's not so much about the *size* of the instrument as how they use it."

"Yes," Piper nodded. "If these paintings reflect their mastery in certain other areas, then I'd have to say some of these men are already masters of their craft."

"So it would seem," Madison said. "But there can only be one winner. Let's show our appreciation for their work by clapping while we appraise each piece. We'll begin with Marco's drawing."

The women clapped softly, wrinkling their foreheads at his messy stick figure.

"At least he tried to put some *meat* on the bones before he finished," Emma chuckled.

"What about Neil's piece?" Madison said, swinging her arm around to the next easel.

"His *heart* was in the right place," Trinity joked while the rest of us giggled at her double entendre.

"How about Ryan?" Madison said, turning toward his drawing of the naked mudflap girl.

"It's actually not a bad reproduction of the familiar icon," Lily said, tilting her head to the side. "But I don't know about you guys, I always *flinch* when I see that picture on the back of a trucker's rig."

"I agree," I said, peering at his picture with a scrunched face.

"Some of you seemed to appreciate *Diego's* drawing," Madison said, continuing to sweep her hand clockwise around the room.

"It's beautiful," Bonnie said as the rest of us clapped in approval. "Echoing Georgia O'Keeffe, it's beautiful and sensuous at the same time."

"And special marks for his flattering commentary," Elle nodded, smiling at Diego.

"What did you think of your *husband's* composition?" Madison said, pointing toward Toby's easel.

"It's pretty impressive, given the limited time he had to work with," Elle smiled. "I had no idea he was so versatile with his penis."

"I'm sure he'd jump at the chance to paint you with some *other* creamy substance if you'll let him," Laura grinned.

"Something tells me he's going to have plenty of chances before the night is over," Elle chuckled.

The women applauded loudly, smiling at Toby while they stared at his bobbing penis.

"What about *Shae*?" Madison said, pointing toward her pictogram.

"I like what her symbol represents," Trinity nodded while the rest of the women clapped softly. "It just doesn't have the same level of *detail* as some of the others."

"That only leaves *Lincoln* then," Madison said, turning toward Linc's easel.

Everybody paused while they took turns staring at his etching and his enormous erection.

"It demonstrates remarkable penmanship," Emma nodded.

"Or *pricks*manship," I chuckled, staring at his angled hard-on, dripping purple paint down the side of his long shaft.

"And the *message* is beautiful, also," Elle said while the rest of us clapped loudly.

"Alright, then," Madison said, turning back toward the men. "It seems to be a pretty close contest between Lincoln, Diego, and Toby. But based on the enthusiasm of your applause, I'd have to give the nod to *Toby*."

Each of the women stood up and cheered, clapping loudly while they peered at his Monet-inspired landscape.

"So, how do we decide which of us gets to clean him up?" Piper said, licking her lips.

"I suppose we could draw lots," Madison said, reaching into her game bag. "But I just happen to have this game wheel left over from one of my other parties. Why don't I spin the needle and see who it points to?"

Madison placed the spinner in the center of the coffee table in front of the sofa, then everyone leaned forward while she flicked the needle with the tip of her finger. After spinning around a few times, it finally stopped, pointing in the direction of one of the easels. The women followed the line of the arrow, tilting their heads slowly in the direction of Brad.

"It's pointing towards *Brad!*" Bonnie said. "I thought you said one of the *women* would have a chance to partner with the winner?"

"I didn't say that exactly," Madison grinned. "I only said it would be a randomly selected participant."

"But I've never been with a man that way before," Toby said, glancing uneasily at Brad.

"Neither had Brad before our last party," Maddy smiled. "But he seemed to warm up to the idea pretty quickly after the completion of the *Joystick Jenga* contest."

"It looks like you'll be kneeling in a slightly *different* position this time," Laura grinned at her husband. "You should be getting pretty used to it by now."

"What exactly do you expect him to *do* with me?" Toby said, peering at Madison with a wrinkled brow.

"Well, technically," Maddy said. "You only need to let him lick the dye off your penis. But depending on how much each of you *enjoy* the experience, there's no reason to stop there."

Elle suddenly cleared her throat, glancing up at her husband with a Cheshire Cat grin.

"We *did* say that we were coming to this party to spread our wings," she smiled. "I've had my chance, now it looks like it's going to be yours."

Toby sighed as he crossed his legs defensively.

"I didn't think when I drew two butterflies," he frowned. "That it might be two *male* butterflies."

———————

8

"So where do you want me to do this?" Toby said, crossing his arms over his chest.

I found it interesting that as much as he pretended to dread the idea of receiving a gay blowjob, that his green-cream-coated dick was still standing straight up and bobbing excitedly overtop of his splattered stomach.

Looks like his little head is winning the battle with his big head, I chuckled to myself.

"Well, you've been standing up for the past ten minutes," Madison nodded. "Why don't you take a rest on the sofa, where Brad can get comfortable with you?"

"Okay..." Toby grumbled, walking slowing over to the couch as his hard-on swung from side to side.

When he sat on the cushion next to the side armrest, the rest of the group retreated toward the fireplace while Brad sat tentatively next to him, a few inches apart.

"How would you like me to do this?" he said, peering at Toby anxiously.

"I have no idea," Toby said, sitting with his knees clamped tightly together and his erection jutting up between his legs. "I've never done anything like this before."

"Not with a *man*, perhaps," his wife grinned, slipping her fingers between her thighs while she stared at Toby's dripping hard-on from the edge of the fireplace hearth. "Why don't you close your eyes and imagine it's me licking your cock instead of Brad? You might even *enjoy* the experience if you open your mind a little bit."

"Yes," Bonnie nodded. "Like Shae suggested with her drawing, we *all* have some degree of attraction to the same sex. Didn't you experiment with some of your friends when you were younger?"

Toby took a deep sigh, refusing to answer the question, then he closed his eyes and tilted his head on the back of the sofa, spreading his legs slowly apart. Brad peered at his bobbing prick and paused while his own yellow-coated erection slapped up against his stomach.

"What are you waiting for, dear?" Laura teased. "You already had a little practice giving head to *Diego* at Madison's last party. This one should be even *tastier* with the creamy food dye coating Brad's cock."

Brad tilted his body slowly to the side and lowered his head toward Toby's erection, beginning to lick the side of his shaft with the end of his tongue. When his tongue reached the tip of his organ, Toby took a deep breath in, gripping the armrest tightly with his left hand.

"That's it, baby," Laura smiled, taking a seat next to Elle on the fireplace hearth so they could watch their husbands together. "I think Toby kind of *likes* it."

Brad darted his eyes at the two women rubbing their legs together on the fireplace, then he pressed his head forward a few more inches, angling his face to lick the other side of Toby's dick.

"Mmm," Laura groaned, staring at Toby's flaring erection. "That's fucking *hot*. Are you savoring this as much as I am, Elle?"

"I didn't think I'd enjoy watching two men having sex this much," Elle nodded, placing her left palm on top of Laura's knee while she watched the action. "Although I'm not sure Brad's going to be able to clean all the paint off Toby's dick from that position."

"I think she's right, honey," Laura said, slipping her hand inside

Elle's parted thighs. "Why don't you *kneel* between Toby's legs so you're in a better position to lick it off?"

"Hmm," Brad nodded, growing increasingly excited watching the two women touching each other.

While Toby squinted with one eye half-open toward him, he slid off the sofa and positioned himself in front of his parted legs.

"*Yes*, baby," Laura hummed, sliding her hand further between Elle's thighs. "Lick his hard-on like it's a *popsicle*. A nice, juicy lemon-lime-flavored one."

Brad flattened his tongue and swiped it up the underside of Toby's pole, and Toby groaned, opening his eye a little further.

"Do you *like* that, sweetheart?" Elle grinned, pulling her left hand closer to Laura's dripping crotch. "Nobody said you couldn't *watch*. Why don't you open your eyes all the way and enjoy the show? Everybody *else* seems to be."

Toby raised his lids, glancing at the gallery of naked party guests touching themselves while they watched the two men on the sofa. When he saw Laura's and Elle's hands buried between each other's thighs, his eyes flared when Brad slid his tongue over his glans.

"*Mhhh,*" he moaned, lowering his eyes to watch Brad sucking the head of his dick.

"*Fuck*, yes," Elle grunted, rocking her hips in concert with her husband while the two women slowly fingered each other. "Suck him hard, Brad. That's fucking insane."

"Don't forget his *balls*, honey," Laura nodded, spreading her knees further apart while Elle slipped two fingers into her hole. "The paint is dripping down his shaft. I know how much you like it when I lick you there."

"Mmm," Brad nodded, lowering his head and sliding his tongue around Toby's tightening balls with mounting enthusiasm.

While he leaned over, licking Toby's cock and balls, I noticed his erection swinging between his legs, dripping yellow strings from his glans.

"Is that *paint* you're dripping onto the floor, Brad, or *pre-cum?*" Laura grinned, rocking her hips against Elle's probing fingers while she watched the erotic show on the sofa. "Because you seem to be enjoying this operation almost as much as Toby is."

"Mm-hmm," Brad nodded, placing his hand around his dick while he raised his head to suck on Toby's helmet again.

By now, Toby had both of his eyes wide open, alternating his gaze between the sight of the two married women fingering each other's dripping pussies and Brad's bobbing head over his hard-on. But this time, he moved his hands overtop of Brad's head, encouraging him to keep his focus on his sensitive glans while he groaned with increasing volume along with the women.

"Oh my God," Elle panted, raising her free hand to Laura's right breast and squeezing it hard. "This is the hottest thing I've ever seen. I'm going to come soon, watching this. Are you getting close, baby?"

"I am *now*," Toby grunted, pushing Brad's head further down over his cock.

"Take him *all the way*, like you did with Diego's cock," Laura groaned, circling her hand rapidly over Elle's darkening vulva while Elle finger-fucked her pussy. I think everybody is ready to come now. Show Toby what it's like to get a *real* gay blowjob."

Brad hesitated for a moment, then he relaxed his throat muscles while he lowered his head all the way down Toby's shaft, until his lips encircled the base of his pole just above his balls. While Toby throat-fucked him with white knuckles, Brad began to jerk his own dick faster while everybody in the room moaned in increasing excitement. When Toby suddenly lurched forward and began convulsing over Brad's bobbing head, Elle and Laura moaned out loud, pressing their fingers hard against each other's cunts while they jetted their juices over our thighs. Before long, everybody in the room was gasping and grunting as they climaxed along with the others.

When I saw Brad squirting thick strings of cum against the side of the sofa while he held his mouth over Toby's pulsing organ, I had to smile at Madison's suggestion this might actually clean things up. Between the splattering food dye from the men jerking their dicks while they watched Toby and Brad, and the women's dripping juices running down the insides of their legs, we'd only succeeded in making even *more* of a mess.

But what a beautiful mess it was, I smiled, watching the juices dripping out of Laura's and Elle's pussies while they squeezed each other's hands tightly between their legs.

"Well," Madison smiled after Brad lifted his head off Toby's dripping organ. "It looks like you managed to lick all the paint off his cock, but it seems that we've got a *different* kind of mess to clean up after now."

She reached into her game kit and pulled out a stack of hand towels, asking everyone to pass them around.

"If you could be so kind to clean up your mess, I'm going to go into the kitchen to prepare some more refreshments, then why don't we take a short break while we prepare for the next round?"

After a few minutes, the party guests began trickling into the kitchen, where we gathered around the island, nibbling on hors d'oeuvres.

"So," Elle said when she noticed her husband entering the room with a sheepish grin on his face. "Was it as awful as you imagined?"

Toby nodded with a lopsided smile, trying to avoid direct eye contact with Brad.

"Judging by how long he kept his dick planted on my husband's face when he came," Laura chuckled. "I'd say he enjoyed it just fine."

"Was it as good as the blowjobs you usually get from *me*?" Elle said, raising an eyebrow.

Toby cocked his head to one side and simply smiled, signaling his satisfaction with the experience.

"It looks like I've still got a few things to learn," Elle grinned, nodding toward Brad. "Maybe same-sex partners really *do* know how to please one another better than mixed couples."

"*You* two certainly seemed to enjoy yourselves enough taking in the show," Toby said, nodding toward Laura and Elle. "Maybe you'll have a few more chances to hook up before the night is over."

"Speaking of," Bonnie said, peering toward Madison. "Isn't it the *women's* turn for some fun in the next contest?"

"Right you are, Bonnie," Maddy nodded. "In our next game I'm calling *Bobbing for Peaches*, each of the men will be competing to see who can get their partners off the fastest."

I couldn't help laughing at some of the names Madison had given the contests.

"I'm guessing based on the name of this one that they'll be doing this only with their mouths?" I chuckled.

"Yes," Maddy said. "Although, for the *winner* of the game, there'll be no limit on how your partner chooses to stimulate your peachka."

"How will we choose our partners *this* time?" Toby grunted. "Another spinning game wheel?"

"I thought to make it a little more interesting," Maddy smiled. "That I'd *blindfold* each of you."

"Both the men and the women?" Lily said.

"Mm-hmm," Madison nodded. "That way, nobody will know who's stimulating whom until it's over."

"Hmm," Laura grinned, peering around the table at each of the men as their penises began to take on a whole new life. "I like the sound of that."

"Once again," Shae huffed. "I seem to be the odd man out. With eight women and seven men, I suppose you want me to be on the *giving* end this time?"

"Not to worry," Madison said. "If you do a good enough job satisfying your partner, you'll have plenty of opportunities to get more involved in the second half of the game. Since you're the proud owner of *two* sets of sexual organs, you'll have more options than most as to how you choose to finish the exercise."

"Mmm," Shae nodded, her rising cock tapping against the underside of the kitchen island. "This contest is sounding more interesting by the moment."

"How will we know who comes first?" Marco said. "What if some of the women fake it?"

"Oh, I'll *know*," Madison grinned. "There are certain telltale signs that are impossible to hide. But to some degree, each of you will be on your honor. Besides, you'd just be doing your partner a disservice if you fake your orgasm. Otherwise, how will men ever learn how to eat pussy the proper way?"

"So we're only allowed to use our *mouths* to stimulate them?" Lincoln said.

"Yes," Madison nodded. "You'd have a bit of an unfair advantage if we allowed you to unleash that weapon of yours again."

"What about our *fingers?*" Brad said.

"Part of the purpose of this exercise is to learn how to use your mouths more creatively," Maddy said. "It's not just about flicking and sucking. It's about teasing and building up the excitement so your partner can enjoy the experience to the fullest."

Laura suddenly chuckled as she peered toward her husband.

"Are you sure you're going to be able to *find* the important parts with your eyes covered, sweetheart?" she said.

"I've never heard you complain before," Brad grinned.

"Can we talk to our partners while they stimulate us?" Piper asked. "If we want to teach them to be better lovers, doesn't it ultimately come down to better communication?"

"Maybe," Madison said. "But there's also something to be said for being more attuned to your partner's *body language*. Oftentimes, the experience is heightened by shutting out some of the other senses."

"Is that why we're wearing blindfolds?" Toby said.

"Partly," Madison nodded. "Besides helping with the random

assignments, I think you'll find it to be a more interesting experience on both sides. Are you ready to get started?"

"Judging by how fast the boys have managed to get their *dicks* up again," Emma chuckled, glancing at the men's bobbing erections. "I'd have to take that as a yes."

10

W hen everybody returned to the living room, Madison instructed the women to sit side-by-side around the large sectional sofa then she gave everyone an individual blindfold, asking them to tie it tightly around their eyes so they couldn't see anything. Then she guided each of the men toward a random partner, pressing gently down on their shoulders until they kneeled on the floor. When I felt someone brush against my parted legs, I felt a dribble of lubrication spilling out of my pussy and trickling down the crack of my ass.

"Okay," Madison said, standing a few feet behind us. "In a few moments, we'll get started. But remember, although the prize goes to the one who climaxes first, that doesn't mean you should try to rush it. Just like in the story of the turtle and the hare, sometimes it's the *slow and steady* one who wins the race."

The room suddenly filled with silence while the redolent aroma of eight dripping pussies wafted under our noses.

"Alright, lady and gentlemen," Maddy announced. "Start your engines."

When I felt my partner's head lower between my legs, it didn't take long for me to recognize the familiar feel of Shae's curvy body pressing up against me. While she slid the tip of her tongue gently up the inside of my parted legs, I felt the ends of her long hair tickling my ankles and the sides of her soft breasts caressing the insides of my thighs.

"Mmm," I moaned, happy that Madison had matched the two of us again.

While she nibbled on the edges of my labia, I flashed back for a moment to the first time we'd bumped into one another at the local supermarket. Recognizing her from a cabaret show I'd attended earlier in the week, we joked about the size of the cucumbers we'd selected from the produce aisle, wondering what we intended to do with them. When I invited her out for coffee, the chemistry between us was undeniable, and it didn't take long for the two of us to head back to my house, where we made love for the rest of the afternoon. When I felt her naked under the covers for the first time, I was shocked and delighted when I discovered she had both male and female fully functioning sex organs. She was skilled and adept at using *all* of her tools, and I lost track of how many times she made me come that day.

But there was something about feeling her stimulating me while we were both *blindfolded* that heightened my excitement even more. While I listened to the sound of her mouth kissing and sucking my dripping pussy, I imagined her big hard-on bobbing between her legs, dripping pre-cum over the crown of her glans while her pussy dribbled juices down the inside of her thighs.

"Unghh," I groaned, as she flattened her tongue and slowly swiped it all the way from my twitching anus to the tip of my folds.

Pausing overtop of my throbbing gland, she nodded her head up and down like she was licking an ice cream cone, blowing softly onto my burning bulb while I panted like a dog in heat a few inches above her body. By the time she encircled my jewel and began sucking on it with her puffy lips, I was already three-quarters of the way to the hardest orgasm I'd experienced in a long time.

As I listened to the sound of the others moaning and panting around me, it hardly mattered to me who came first. I just wanted to close my eyes and savor the feeling of this beautiful transgender woman giving me the sweetest pussy licking of my life. I smiled, imagining Madison standing behind all of us watching the sight of the men's asses raised in the air while each of us squirmed on the sofa, our hardening nipples and spreading sex flushes betraying our rising excitement. I envied her for a moment, but when Shae began drawing figure-eight patterns over my throbbing clit with the tip of her tongue, I grasped the back of her head tightly with two hands, pulling her face harder against my cunt.

Madison had said the *men* couldn't use their hands, but that didn't stop me from giving her some non-verbal feedback to keep doing what she was doing. While I felt my pleasure rising inexorably like an oncoming freight train, I slowly widened my legs, gaping my mouth open as I neared the tipping point. Shutting out the sounds of everything else in the room, when I felt my orgasm wash over me like a burst dam, I gushed my juices hard over her face buried between my legs, pressing her nose so hard against my spasming vulva that she could barely breathe. My orgasm seemed to last forever, and as I slowly began to become aware of the sounds of other women climaxing soon after, Shae hummed happily into my pussy while she cradled my ass gently in her hands.

Madison hesitated until the last of the women climaxed, then she glanced at her smartphone, nodding approvingly.

"That was quite a sight to behold," she said as the women panted in unison on the sofa and the men slowly raised their heads from their pussies, their erections bouncing excitedly between their legs. "Maybe you should practice this technique more frequently with your lovers. Because from *my* point of view, I've rarely seen a group of women more satisfied from the oral ministrations of their partners."

"Who was the winner?" Trinity said.

"Jade," Madison nodded, glancing at her timer. "And it took just over five minutes to get there. I was happy to see each of you taking your time and enjoying the *process* instead of just focusing on the destination."

"How can you be so sure she was the one who came *first?*" Laura said. "Because from where I was sitting, there was a whole lot of moaning going on all around me."

"Jade has a unique way of demonstrating when she climaxes, aren't I right, Shae?" Madison said.

"Mmm," Shae smiled, licking my juices off the sides of her mouth while her breasts glistened from the spray I'd jetted on her chest. "She squirts even harder than *I* do when I come."

Elle suddenly shifted restlessly on the sofa, tugging on her bandana.

"Does that mean we can take our blindfolds off now?" she said. "Because I'd like to watch them finish up, not to mention find out who was sucking my pussy so expertly."

"Absolutely," Madison nodded, eager to move on to the next phase of the contest.

When each of the participants flipped off their bandanas, they smiled at their partners, nodding in excitement with who they'd been paired up with. Once again, Madison had expertly mixed up the matches so everyone had a chance to hookup with a new partner, and I had to laugh at how well she'd organized the whole event.

"Something tells me these pairings you've been setting us up with aren't nearly as *random* as you're leading us to believe," I chuckled.

"Just trying to spread the love around," Madison grinned, revealing a dark stain in the crotch of her jeans as she shifted position.

"It looks like we weren't the *only* ones enjoying that last exercise," I said. "It seems a little unfair that you get to soak it all up while the rest of us are kept in the dark."

"I didn't hear you complaining while you were coming all over Shae's face," Madison grinned, stepping out of her wet clothes. "But now that you mention it, I'm looking forward to enjoying the rest of the show almost as much as the rest of you."

11

"How do you want us to *finish* the exercise?" Shae said, leaning back as a large drop of pre-cum slid down the underside of her bobbing prick.

"It looks like you're about ready to explode along with the rest of the men," Maddy smiled, glancing down at her flaring cock. "It's only fair that *both* of you should have an opportunity to enjoy the experience equally this time,"

"I almost came when I felt Jade squirting all over my face," Shae nodded. "I'd love to dip my tool in her well if she's willing."

"Are you kidding me?" I grunted, leaning forward to lick my juices off her hardening nipples. "I've been dreaming of riding that cock ever since I watched you drawing that picture on the easel."

Brad cleared his throat, peering at his partner Piper's tumescent pussy lips while she dribbled juices out of her slit.

"Are we allowed to hookup with *our* partners too?" he said.

"As much as I'm sure all of you would like to," Madison said. "In the interests of keeping the contest fair, I think we should continue to play by the rules. There can only be one winner this time."

"That doesn't stop us from touching *ourselves* while we watch them make love, does it?" Neil said, caressing the tip of his pole.

"I suppose not," Madison smiled. "But you might want to save some for the next game coming up after this. Because in the contest called *Firing Range*, the more primed your pump will be, the better chance you'll have of capturing your prize once it's over."

"Fair enough," Neil nodded, pulling his hand away from his cock. "Because I'm pretty pumped after licking Emma's pussy."

"Save that thought and you'll have your chance to blow your wad soon enough. But for now, why don't each of us relax while we watch Jade and Shae consummate their connection in a more intimate way."

"Mmm," Shae said, smiling toward me. "Is there any particular way you'd like to have me?"

"I'd like to have you *every* way," I grinned, running my eyes over her glistening breasts, toward her flexing hard-on and dripping pussy. "But right now, I just want you *inside* me. If you don't put that pretty prick inside my pussy soon, I liable to come all over you again just *looking* at you."

"You don't have to ask twice," Shae said, pressing her hips forward, pointing her flexing phallus toward my opening.

I reached out to grasp the tip of it, swiping it up and down my dripping vulva, and she groaned when she felt my soft lips caressing the sensitive glans of her penis.

"Talk about coming just *watching* you," she grunted. "If you keep teasing me like that, I'm going to make almost as much of a mess as you just did."

"Well, we can't have that," I grinned, pushing my hips forward as her crown slipped inside my slit. "I want to feel you coming *inside* me."

"Fuck, yes," Shae hissed, burying her cock slowly inside me. "I don't know which I enjoy more, feeling you squirt all over my *face* or my *cock* when you come."

"I'm pretty sure I can *guess* which you prefer," I chuckled, leaning forward to rub my tits against hers while I drifted my hand around the back of her ass. "I want to feel your pussy throbbing when you come inside me."

"Oh *God*," Shae hissed when she felt my fingers sliding inside her hole. "That feels so good. Play with my pussy while I fuck you."

"Holy shit," Toby suddenly groaned, while he stared at the two of us making out.

"You like that, baby?" his wife grinned, glancing toward his cock straining up against his stomach. "Maybe you'd like to play with a *different* kind of cock next time?"

"Or her *pussy*," Toby nodded, dry-humping the air in front of his partner Trinity.

"Having twice the equipment makes it twice the fun," I smiled, squeezing Shae's tits while she fucked me with her big dick.

"Mhhh," she groaned, pressing her face forward to kiss me. "Keep fingering me like that. I can feel it coming. I'm going to come so hard inside you."

"Yes, baby," I panted, feeling my own pleasure rapidly rising. "I'm going to come with you. Ride me like a horse."

While Shae dug the tips of her fingers harder into the sides of my ass as she pounded her instrument deep inside me, I began to feel the inside of her pussy tenting open, preparing to spasm in orgasmic contractions. Although she had a fully functioning penis, I found it fascinating how she seemed like a woman in every other respect, from her pretty face to her natural breasts to her pulsating pussy. But there was something about having her hard *tool* inside me that took her lovemaking to an entirely new level. I'd enjoyed plenty of strap-on dildos with my lesbian lovers over the years, but feeling a real-life, throbbing, burning erection inside me while I squeezed her pretty tits was something nobody else could duplicate.

Suddenly, she arched her back and threw her head back, gaping her mouth open as a deep flush rolled over her cheeks, squealing in ecstasy while she emptied her seed deep inside my pussy. When we both began squirting our juices between our parted legs, everybody in the room groaned, hardly believing what they were watching. But while the two of us held each other tightly, convulsing in the throes of a powerful mutual climax, I noticed Madison standing a short distance behind us, peering at our two pussies while she thrust three fingers deep into her snatch.

It looks like more than two can play this game, I smiled, happy to see her joining the fun along with the rest of the group.

12

"**M**mm," Madison said, pulling her fingers out of her dripping pussy. "These games are getting more exciting by the moment."

"I thought you said we couldn't *play* with ourselves?" Neil huffed.

"I only said the *men* couldn't," Maddy smiled.

"It hardly seems fair," Marco protested. "I'm about to *explode* from watching that hot hookup."

"That's exactly the way I wanted it," Maddy nodded. "Because in our next contest named *Firing Range*, you're going to have a chance to put all your pent-up energy to good use."

"Are we going to be aiming at another target like in the bullseye contest from your last party?" Linc said.

"You won't be focusing on a specific *target* per se," Madison grinned, peering down at Lincoln's bobbing organ, already rock-hard from watching Shae and me. "In this game, *distance* will be more important than aim. So you've already got a few inches head start on the rest of the field."

"What did you have in mind, exactly?" Diego said, wrinkling his forehead.

Madison reached into her bag and pulled out a thick roll of pink parchment paper, laying it in long strips in front of the fireplace. Then she dragged the sofa back a few feet and asked the men to stand in front of it, side-by-side.

"You guys said you wanted to *touch* yourselves in the last round," she smiled. "Well, here's your big chance. In this contest, we're going to see how far you can shoot your wad. The man who fires the furthest wins the prize."

"What's the prize?" Toby said.

"This time, I'm going to let you *choose* who you'd like to hook-up with. That is, assuming the women are willing."

"Oh, I'm willing, alright," Laura grinned. "I haven't had so much fun playing musical chairs since Kindergarten."

"Who says it has to be a *woman*?" Ryan said, placing his hands on his hips.

"Good point, Ryan," Madison nodded. "We *did* say to park your mental blocks at the door. We've already seen enough boy-on-boy and girl-on-girl pairings to spark everyone's imagination."

Shae suddenly cleared her throat, crossing her arms defiantly.

"Which side of the contest do you want *me* to be on this time?" she said. "I'm not really either a boy or a girl."

"You've got a *cock*, don't you?" Maddy grinned. "Let's see if you've got the right stuff."

"I'm not sure how much more I've got left to deliver after coming so hard with Jade," Shae smiled. "But I'll give it my best shot."

"Speaking of," Brad said. "How will we know who shot the furthest?"

Madison reached into her game kit and pulled out a small pad of Post-it notes, scribbling each contestant's name on the slips and handing one to each of the women.

"Each of you will have a counterpart who'll be responsible for recording the landing points of your cumshots by placing a marker with your name beside the target. I've chosen pink-colored paper to help identify the spots, since the color should change to dark red with the extra moisture. But you better be careful ladies, you might have to sidestep the volleys of spunk if everybody comes at the same time."

"Holy shit," Lily said, shaking her head. "This is insane! Where do you come up with these ideas?"

"I've seen enough guys jerk off in my day," Madison smiled. "I thought it might be kind of fun to compare their technique while we give them a chance to relieve their purple balls."

"Hmm," Laura nodded. "While we come up with a few new ideas for giving them better handies."

"Exactly," Madison said. "If nothing else, I hope this party has expanded your repertoire of skills you can use with your partners."

"To say the *least*," Elle grinned, glancing at her husband standing beside the other men while their flagpoles stood waving in front of their bellies. "I had no idea it would open so many doors for Toby and me when we agreed to come."

"Speaking of *coming*," Madison said, turning toward the lineup of grinning men. "Are you guys ready to get started?"

"I'm not sure I've seen eight men more eager to get started in my whole life," Laura chuckled.

While Madison took up position beside the men to signal for them to begin, I glanced at the row of bobbing erections with a giant smile. Each of them was a different size, color, and shape, and it echoed back to the first contest of the evening, when the men used the Rorschach blots to match each of the women's pussies to their owner.

Marco's and Neil's cocks were uncircumcised, with their pink crowns partially exposed like two piggies in a blanket. Diego and Marco had a warm caramel color to their instruments, making them look like bronze sculptures. Lincoln's huge, slightly curved black organ looked like an enormous sausage, ready for the licking. Only *Shae's* prick looked somewhat out of place, with her dripping pussy sitting under her flaring erection instead of two balls.

But *everyone's* erection looked proud and capable standing at full mast, twitching in the still air while each of the women looked on with fascination.

"Alright," Madison smiled, glancing at their bobbing dicks and lowering her arm. "This contest isn't timed, so feel free to take your time and enjoy the experience to the fullest. As with the turtle and the hare, you might well find that the slower the build-up, the greater the reward."

Each of the men grabbed their hard-ons and began stroking them softly, darting their eyes between the cocks of the other men and the line-up of women who'd assembled at the side of the runway to mark their results. I found it mesmerizing to watch each of their techniques, somewhat surprised by how different they varied from one man to another. Some of the men only stroked the sensitive end of their penis, while others gripped the entire shaft of their organs with a balled fist, jerking their poles hard while they rocked their hips forward and back. And some of them caressed their balls with one hand while they stroked their penis with their other, while some of the better *endowed* men held their cock with two hands as they flexed their buttocks, poking their dripping heads out the end while they stared at their manhood, moaning softly.

It didn't take long for each of the *women* to get into the mood along with the men, and before long, we were rolling our fingers absent-mindedly over our clits while we watched the men fapping their dicks.

"Don't get too distracted by the entertainment, ladies," Madison kidded. "Remember, you're going to have to act quickly when your partner pops off."

"We can do two things at once," I grinned, glancing at the other women standing on opposite sides of the parchment paper. "It's kind of like watching porn on a slow day at work. We've got to find *something* to do while we wait for the big finish."

"It shouldn't be much longer now," Neil huffed, jerking his darkening tool faster while his balls slowly tightened around the base of his shaft.

"Mmm, yes, baby," Bonnie purred, holding his tag softly in her hand. "Let it rip and show us what you've got."

"Nnghh," he suddenly groaned, pressing his hips forward while he squeezed his shaft, jetting a string of jizz in a long arc toward the fireplace.

When his first volley landed halfway down the landing strip, Bonnie paused until each of his successive spurts plopped in progressively shorter distances down the runway. When he finally finished spurting, she stepped gingerly onto the pad, placing her note beside the first shot, then she quickly stepped back to the relative safety of the viewing gallery.

"I might be the lucky one having my partner shoot first," she smiled, nodding to the paper, stained with seven dark blotches. "Things could get pretty *slippery* over there in another couple of minutes."

"Oh God," Marco suddenly growled, gripping his dick tightly between two hands, his glans now fully exposed from his retracted foreskin. "I'm going to come–oh *fuckkk...*"

This time, his spunk jetted out in a straight line while he held his throbbing dick level with the floor, his semen sliding along the paper as it landed, leaving a trail like a slug.

But his marker Emma made the mistake of stepping onto the mat too quickly, and as she bent over to mark his first landing spot, his second shot caught her square on the side of her cheek.

"Ew!" she squealed, quickly recoiling and wiping her face with the side of her arm while she retreated back to the side of the runway.

"You better wait until they finish dropping their load next time," Laura chuckled, winking toward Emma. "It looks like their first shot isn't always their *best* shot."

"I'll have to remember that," Emma grinned, wiping her slippery arm against the side of her ass.

One by one, each of the men grunted and groaned in succession, tightening their faces and tensing their bodies while they spurted their spunk in a volley of streams along the runway.

"This is better than watching the Bellagio fountain in Las Vegas,"

Laura chuckled, sprinting between the salvos to mark her partner's shot.

"And the canvas is almost as interesting as a *Pollock* painting," Trinity said, nodding toward the pattern of random speckled dots on the paper.

"This is absolutely brilliant," Bonnie agreed, watching the men's cocks spasming as they spurted long ropes of jizz all over the parchment. "Who would have thought it would be so much fun watching a group of men jacking off together?"

"Yeah," Piper said. "Screw the *circle jerk*, it's way more interesting watching them trying to outdo one another."

"That only leaves Toby and Lincoln left to pop off," I said, glancing toward the two remaining men still stroking their hard-ons.

The women's gaze turned back toward the sofa, where Toby and Linc were holding their breath as a deep flush began to roll over their flexing pecs. It was interesting to see Lincoln pounding his big dick between his hands almost like he was fucking an inanimate object, while Toby rolled his right hand softly over his purple crown while he squeezed his balls with his other hand. Before long, Lincoln began grunting like a wild boar, squirting his first shot all the way to the base of the fireplace hearth. I waited until he finished coming, then I quickly placed my marker beside his wet spot near the fireplace, rejoining the rest of the women as we watched Toby's face becoming redder and redder.

"It looks like you're going to have an *aneurism*," his wife said, peering at him with wide eyes. "Just let it go, baby. You're starting to worry me."

His entire body tensed up, then his mouth slowly yawned open while he stared straight ahead in a catatonic trance. When his cream finally flew out of the tip of his cock, the first shot landed with a loud plop on the face of the fireplace just below the mantle. Most of his strings landed further than the other men's, even Lincoln's, until his spurts slowly began to subside, landing closer to his feet. By the time he finished, I counted twelve new spots on the canvas, nodding approvingly.

"Holy *fuck*, Elle," I said, turning toward his wife. "Your husband is a beast. Does he *always* shoot that hard?"

"Not that I've noticed before," Elle grinned. "Maybe the sight of eight women watching him jerk off gave him a little extra motivation."

"Or maybe he's already thinking about who he'd like to hook up with in the next round," Laura smiled.

13

W hile the men stood next to each other with their half-erect penises dripping strings of cum onto the floor, Madison turned toward the women and smiled.

"I don't think we need the markers to tell us who won," she grinned, glancing at the large stain on the front of the fireplace. "That was a pretty impressive performance, Toby. I don't think your swimmers even need *tails* to find their way to their target with a cannon like that to shoot from. I'm surprised you and Elle only have two children!"

"It's a good thing I'm on birth control," Emma nodded. "Although after that demonstration, I'm thinking maybe we should *double up* on our protection."

Madison laughed, then she turned toward Toby.

"Do you think you've got enough gas left in the tank to run a few more laps?" she said. "Who would you like to partner up with to claim your prize?"

"I think I need a few more moments to recover," Toby said, holding his hands on his knees while he bent over, panting heavily.

"Not based on how erect your cock is," Elle joked, peering

between his legs at his flaring erection. "You must have somebody *special* in mind if you're still this hard after coming so strong."

"Maybe he's thinking about another gay blowjob," Trinity laughed.

"I'm thinking about someone with a *cock* alright," Toby grinned. "But not another man. I'd love to have a chance to hook up with Shae if she's still up for it."

"I *knew* it," Elle chuckled. "The way you've been staring at her all night, it's hardly a surprise."

"But it's not so bad if it's with another *woman* this time, is it?" he said with a lopsided smile.

"Perhaps you'd like to *join* the two of us?" Shae said, glancing toward Elle. "With all of my body parts, there's more than enough to go around."

"Really?" Elle said, raising her eyebrows at the thought of having a three-way with her husband and the sexy ladyboy. "How would we do that exactly? Won't we be tied up like a *pretzel*?"

"Well, we'd have to position ourselves carefully," Shae laughed. "But it's not like I haven't done this before. I'm equally adept at making love with both men and women."

"Jesus, babe," Toby said, bulging his eyes as he peered toward his wife. "That sounds fucking hot. Plus, it's not cheating if we do it *together*."

"I'm game if you are," Elle smiled, noticing Shae's organ slowly rising again between her legs. "But who's going to put what *where*? With so many cocks and holes to choose from, it seems like a bit of a crap shoot."

"Well, Toby's already experienced what it's like to be with another man," Shae said. "How about if he samples my lady part this time, while you go for a ride on my cock?"

"Okay," Elle said, furrowing her brow. "But I'm still having a hard time picturing it..."

"Tell you what," Shae smiled. "Let's make this simple. Why don't we have Toby lie down on the floor face-up while I sit on his cock, facing toward his chest. Then you can in turn sit on *my* cock, facing in whichever direction you prefer."

"Mmm," Elle hummed, picturing the scene as a dribble of lubrication trickled down the inside of her thigh. "That sounds hot. Which way would you like me to face, sweetheart–toward Shae or towards you?"

"Hmm," Toby nodded, pausing for a moment while he considered the options. "As much as like the idea of you two rubbing your tits together while Shae fucks you, I think I'd enjoy it even *more* watching the expression on your face while she fucks you from behind."

"Works for me," Elle said, sliding her fingers over her dripping pussy and raising them to her mouth to lick them teasingly. "But you better assume the position quickly, because I'm already dripping like a faucet imagining what this is going to feel like."

Toby glanced at Madison to make sure she was okay with the slight change of plans, and when she nodded silently, he brushed the sheets of parchment paper off to the side of the fireplace, then he lay down on the hardwood floor with his bouncing prick pointing toward his face.

"I'll have some of that," Shae nodded, taking this as her invitation.

She walked over in front of him and placed her feet on either side of his hips, then slowly lowered her pussy over his throbbing erection.

"Mmm," she groaned, taking Toby's dick all the way inside her hole. "I don't often get enough attention to my girly parts. Everybody seems to only want a piece of my *cock.*"

"Well, it's a very pretty one indeed," Toby said, tilting his head forward and grasping it gently with two hands. "To match the *rest* of your beautiful body."

"Ohh," Laura sighed, staring at the handsome couple joined at the hip. "That's so sweet. Are you guys sure you don't want *another* one in the mix?"

"Back off, bitch," Elle joked, pushing Laura aside playfully. "She's mine. My husband won her fair and square. Just sit back and enjoy the show."

"Mmm," Shae purred, watching Elle strut in front of the fireplace. "That is one *sweet* ass. No wonder Toby shoots as far as he does. I would *too* if I had that to come home to every night."

"Well, *tonight*," Elle grinned, stamping her feet on either side of Toby's torso while she dripped her juices onto his bare chest. "He's going to be coming home to something different. And I'm going to be there to *watch* him."

She bent slowly forward at the waist, angling her pussy toward Shae's face, and Shae leaned toward her, licking her tongue between her legs, swiping it softly all the way from the base of her mound to her tight pucker.

"Mmm," Elle groaned as she grinned at her husband. "Are you sure I can't sit on her *face* instead of her cock while you fuck her?"

"Whichever you prefer, babe," Toby smiled while squeezing her swinging tits. "I can bring it home either way."

"Well, we can't let *you* have all the fun, can we?" she smiled, lowering her hips until she felt the tip of Shae's hard-on pressing up against her lips.

Shae grabbed the side of her ass and guided it further down, slowly inserting her erection in Elle's pussy while Elle spread her knees over Brad's stomach.

"Oh, *fuckkk*," Elle groaned, flaring her eyes while she stared at her husband. "This is insane. We've got to come to these parties more often."

"That's fine by me," Madison moaned, circling her clit as she watched the three lovers making out on the floor.

"And *me*," Laura nodded.

"And me..." Piper agreed.

"I think it's *unanimous*," Madison laughed, glancing around the room at the group of men and women nodding enthusiastically while they rubbed their crotches in growing arousal.

"*Fuck* me, Shae," Elle suddenly grunted, placing the palms of her hands on Toby's flexing pecs while Shae rocked her hips from behind. "I want to watch the look on my husband's face while you pound me."

"And while he pounds *me*," Shae groaned, gripping Elle's ass tightly in her hands.

"Yes," Toby moaned, watching the two women rolling their bodies over his hips. "This is the hottest thing I've ever seen."

"Even from your porn stash?" Elle joked.

"It's a million times better in real life," Toby nodded. "I didn't even know it was *possible* for three people to hook up like this."

"That's because I'm one in a million," Shae panted, slipping her hands around the front of Elle's body and squeezing her breasts while she fucked her tight ass. "There's not many transgender girls that have both a cock and a pussy."

"Are you sure we can't take you *home* with us to play with you more often?" Elle grunted, curling her fingertips into Toby's skin while she felt her pleasure slowly beginning to rise. "Because I can imagine a whole *slew* of sexy combinations the three of us could get into if we had more time."

"Just give me the word and I'll be at your doorstep in a flash," Shae nodded, feeling her own orgasm beginning to build inside her.

"Mmm," Toby said, rising up off the floor and bending forward to kiss his wife while he and Shae rocked their hips together in unison. "I'm going to come again soon, baby. Do you think you can come with me?"

"*Fuck* yes," Elle panted, sliding her hands around his back and squeezing his flexing buttocks. "Empty your seed in Shae's sweet pussy. I'm just about there."

"That makes *three* of us," Shae grunted, gripping Elle's tits tightly in her hands as she passed over the tipping point.

"*Mmftt*," she suddenly hissed, slapping the sides of her thighs against Elle's buttocks while she exhaled heavily on her back.

"Oh God, Toby," Elle rasped. "I can feel her cumming inside me. Let it go, baby. I'm ready to come. It feels so good..."

Toby stretched his arms around the back of Shae's shoulders and pulled the three of them tighter together, then he grunted into Elle's mouth while he kissed her passionately.

"Nngah!" he growled, feeling his cock pulsing hard inside Shae's dripping pussy while his wife convulsed over Shae's organ.

I was so busy watching the three of them have the hottest sex I'd seen in a long time, that I completely lost track of where I was. But as I listened to the sound of the other party guests climaxing while they played with their cocks and pussies, I smiled, happy to savor the sight of everyone else lost in a moment of rapture while I experienced my own version of quiet nirvana.

14

"That was crazy-hot," I grinned after everyone came down from their highs.

"It *was* kind of fun, wasn't it?" Madison said while streams of lubrication dribbled down the insides of her thighs.

"I can't imagine how you're going to top the last contest where all the guys shot off together."

"What if *everyone* has a chance to come this time?" Maddy smiled.

"I don't know how you could possibly arrange that," I said, pinching my eyebrows together.

"Well, half of the fun in the last contest was watching the men while they stimulated themselves. What if we could see *everybody's* faces while they hooked up? In this next contest named *Orgasm Face*, we're going to do just that."

"You mean everyone's going to have a chance to hook up with each other at the *same time*?" Piper said.

"It's starting to get a bit late," Madison nodded, peering at her watch. "I think the best way to end our party with a bang is to finish with a *different* kind of big bang."

Then she peered at some of the men still standing with their dicks in their hands.

"But to get started, I first need a couple of volunteers to help me move a few things around."

Ryan and Marco nodded their heads, then Madison escorted them up to the second floor, where she asked them to carry the large stand-up mirror in her bedroom downstairs. When they returned to the living room, she instructed them to lay it horizontally at the base of the fireplace, then she placed eight cushions on the floor a few feet in front of the mirror.

"I'm guessing it's the *women's* turn to get on their knees this time?" Trinity said, inspecting the unusual arrangement.

"Actually, *everybody* will be on their knees in this final game," Madison smiled. "While the women rest on their hands and knees facing the mirror, the men will crouch behind them, watching their faces while they fuck them doggy-style."

"And while we watch *their* faces," Emma nodded.

"Exactly," Madison said. "It's a little bit like the house of mirrors at the county fair, except in *this* case you'll have something a little more interesting to keep yourselves amused."

"How will we choose our partners this time?" Bonnie said.

"To keep with the theme of random pairings," Madison said, scribbling some notes on a Post-it pad and handing the slips out to each contestant. "I've marked each of your slips with either a number or a letter. Number one will match up with letter A, number two will match up with letter B, and so on."

Everybody glanced at their slips, then they peered curiously around the room, wondering who they were going to be paired up with.

"Are the women designated with *letters or numbers*?" Shae said.

"Letters," Madison nodded.

"So that means I'm joining the *men* again?" she frowned.

"Only because there's eight women and seven men," Maddy smiled. "Otherwise, you'd be the odd man out."

"Story of my life," Shae chuckled.

"What will *you* be doing while all this is going down?" Laura said. "It doesn't look like this game requires any *officiating* this time."

"I'm just going to stand back and enjoy the show," Maddy grinned. "I'll have a unique perspective none of the rest of you have. While you're watching each other's *faces* in the mirror, I'll be watching your pussies and asses while the men pound you from behind."

"I'm beginning to see why you planned these parties," Elle chuckled. "You get your pick of the premium viewing spots."

"And with an odd number of *men and women*," Shae nodded. "When she gets to slip into the *action*."

"What can I say?" Madison grinned. "I'm just a lonely girl looking for some new ways to spice up my love life."

"Well, feel free to join us any time," Shae said. "I'm sure we can find some way to accommodate one more in the mix to make sure *everyone* walks away with a happy ending."

"Maybe I will," Madison smiled, peering down at the cushions. "But for now, I want each of the women to kneel on the cushions from left to right, starting with letter A. Then the men will take up position behind them, matching the correct numbers with the letters."

After all of the women rested on the cushions, I was excited to see Toby kneel behind me, eager to feel his pulsing tool inside me.

"Are you sure you're going to be able to get it *up* one more time?" his wife Elle kidded. "What will this be, the *third* time you've come tonight?"

"Four, actually," Toby smiled, peering at my dripping pussy. "But after seeing how Jade squirts when she comes, I'm *already* getting excited just thinking about it."

"Enjoy, baby," Elle grinned, glancing in the mirror while Brad kneeled behind her. "It looks like it'll be *my* turn to pair up with Brad this time. Let's hope he's as talented with his *dick* as he is with his mouth."

"Mmm," Laura hummed, widening her eyes when she saw Shae nestling up behind her with her dripping cock. "Looks like I'm finally going to have a chance to hook up with Shae. I have to hand it to Madison, she really knows how to encourage *mingling* at her parties."

Everybody chuckled while they smiled at their partners, then Madison gave the go-ahead to get started.

"Alright," she smiled. "What are you guys waiting for? Those pussies aren't going to fuck *themselves.*"

The men peered down at their partners' asses, then they grabbed the tips of their cocks, pointing them toward the women's dripping holes. When they inserted them inside their pussies, each of the women moaned, watching their partners in the mirror as their faces began to flush. While their bodies began to rock back and forth, I darted my eyes along the length of the mirror, watching their tits shaking on their chests and the men's abs flexing while they pounded their pussies from behind. Everybody seemed just as interested in what everyone *else* was doing, and as their eyes flitted between the twisting bodies, it seemed like a voyeur's dream.

But when I noticed Madison standing alone, rubbing her pussy gently while she watched everyone grunting and moaning, I signaled for her to join Toby and me in front of the fireplace. When she strolled over next to us, I instructed her to sit on the raised hearth in front of my head, then I buried my face between her knees, eagerly lapping up her juices. Before long, everybody in the room was panting and groaning, edging closer to another collective orgasm.

Laura was the first one to climax as she stared at Shae's bouncing tits while she tilted her hips, pressing her pulsing organ deep inside her pussy. Then Brad came soon after, watching his wife groaning on the end of her dick, and before long, the entire room was filled with the glorious sound of seventeen friends climaxing together while they watched each other's faces twisting in delirious pleasure. Madison waited until everybody else climaxed, and when I felt her hips begin to convulse over my face, I too lost all control, jetting my juices all over Toby's tightening balls while he gripped my ass, shooting his wad hard inside me.

When everybody finally finished shaking and groaning, we all collapsed in a giant heap on top of the cushions, laughing and caressing each other's dripping bodies. Madison's carnival-themed party had been a giant hit, and I was already thinking ahead to what she would dream up next.

MORE FROM VICTORIA RUSH:

Choose your next toe-curling fantasy from over thirty-five spicy stories in Jade's Erotic Adventures. Browse the full collection here:

Click to scan your favorites...

FOLLOW VICTORIA RUSH:

Want to keep informed of my latest erotic book releases? Sign up for my newsletter and receive a FREE bonus book:

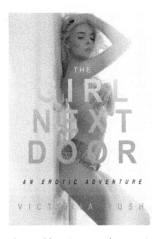

Spying on the neighbors just got a lot more interesting...